Richard Tregaskis
Classics Collection

Last Plane to Shanghai

Richard Tregaskis

Last Plane to Shanghai

Published by JMFdeA Press

For information address:
JMFdeA Press
P.O. Box 235737
Honolulu, HI 96823
www.jmfdeapress.com

Paperback ISBN: 978-1-7362954-8-9
E-Book ISBN: 978-1-7362954-9-6

JMFdeA Press chose to keep the content and punctuation in the Richard Tregaskis Classics Collection as RT originally wrote it. We feel RT's flavor would have been diluted by making changes to adhere to modern rules. There are certain words RT used that will show the reader the era in which RT lived. Richard Tregaskis was a kind, generous, big-hearted man who continuously put himself at great peril to tell the stories the world needed to know. He used some terms that are not acceptable today. Richard meant no malice. He was writing about his enemies. JMFdeA Press did not alter RT's works out of respect for him, and to also show how far as a society we have matured *some*. On Sept.18, 2021 there was a rally "Justice for J6" in Washington, D.C.. Have we really evolved in today's time to be a more tolerant society?

"As a young boy, I enjoyed reading about the heroes of our Nation. In reading the Landmark book version of Richard Tregaskis' *Guadalcanal Diary*, I was inspired by the courage and sacrifice of the Marines and sailors who fought and persevered in that very difficult battle—the first land offensive of the US in WWII. It inspired me to serve later in my life, but more importantly, taught me about the importance of exhibiting will, courage, and resilience when things were hard. Thanks RT for telling the story of these great Americans and so many others over the course of your life and career."

Robert B. Neller
General USMC retired
37th Commandant of the Marine Corps

Contents

About the Author

After graduating from Harvard in 1938, *cum laude*, Richard Tregaskis was a journalist and a staff member of the International Service. RT was anxious to get to the heart of the action to be able to tell the heart stories of the valiant men putting their lives on the line for our country. He was sent as a correspondent to cover operations of the Pacific Fleet at the outbreak of World War II. His experiences in the South Pacific became his first book. He wrote about war in a unique way and *Guadalcanal Diary* earned him a permanent spot in American literature and set the genre of war correspondence. It continues to be essential reading by U.S. military personnel.

Tregaskis was also in the European theatre following the Allies of the invasion of Italy, and then the American forces from Normandy into Germany, from which came *Invasion Diary* and *Stronger Than Fear*. While he was in Italy, he was hit by German shrapnel. A piece went through his helmet and head and out the other side of his helmet. After learning how to speak and use his right hand again, he continued writing.

In 1947 he journeyed for two years around the world. He spent most of that time observing the Nationalist-Communist war in China, from which he barely escaped. From those amazing experiences came *Seven Leagues to Paradise*, *Last Plane to Shanghai*, and *China Bomb: A Novel*. RT was compelled to write about the dangers of indirect insurgencies why they are successful. Since WWII we had constant emerging enemies who brought new kinds of war. Tregaskis wrote about all of them.

RT felt compelled to pen *X-15 Diary: The Story of America's First Space Ship*, which describes the full story of the X-15 hypersonic manned rocket ship, first of its kind in the race to space. There are the many stories of the men and women who worked tirelessly in this great chapter of American history.

Vietnam Diary, another seminal war correspondence book, was the first definitive eyewitness account of this new style of guerrilla combat. Tregaskis was on the frontlines for four months to share the compelling stories of courageous men fighting in these vicious battles. Due to his special skills and extensive travel in Vietnam, RT was contracted to write about one of the largest war-time construction efforts in history. His book, *Southeast Asia: Building the Bases The History of Construction in Southeast Asia* was an incredible undertaking which only he, with his talent and expertise could write. It covers every major construction by the U.S. Navy Construction Battalions (Navy SEABEES), and other military and civilian engineers and their stories as the events of the war evolved.

Amidst writing for motion pictures and television, RT delved into fictional biographies. *The Warrior King: Hawaii's Kamehameha the*

Great was created out of his love of Hawaii after he made it his home. It is an exceptional historical story of the legendary leader of the Hawaiian Islands. Tregaskis transports the reader back in time to when the Hawaiian Islands were under the rule of many kings and the events that transpired to create a one Hawaiian Nation, governed by one ruler for the prosperity of all of the Hawaiian people.

RT left behind a halfway finished love story, *The Secret of the Taj*, about Mumtaz Mahal who inspired the creation of the Taj Mahal. It was out of his passionate love of his wife, Moana, and their assignments to India, that this manuscript came to fruition.

In 1964, Richard Tregaskis was awarded the George Polk Award for reporting under hazardous conditions for the book that became Vietnam Diary. The helmet he wore in 1943 in Italy when a shell fragment pierced through it and into his skull is on display at the National Museum of the Marine Corps, along with a copy of *Invasion Diary*. Although RT had challenges with Type I diabetes, he never complained and it never stopped him from telling the important stories of the times as they were happening. During his life Richard Tregaskis clambered in and out of jeeps, fighters, bombers, trucks, and choppers while carrying his pack and notebook into the battles of nine wars. He was a special war correspondent who was able to sense the problems of the men on the front lines, while having an extraordinary ability to understand the strategy of war.

Introduction

RT wrote the exciting novel, *Last Plane to Shanghai* in 1960 before we met. Just as sometimes fiction turns into reality, it did so in this case. The character, Scott, has many attributes of RT. He's tall, a swimmer, appreciates Polynesian culture, and is a hardened war correspondent. I have many attributes of Martha, although physically we are not alike. She's blond. I'm brunette. She has short legs and arms. Mine are tall and lanky. We both are unafraid of being in the thick of war and have a yearning for adventure. I think it's interesting how RT asked me to learn photography after I met him in 1962. I did and we traveled together to Vietnam to cover the war. I wanted to go. He was the war correspondent and I, the photographer. It was harrowing and fulfilling all at the same time. I learned much from him and in future years, covered other wars on my own.

Although this is a fictional novel, one cannot mistake the realness of the war scenes. When one reads it, they understand the author is well versed in the details of war. It is clear he knows this from experience. RT was excited to put these aspects into fiction. It's entirely different than his non-fiction books about war. One feels they are there. It surrounds the reader who feels as the characters do. I am including the prologue that was cut from the book. There is much to learn from it.

In this novel, the main characters are forward thinkers. They do not fit into molds of that time. Yet there are racist and sexist views by some characters that are telling of the times when RT wrote it. Reading it again for this new edition has caused me to reflect on how much we as a global community have changed. The way women were seen then and how they are now are stark contrasts as is the way people commonly joked about other races. *Last Plane to Shanghai* is a great tool to reflect on how far we've come in respecting others in a short time.

RT did not believe women were the weaker sex. It is obvious in this book and others. That was one of the many things I loved about him. If he were to write this book now, the characters and the war would be different. Our enemies are different now and inside our own shores. We have the enemy of the COVID-19 virus. There is the enemy of fear and hatred because of different melanin levels in a person's body. Why that is, RT never understood, nor I. And there is also the waring of the political parties based in fear and hatred. My hope is that we unite and become the Great United States of America again. Americans were united against communism when RT wrote this novel. My hope is that we can learn to unite in love and peace, in the UNITED States, and include in that unity with all countries spanning the globe.

RT's first book was *Guadalcanal Diary* which set the genre for war correspondence books. No one knew about the tins of sardines crammed in his backpack. If anyone asked about his copy of a manual authored by the founder of Boston's famed Joslin Diabetes clinic, RT would say it was autographed by a special friend. Leaving Guadalcanal, RT returned to Pearl Harbor to write. In the field he filled a small notebook, and when at camp would transcribe them into a larger journal. When his adventure was finished, he had several. Daytime, the Navy locked him up to work with his notebooks and locked up the notebooks at night. The bloody experience of Guadalcanal changed him. He was stunned to be alive, and glad for it. The battle on that feverish island changed all those who survived it, yet these men couldn't bring themselves to talk about their experiences. RT told their stories. He saw, felt, and brought readers into the pangs of homesickness, the tales of scrounging, or the moments of humor.

Leaving the Pacific, RT went to the European theatre. The size fourteen boots Marines called his PTs, for "Patrol Tregaskis," went along. Eventually, luck deserted him. In a battle in Italy, on a hill called Mount Corno near Cassino, RT was hit by German shrapnel. A piece went through his helmet, a part of his head, and out the other side of the helmet, leaving a gaping jagged hole. Somehow, he staggered to the lines of the American 38th Evacuation Hospital, dragging along the helmet. There, managing to convey the word "diabetic" to a doctor, Major William Pitts of Charlotte, N.C., who performed the tedious, massive surgery. Within a few months, RT had learned again to talk. RT read poetry to practice speaking. He again learned to use his right hand, and was back to duty writing *Invasion Diary* and immediately afterward, *Stronger Than Fear*. The helmet he wore is now displayed at the National Museum of the Marine Corps.

The fear of communism in America started right after WWII. There was a heightened sense that communists were infiltrating America and converting people. That led to hysteria and many false accusations and blacklists, which was fueled by a political power struggle. Once Senator McCarthy was censured by the Senate in

1954, this upheaval started to quiet. But great damage was done. And at the same time, the Cold War was amplifying.

RT needed a change of pace. He was dedicated to report realistic lives of soldiers and their experiences. Yet it was time for something different. RT traveled around the world for True Magazine in 1948 for two years. *Seven Leagues to Paradise* was the book he wrote from that big adventure. On his travels, he discovered that Russians brought leaders of Third World countries to Russia for indoctrination. They then returned to their homeland to spread the values of communism. It worked by what he called the remote control method. There were few actual Russians living in those countries, so they could not be blamed for interfering. The conflicts that were created were by their own people, not the Russian army on the surface. The communist ideals seemed appealing with talk of equality for everyone. In reality, it doesn't work and is oppressive for the masses while government leaders enjoy the life of luxury. Freedom of expression, choice of career or being able to decide how many children to have are controlled because everyone has to be shoved into the same box. It doesn't matter if the person doesn't like it—they have no say in the matter.

RT wanted for the US to adopt this successful method to share our American values. After foreign leaders lived in America for a while, they would see how the US lifestyle is better than the communist way of life. They would return home and spread American ideals, not Communist propaganda. RT had other astute ideas to copy the methods of communist propaganda for the spread of American principles. He wrote *Last Plane to Shanghai* as a result of these concerns that would not let him go. RT said that fiction was a way to sweeten a harsh message. He was stunned how these dangers seemed to amplify as he wrote the book.

In 1955 the US became official supporters of South Vietnam. Although their paths did not cross in the Solomon Islands, a man he knew in college days was at sea in the waters of Guadalcanal at the same time RT was on the island. This man was President John F. Kennedy. While President Kennedy was in office, RT wrote *John F. Kennedy and PT-109*. The President loaned RT his personal logs and notes for research. At Harvard, RT and Jack Kennedy were swimmers, and close friend Torbert MacDonald captained the Harvard football team. At competitions for the varsity swim team backstrokers, RT trounced Kennedy for a slot on the team; it was a special year—they beat Yale. As press secretary Pierre Salinger took RT into the Oval Office, the first thing the President said was, "Pierre, RT beat me out for the Harvard Varsity Swim Team." RT replied, "Sir, if I'd known you would be President, I would have let you win." Amidst the laughter, one could note that neither President Kennedy nor Congressman MacDonald ever forgot that competition.

RT also delved into the race for space with *X-15 Diary*. He was fascinated with the execution of the plan to go into new territory. He covered the entire process of the US inaugural flight to space; the good and the bad—all of it thrilling. Both *X-15 Diary* and *Last Plane to Shanghai* were published in 1961. The same year President Kennedy added additional support in Vietnam.

In 1962 I was introduced to RT at the beach by my neighbor. The next day, I started working with him as a secretary. He was already researching *Vietnam Diary*. He left for Vietnam a few weeks later.

From 1963 until the end of the war, we went several times together. I took the photographs, and he wrote the stories.

A few years later, RT and I tackled the communist regime in *China Bomb: A novel.* RT felt a great urgency to share how such indirect insurgencies happen and why they are so successful. Set in the near future, it explored what every American in the late 1960s feared—China building a nuclear bomb. Americans were all war-torn with Vietnam continuing, and here was an enemy emerging with a new kind of war with more dangerous weapons. It was vital for people to understand the importance of this instead of being lackadaisical, despite our weariness.

RT and I went to many places and had innumerous adventures while writing books, magazine and newspaper articles, and screenplays. A scrupulous taker of notes, meticulous researcher, and diligent questioner, RT shared in the ordeals of the men he chronicled. While participating, he was uncommonly brave, and two generations of American fighting men accepted him as a member of their team. They talked about him, angular and tall, a bit over six foot six, soft-spoken and very thin, always writing, watching, questioning, and taking photographs at the height of battle. In addition to these traits crucial to the military historian, RT brought another quality to the battle lines—it distinguishes the great in both soldiers and civilians—he cared deeply about the affairs of the everyday man. I was never happier than I was with him, even in the uncomfortable bush being eaten by insects with the enemy nearby.

Over our many trips to India, we went to Agra. RT became enamored with the woman who inspired the Taj Mahal. He wrote a complete outline and half a manuscript of a fictional biography called *The Secret of the Taj* about Mumtaz Mahal, but did not finish it.

In 1964 RT and I were on an assignment in an area called Ladakh. It is the famous roof of the world where the Himalaya and Karakoram of India nearly meet the Pamirs of Russia. It is a high, cold, desolate moraine. Indian soldiers peered through binoculars at Chinese soldiers who peered in return over their own sandbags. We flew over the Karakoram in an unpressurized Indian Air Force plane, with oxygen bottles, then landed at the lowest elevation—11,000 feet.

We carried RT's insulin kit and an odd assortment of food and drugs. He acquired a blister on his foot from a faulty stirrup adjustment. We flew immediately to Kashmir. There, in an Army hospital, the gangrene set in. He went into a 4-day coma and his foot turned black. The doctor told me there was no diabetes of this severity in India. I thought – I know, they just die. I never left his room and helped my husband. They evicted me, but I went right back anyway. He recovered—I believe due mostly to that RT will-power that was so powerful. He immediately returned to writing.

RT and I had a rare, special relationship. We learned to play out our minds back and forth and the mental stimulation was exhilarating and I was grateful to always be in synch with my husband. RT was a man of courage. He inspired me to travel on assignment with and without him to cover the 1971 Indo-Pakistani War.

One of his favorite books to write was The *Warrior King; Hawaii's Kamehameha the Great* for he was much taken by the story of Kamehameha. RT was thrilled to share more about his home, beloved Hawai'i. He needed to exercise for his diabetes. Hawaii was ideal to do his daily exercises of swimming. Who wouldn't want to swim in the warm Pacific Ocean with the Hawaiian trade winds tickling you every day? RT went to Grey's beach and liked chatting with the regulars. In the tropics, he loved wearing as little as possible at home because the temperature rarely dipped below 66°. Living in Waikiki, we walked almost everywhere because everything was centrally located. Often, we visited Don the Beachcomber who was my first employer in Hawai'i. Friends constantly stopped by our home at any time. Once John Steinbeck spent the whole day with us lounging on our large lanai with a mural of a beach although we were two blocks away from the real thing. Those years were truly special.

In 2000 I reprinted some of his books. In 2016 a publisher approached me to turn a few of RT's books into e-books and audio books. It was a great success. Now I am thrilled to introduce The Richard Tregaskis Classics Collection through JMFdeA Press to share his complete legacy in audio and digital format as well as print while providing new personal stories and memorabilia. Look for *The Secret of the Taj* as well, for I am trying to finish it for my love.

RT was one of the few civilians to receive a purple heart for bravery in combat. He was a courageous man who made it his mission to share the reality of war as it was happening with details that was not normally covered. In 1964, the Overseas Press Club presented Richard Tregaskis with the George Polk Award for first-person reporting under hazardous circumstances for the book that became *Vietnam Diary*. In 1973, Marquis' "Who's Who in America" asked for a quote; RT sent these words: "Reverence for truth, thank God, continues to be a great American ideal. Beauty makes life most pleasant, and humor cushions the worst moments. But courage remains the most valuable of all. My life in many wars has shown me that America has ample stores of all of these values in the face of the most severe mortal dangers."

I want to extend my deepest aloha to the American Heritage Center at the University of Wyoming where the Richard Tregaskis Papers are housed. I have sent them a large part of RT's correspondence and research. They provided me scans of some of the memorabilia I am sharing with you. It is my hope to have his entire collection scanned to aid researchers with their work.

Please visit the estate's website about RT at richardtregaskis.com to learn more about this fascinating man who I loved deeply and his extraordinary books. Visit jmfdeapress.com to add to your collection of his compelling historical works.

Much aloha,
Moana
March 2021

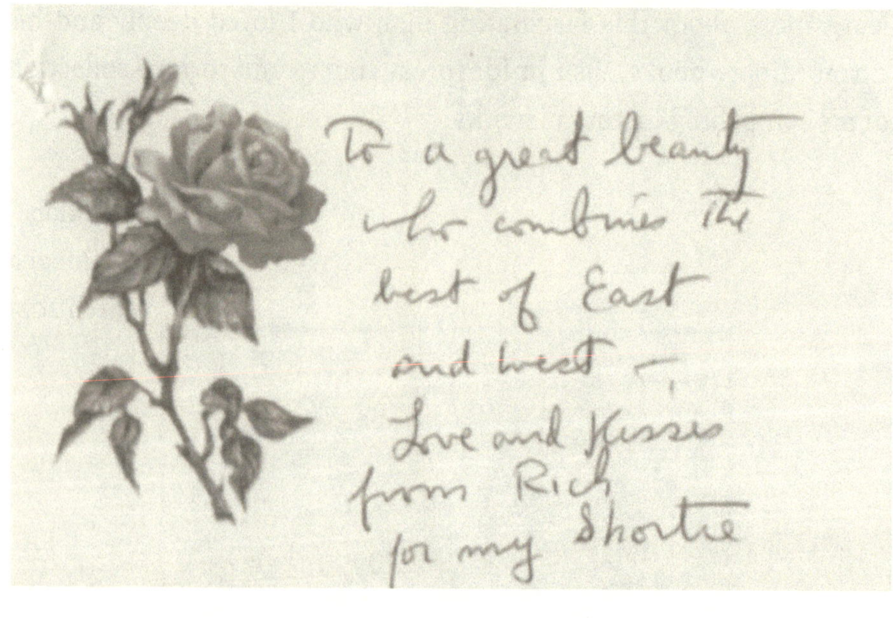
To a great beauty
who combines the
best of East
and west —
Love and Kisses
from Rich
for my Shortie

Photographs & Archives

PROLOGUE

SHANGHAI DIARY

There was a fever about Shanghai in the hot dog days
of May, 1949. The city lay crippled like the severed tail
of a serpent still twitching with remnants of life. Shanghai
was in fact a severed extremity, the remaining corner of
China's population axis in the Yangstze delta. The Reds had
lopped off the rich, green rice land surrounding Shanghai,
and the refugees fled before the advance until in the city
they could flee no farther. Here they hit the East China Sea,
land's end, with only the Pacific beyond. Millions of
Chinese, who might even be Mongols driven clear across the
Eastern Asian loess by the new religionists of Communism,
were backed against the Bund, the muddy Whangpoo waterfront.
Shanghai had been swollen into malignance, its overcrowded
streets carried seven million people. In its forced tumescence it became, unnaturally, the fourth largest city of
the world, bloated and overgrown by comparison with its
healthier and more muscular brothers, New York, London, Tokyo.

With unrelieved tumescence came fever. There was
no place for the back-pressure to go. The Red armies pressed
in from the north, south, and west, following their classic

technique of seizing the agricultural lands, which could
produce wealth, and leaving the barren trading centers,
swollen with refugees, to Chiang and his Nationalists.

The Communists in fact had sliced Chiang's China
into ridges of isolated scar tissue, centering around the
cities, so that the only remaining communication amongst
most of the islands of population was by plane.

And in each island--the island-axis that ran from
Shanghai to Nanking, the northern island including Tientsin
and Peking and Tsingtao, the southern group centering around
Canton--the same illnesses of tumescence occurred.

There was a food shortage, and that was basic, because China, with the biggest population in the world, lived
close to starvation even in good times. Now, with the Reds
cutting deeply into the lands that produced rice in the
south, sorghum in the north, food was high priced and scarce,
and the Americans had to bring in millions of dollars worth
of bulk and canned goods under the UNNRA banner, and much
of that ended in the Thieves' markets for the benefit of
fat politicians who drove black Cadillacs in Shanghai.

The cumshaw madness had seized China. The word carried
over from English, commission, violently twisted into pidgin
Chinese, had become the dominant economic modus operandi.
There were two business worlds--the upper, formal and old-
fashioned world, the lower world of key money and under-the-
counter payoffs. And in Chiang's China, "squeeze", the method

of the unofficial payoff, lurked increasingly, transparently
close to the surface of formal relations in business and
government. Why should a Chinese Army doctor endure the
rigors of life at the front for a devaluated pay check worth
five dollars a month, when he could pay a sergeant two dollars
to sign the necessary papers up north in Weishein, and meanwhile enjoy the fruits of private practice in Shanghai?

What had happened to Chiang Kai-shek's government?
How had the Reds managed to pile up such an advantage?
Why had the enemy, obviously devoted to repression of freedom, so obviously feared and so consistently fled by refugees
who left all their worldly goods behind so that they could
escape at all costs--why had that enemy gained enough strength
to bowl over the well-equipped, frequently well-trained
Nationalist forces? What was wrong with the Nationalist morale?
Why couldn't the American Military Advisory Group, set up
with all the modern advantages in Shanghai, make the Nationalists want to fight?

The answer came in the fever that gripped Shanghai
and the other cities. In the time of decadance, when men
still preferred freedom but didn't have the strength of mind
to want to fight for it, when the leaders were out to get
theirs and to hell with the rest of the world, and that psy-
chology spread downwards and outwards like brain sickness,
a dystrophy seeping into the extremeties with paralyzing rap-
ture--then like a ripe orange on the bough, freedom fattened
itself, made itself a fit prize for Communism, surrendered to
the forces of gravity.

Is there a lesson in it for the rest of the world?
A terrible lesson, when the world's largest nation, one
fifth of the world's population, an old and honored civilization that once brought us art, beauty and philosophy,
and the freedom these things need to breathe and live, should
give itself up almost individual by individual, to barbaric
Statism, the life of the barracks and the prison. And an even
greater lesson, that the world-wide Communist foe is powerful and relentless.
But in the tiger heat of 1948, in the confusion of
Armageddon, no one knew how China's fever would end. Some
thought the Reds and Chiang's Kuomintang would yet end their
differences with compromise. Others, knowing the Communists
better, said that religions never end their differences
without being absorbed, one by the other: that an aggressive
religion like Communism will think of any compromise as only
temporary, only as a step on the way to final victory.

And there were still others, perhaps the majority,
who drifted along with the current, enjoying it as much as
they could, taking what profit they could for themselves,
and finding it amusing that in Shanghai's devaluated currency,
it cost you $40,000 for a newspaper, and $10,000,000 to take
your girl out to dinner. To these people, the fever of 1948
was a last dizzy whirl, a delirious fling on the edge of the
precipice, before the curtain was drawn.

July 25, 1950

Mr. Louis Ruppel
Editor
Collier's
New York

Dear Lou,

It was swell of you to be so understanding about the Korean assignment. When I thought it over, talked to my doctor, and listened to what Marian had to say about it, I was convinced that after all it wasn't such a good idea for me. It also wouldn't have been fair to Twentieth-Century Fox to pull out in the middle of a project they had assigned me to, even though I was being hired on a week-to-week basis and they weren't too sure they were going on with the project.

The biggest reason, though, was in the matter of health. During World War II, although I had diabetes then too, I didn't have to take insulin. I handled the disease with diet. Now, on an insulin regime, I seem to have more difficulty keeping the thing under control. It seemed wise to me to wrestle with the diabetes a bit longer before going out on a deal as rugged as the Korean war. Maybe I can whip the thing down somewhat before the next Little Hot War breaks out, or at least before the big war in 1953. I hope when there are further developments in Southeast Asia or the Iran-Iraq-Arabia area, you'll send me out to do a job for you.

Meanwhile, I'd like to suggest a piece along this line: How to Beat the Russians At Their Own Game. On the trip around the world I made for True in 1948-49, I was struck time after time with the expert methods the Russians were using everywhere to engineer their world revolution---a shapr contrast to our own bungling. Everywhere I went is seemed that the Russians were carrying on the Third World War by starting civil wars--but they were doing it cheaply, by remote control. One saw few Russians in Chian, Siam or India or in Western Europe, but when you checked, you always found out that the revolutionary leaders were being sent or had been sent to Russia for indoctrination, then sent back to do the Communist business. If anyone objected that the Russians were interfering in foreign affairs, the Russians had--and have-- a good answer: therevolutionaries are nationals, not Russi

2

 In contrast with the Russian method, our technique seemed inept and ~~with~~ ineffective. We sent American advisory groups in, and the nationals, like the Chinese, disliked and distrusted us for this rather obvious insult to their touchy national pride.

 Instead of sending in droves of Americans, who always look like imperialists, we should do what the Russians do: we should take the small groups of literate men, intellectuals and patriots who are the leaders in any given country, and bring t them to the U.S. Here they would see how well men live, how automobiles, refrigerators, handsome houses, television and radio sets, clean and healthful food are available to the average person. They should be given fellowships at American universities--because most of the leaders are serious, earnest men--and they should have all their expenses paid so that they could roam around the country at will. After a few months they would be able to see for themselves how much better the U.S. way of life is than the Russian. Then, going home, they would lead their countries towards our way. No coercion would be needed, and the Russians would be beaten at their own game.

 Another Russian method could well be copied by us: the paper war. A Tass correspondent whom I had met on the Western Front told me in 1948, in Shanghai, that the biggest import from Russia into China was newsprint. It was being shipped into China at giveaway prices; you saw it in processed form, in the mountains of pamphlets and leaflets and broadsides which the Chinese intellectuals disseminated to further the leftist cause.

 Our propaganda efforts ~~could~~ in other media could also benefit from some imitation of the Russians. The Commies in China offered specific, ~~concrete~~ concrete examples as benefits of their system: like raises in the pay of labor, more land for farmers, etc. In Europe I was told many times that the Voice of America is a fizzle because it is not as direct in its propaganda as the Russians. Europeans often told me that the Voice of America programs of music, intermingled with ~~prana~~ laudatory accounts of American history, are ineffective. Programs, I was told, should tell how much the average man makes in America, should emphasize the fact that he has a refrigerator, car, and a good house with a bath and hot and cold running water, works only forty hours a week, lives on plenty of butter and meat. These things, it seems, are more interesting to hungry and poor people than political ideals.

 I have a lot of material on this subject gathered on th round the world trip. The stuff seems ~~dun~~ especially importan nowadays. Do you think so too?   Best,

January 19, 1961

Mr. Monroe Stearns
Managing Editor
The Bobbs-Merrill Co., Inc.
717 Fifth Avenue
New York 22, New York

Dear Monroe:

I'm glad you sent the cover along to me right away, and I think it is a bright design and that the jacket material covers the characters.

However, I hope it's not too late to change some of the jacket blurb. One minor item is that Ostermanns name is spelled with one "n", where I spell it with two in the book.

Also, It seems to me there is a fundamental omission in the blurb: First, and prominently, it should say something like this:

"This story is a major publishing event, wherein, through a tender and effecting love story, a theme of great consequence is unrolled for the American people -- perhaps not too late to save us in the generally unrecognized war which shakes our world

"The setting is the China civil war, which placed one fifth of the world's population in the Communist camp. The China war was the prototype of Cuba, the Congo, Laos, the prototype, the first and the greatest of the civil conflicts, the revolutions, the bush wars through which the Reds have been conquering the world." Then the jacket material can begin as is.

I think this short introduction absolutely oblig-
itory, because it sets the key of the story and clearly
states its importance.

I know that reviewers do their most careful reading
in the blurb material and this determines their approach
to the book. Without the type of introduction I have
written, the book sounds like one of 5000 novels, no more
deserving than that. I want to give the reviewers a clue
to the importance and value of the book, besides saying
at the end of the blurb that it is valuable.

Also, I would add a phrase after "repulsive husband"
(line 10): "repulsive husband who was part of the corruption that gathers when lazy and venal people handle
our foreign aid."

On the back flap, after line one "hope and confidence", add: "the kind of resolution Americans must reach
in a world tragically divided."

In the biography, I believe it is very bad selling
to say, five lines from the bottom: "For the last ten
years he has been writing principally for the motion pictures and television". That sounds as if I have been
sitting in Hollywood, whereas actually I have been spending
most of my time and effort travelling as a correspondent,
confirming my views on the world conflict between Communism
and the West, and for the last five years, working on the
present novel.

There is a strange flavor of antiquity about the
blurb, which makes and book and author sound out-of-date.
The material should say in effect "This is an UGLY AMERICAN
told in a love story." I was hoping that the copy of the
galley sent by Dan Green to Bill Lederer would elicit such
a quote from Lederer, and that it could be printed prominently
on the jacket. When I saw Lederer in Hawaii, he said something close to this after I had told him this was a love
story with the same theme he expounded. He said: "That's
what I should have done."

Can't we get some such quote onto the jacket? I wrote
about twenty letters to likely sources for this. I am
afraid that without some such powerful send-off the book
will wither on the vine.

As ever,

Richard Tregaskis

ESTABLISHED 1838

THE BOBBS·MERRILL COMPANY·INC. · PUBLISHERS

1720 EAST 38TH STREET · INDIANAPOLIS 6, INDIANA

MONROE M. STEARNS
MANAGING EDITOR
717 FIFTH AVENUE, NEW YORK 22, N.Y.

August 30, 1960

Mr. Richard Tregaskis
234 San Vicente Boulevard
Santa Monica, California

Dear Mr. Tregaskis:

Henry Morrison has just delivered the manuscript of SHANG-
HAI DIARY, and has told me that the revisions are not entirely complete.

I intend to read the novel again over the coming weekend
and then to write both you and Henry Morrison my opinions
of what, if anything, I think should be revised.

I shall be at the Beverly Hills Hotel from September 9
until approximately September 15. In the first place,
let me invite you most cordially to a little party we are
giving for our California authors at the hotel on September 9 from 5 p.m. on. Not only do I wish to meet you in
person, but I know that the President of the company, Mr.
M. Hughes Miller, is also very eager to be introduced to
you at that time.

Would you please try to arrange your schedule now so
that we can have several hours of conference about the
manuscript during my California visit. We have planned
to make the novel our lead fiction title in our Spring
1961 List, and I am sure that both you and we want it in
the best possible shape not only for hard cover sales but
also for book club and reprint subsidiary sales.

Let me assure you of my great interest in the book and
in working with you and send you my kind regards.

Sincerely,

Monroe Stearns

Stearns:lt

October 17, 1960

Mr. Monroe Stearns
Managing Editor
The Bobbs-Merrill Company, Inc.
717 Fifth Ave.
New York 22, N.Y.

Dear Monroe,

I was glad to have the quick word on the rewrite of SHANGHAI DIARY,
and I agree that some other title would be better for fear of
confusion with my non-fiction works.

I thought about this title business for a long time during the earlier
drafts of the book, and I believe the best I came up with ,by far,
was LAST PLANE TO SHANGHAI. I still like that best of all and I believe
it's very dramatic and hits the core and locale of the story precisely
add with the right degree of subtlety. I think your suggestion about
the Givers and the Takers is a good one, it comes close to the heart
of the story but it isn't strongly enough oriented in locating it
or hinting at the background or the drama in which the protagonists
are involved.

I'm glad we are in such general agreement on the book and believe as
you do that it should succeed as a paperback project (and probably
as a movie too) One line in your letter I did worry about was to the
effect that you thought the stiffback people would buy the book. The
context seemed to indicate that there was some other stiffback publisher
beyond Bobbs-Merrill. Maybe that apparent meaning was just a
transcription mistake by your secretary. Please let us know about it
if you have a moment.

One point I'd like to reemphasize: I would be happy with the title
LAST PLANE TO SHANGHAI and I think it's the best of all the titles
I've considered.

                         Best,

P.S. I'm enclosing an updated biog. to add to your exploitation and
jacket material. Walton will print some 8x10 pix of me them in
the next day or two and send them off to you, in case you should need
them for the jacket or otherwise. I'msure you noticed the dedication
FOR WALTON. Again, thanks for being polite and perceiving.

                         R.

RICHARD TREGASKIS   234 SAN VICENTE BLVD.   SANTA MONICA, CALIFORNIA

September 4, 1960

Mr. Monroe Stearns
The Bobbs-Merrill Co.
717 Fifth Ave.
New York 22, N.Y.

Dear Mr. Stearns,

I was glad to have your note and will be very happy if we can
have several hours of conference about SHANGHAI DIARY when you
are here in California.

As I think I indicated in my last note to you on July 12, I wondered
what had happened with the supplemental material I had sent you
via Scott Meredith on January 25. This material consisted of a third-
person version of the first 100-odd pages of the MS, with an outline
of the rest: and a frame which could be used with the existing first-
person version which originally interested you.

These two pieces of MS--the frame for the first person narrative and
the projected third-person approach and outline---were two different
approaches toward the problem of meeting the objections you voiced
in your letter of Dec. 30, 1959, to Henry Morrison. In this
letter you had said that the present MS needs conflict, motivation,
growth of characters, a "point". You felt Martha should be more
fully developed, Scott's and Martha's love affair rationalized,
Martha made less of a pushover, Scott a more despairing character at
the outset and changed by the experience in the story, and lastly,
another ending, possibly Martha's death.

The two major emendations I constructed I believe took notice of
most of your points, as well as I could realize them. The third-
person version, and outline of the rest, was to be the more thorough-
going rewrite. The frame which was designed to utilize the first-
person version, and give it more depth and in fact an ironic twist
centering in Scott's character change, would achieve a considerable
gain, I believe, and it would be to my liking, since it would make
it possible to use the first-person narrative almost as is, with the
exception that the end of the escape sequence in North China
would be changed so that Martha would die. In my first few versions
Martha died here, and I changed it because my friends who read the
manuscript wanted her to live. The frame extends her death and the
character change in Scott to their logical and I believe real
conclusion.

RICHARD TREGASKIS   234 SAN VICENTE BLVD,   SANTA MONICA, CALIFORNIA

I explained all this in the covering letters I sent toScott on January,
and requested that the whole be sent on to you.

Subsequently I inquired several times about your reaction to all this,
and on my last trip east in July, I asked Morrison (Scott was on
vacation) what if anything had happened to the rewrite efforts. He
said you had been terribly busy with a group of books you were
pushing through for the upcoming fall list, and hadn't yet got to
the Shanghai Diary project. Flying back to the West Coast over
Indianapolis , I was reminded that I wanted to drop you a line,
and did. I believe I mentioned on the card that Henry had tried
to reach you by phone during my brief stay in New York, but
you were not in town.

Anyhow, thamavery glad tolhear from you now, and am looking forward to
seeing you and talking about the book, also to meeting your Mr. Miller.

Yours sincerely,

Richard Tregaskis

THE WHITE HOUSE

WASHINGTON

April 10, 1961

PERSONAL

Dear Mr. Tregaskis:

Your publisher has kindly forwarded to the
President your letter and an advance copy
of "Last Plane To Shanghai" that you wanted him to have. He is, of course, delighted
to receive your novel dealing with the China-
Communist problem and looks forward
eagerly to an early opportunity of reading it.

With the President's thanks and warm good
wishes,

Sincerely yours,

Evelyn Lincoln
Personal Secretary
to The President

Mr. Richard Tregaskis
2185 State Street
Costa Mesa, California

PERSONAL

OUTLINE OF REST OF STORY

At the Wagon-Lits Hotel, Mark phones Frank Von Reno, the local AP man, asks him to send a message to Harold Hampden in Shanghai: please forward any cable from Brundidge, Mark's editor in New York. Mark expects the next message from Brundidge will have word about Geordie's condition.

Mark also locates Jack Nelson, the American buccaneer-type flier he heard about from Carver; the story about Nelson's exploits during the fall of Keishien will be a good "spare" story in case everything else falls through. He makes a date with Nelson.

In the hotel lobby, Mark sees Carl Shoon meeting with several large and sinister Mongol-type Chinese. He also notes that another Chinese is covertly watching Shoop and his friends.

Mark is called to the Nationalist Press Office, in a Nationalist office building. In one of the corridors he sees the same Chinese who was spying on Shoop. The spy or agent is apparently reporting to the Nationalist Intelligence Office.

At the Nationalist Press Office, Jimmy Way introduces Mark to the head man, an Americanized Chinese named P. Brooks Young. Mark has a hassle with Young and Young's conservative old assistant, Chun Li Jen, and Major Lu, about going up to a front-line area. It seems unlikely Mark will make it, though Jimmy Way pitches in to help. The press people are trying to

EARLY EXPERIMENT WITH STREAM OF CONSCIOUSNESS P.O.V. (abandoned)

CHINA FAREWELL
retitled SHANGHAI DIARY,
Then LAST PLANE TO SHANGHAI

LING

Ling looked up the alleyway by the customs shed. The
first of the Big Noses were beginning to come out now, with their
baggage. The customs people had kept them a long time. Maybe they
had found a smuggler, maybe that had caused a delay. Maybe they were
just slow and lazy because it was hot.

Ling had been waiting with his old Dodge cab for an hour on the
street called Broadway, though the real name was Lotus Water. It had
been more than two hours since the big gray ship had put out her fat
ropes and the big wooden stairway that came out of a hole in the
side.

But the fare would probably be worth the wait. If Ling could get
a rich Melikan, he could charge double and get good cumshaw too.
Strangers, foreign devils like this, new to Shanghai, didn't know
the CNC currency. You could charge them two or three million instead
of one million, they wouldn't complain. They would only laugh, because
it was figured in millions, and in their money a million was only one
buck. One buck, they always laughed when he said a million was one
buck.

Now came a big foreign devil, a very tall one, with three coolies
carrying his luggage behind. With so much luggage behind him, he
might be very rich. You couldn't tell from the luggage: all the
Americans had wealthy luggage.

How big the foreign devil is, Ling thought. He is too tall. He's
as tall as the White Dagoba in the Forbidden City, his face is not
so evilly red as usual with the Big Noses. His features are nearly

For Walton

1

THE THING THAT GOT ME ABOUT SHANGHAI IN THE SUMMER of 1948 was that nobody thought anything was going to happen. It was happening all around them and still they said nothing was going to happen.

When I got off the ship that day in July I didn't know either. I went in there trying to keep my eyes open, trying just to look for a good adventure story, because adventure stories were marketable— and because my exchequer was sadly in need of marketable writing. I should have been more knowledgeable, then, about the great political story of China falling apart. But simply enough, I needed money. A woman had led me to this situation. Another woman was about to lead me to a more gratifying one.

That first day I saw her I knew what kind of a girl she was—and I knew I was going to be involved with her, at least.

I had just got off the President Wilson, the big A.P.L. liner, and grabbed a rickety taxi. The cab rattled down the grubby little street then called Broadway, past the sailor joints with signs that said

Sanitary Cafe, Suvenir and Bar Ber, then over the Garden Bridge and into a snarl of traffic on the Bund.

My little cabbie had already asked me if I wanted a zig-zig girl—the standard first question to a visitor in disintegrating Shanghai—and I had declined with thanks, saying that I was too tired. Then he stopped, suddenly, at the foot of the Garden Bridge.

I could see what the holdup was. Where Nanking Road connected with the Bund, a mob eddied. They carried wide paper banners, the kind we sometimes use at political conventions. There were several hundred in the crowd, and when I took a good look, I decided they were students. I could hear their chanting, a regular chorus like katydids in the mating season.

The Commies, following their usual pattern, were stirring up the boys and girls, appealing to their nationalistic instincts, a very workable mechanism to the Communists, then as now. Most of the parades in Shanghai then, as they have been in the rest of the world, were protest-meetings, pep sessions directed against the imperialists—that was the Americans and the British, French, Dutch, and Belgians. The katydid mating chant translates roughly as "Imperialists Go Home and Leave Us Alone," and naturally these young punks, full of sex juice mostly sublimated into nationalism, don't know the sequel to their chant can be easily supplied: ". . . so the Communists Can Put Us In Jail." In the case of Shanghai, 1948, Chiang, like the other nationalist dictators of our world-in-flux, let this kind of activity go almost unimpeded because it masqueraded as patriotism. Like any other politician, Chiang wanted to be patriotic above all else.

At this point, though, I didn't know much about the Chinese Communists, and I was just excited by the thought of watching a riot, and maybe getting an eyewitness bit for a magazine story. I had already covered quite a bracket of the new type wars in Asia and the Middle East, the civil-war kind which the Commies find a cut-rate way to subvert a country. I knew that if there was a parade, it was probably directed against Americans and their Allies, the Imperialists. If there were any Americans in the vicinity, a riot was apt to come about. The magazine I worked for, *Beacon*, was non-political. But wars could still yield good adventure stories, and today looked promising.

So I told the cabbie to wait—he was jammed in traffic and couldn't move anyhow—and went down the slope of the bridge to the Bund on foot.

Down there, a crowd of maybe two hundred pedestrians, a small crowd in terms of China, had stopped on the sidewalk to peep at the excitement. I found out later that they habitually waited there to watch the Shanghai police administer mild billy-club discipline to the marching students. The students, all worked up at the end of their parade, were trying to go on up the Bund and across the Garden Bridge, then to picket the big modern apartment building called Broadway Mansions.

Broadway Mansions was the headquarters and billet of the MAG, the American Military Advisory Group, and the students (as I found out later) liked to chant "Go Home, Melikan" at whatever Yankee they could see, or scrawl "Go Home, Impelialist" or "Running Dog of Capitalism" or some such witty saying in chalk on the granite facing of the building. So the Shanghai police, to prevent this sort of occurrence, usually set up a picket line between the Garden Bridge and the Bund. Inevitably, some of the students were hit over the head, and the Chinese mob liked to gawk at the bloodshed.

This day, I saw the picket-line ranged at the foot of the bridge, tough looking bully-boys with white helmets and leggings, the formidable night-sticks—and of course, the real badges and threats of the world's bully-boys, pistols.

Down the Bund, a couple of hundred feet away, the students came toward the cops in a solid wall of white shirts and black pants, like a mass of ambulant piano keys. Probably to keep up their courage, they chanted more loudly than ever. They straightened their cockeyed paper banners, and on our side of the Bund, I saw a couple of cops pull guns. They would be the nervous ones. It seemed to me that somebody was going to get hurt this day.

Then I saw her: the light blonde hair, the boyish figure in khaki pants and shirt, taller than most of the surrounding Chinese. She stood quite close behind the skirmish line of cops, and she was making pictures as the line of the students advanced. She had a 35-mm. camera, and it looked to me as if she were well placed to get good pictures. She could shoot through the picket line, framing a banner or two between cops. I admired her placement professionally, just as a pro might admire good stance in a golfer, and I also respected her nerve. I had seen enough of Asia to know how quickly you can get hurt in that kind of a situation.

The marchers came closer, and their chanting louder. I could hear a drum beat distantly, somewhere in the back of the mass of students. And I saw her move. Still moving with the savvy footwork of a good photographer, who will always be close to the right place for the best pictures, she strode toward the sidewalk, where the pedestrians gawked at the impending police action.

I figured she knew that the mob, panicky and scatterbrained, would start pulling and hauling at each other the minute they thought danger was close. But she apparently wasn't thinking of that. Her plan was evidently that from the sidewalk she could cover the cops, the students, and the spectators.

But she would also be taking a chance of getting knocked over. If she were knocked over, she might be badly hurt, might be trampled to death by the mob. Even if she weren't knocked down, she might lose the camera, and the pix, to a pickpocket in that crowd. She had nerve, or else she didn't know any better. I didn't know then which it was.

Then, over on the left, I caught the flash of a billy-club, two rapid strokes. I saw a couple of people fall. The black and white mob had hit one part of the picket line, and the sparse line of cops was falling back.

Behind them, though, a squad of fresh cops was moving up, in a kind of flying wedge. I saw some more clubs flash, saw a little knot of white-skirted students struggling with a couple of cops, a violent swirl in the current of people. Two more cops came up with clubs flailing, and I heard the bursting outcry of a group under sudden stress. The outcry, a sort of sigh, seemed to pass across the crowd. Clubs flickered across the line, like low surf at the shore, where the paraders and the cops had come into contact.

I looked back for the girl, and saw her scooting around, squatting to get a low angle of a cop beleaguered by three students, and swinging his club. But she didn't seem to realize how the spectators were pressing toward her, wadding up at the point of action.

I could have stayed right where I was, and maybe stopped to make a note or two, but it impressed me that the girl was all alone down there. Not another Westerner in sight. I found that I was drifting down in her direction, almost automatically. There must have been some presentiment of trouble, some compulsion to be more than a spectator if something was going to happen to her.

Then it did happen. I heard a shot, and another, and turning toward them, saw a cop with his gun in the air. He seemed to be off balance as three or four students heaved at him. I saw the gun barrel etched in the air next to the white helmet, saw it puff smoke and heard the report. The students pulled back, the crowd of spectators behind the cop pushed and shoved each other to get away from the danger, and the pushing and shoving spread like a fast wave across the crowd, swept into the corner where the girl had crouched to make a picture.

The small khaki body moved under the trampling feet, and I started to run toward her. I knew what could happen in a few seconds. It could happen to one of their own kind who had the misfortune to fall under their stampeding hoofs, but it could happen faster to a Westerner. It wasn't often the Chinese had a chance to kick an Imperialist physically. Now they could do it almost accidentally while also scrambling for their lives.

The worst was that wrestling matches of the impromptu sort also broke out, as the more panicky struggled too hard to get out of the crowd. From somewhere on the picket line another couple of shots hit the air, and that sound was a shot of adrenalin to the mob.

In this kind of thing you don't have much time for thought. If you could call it a thought, I thought about a British woman I had seen caught in a riot near Hong Kong's Kai Tak airport. I could see in my mind her body twitching on the ground, only a thing moving, blood obscuring the fact that this thing had been, once, mammaries and a face.

Something like that flashed across my imagination, and then in a couple of seconds I was in that crowd. The Chinese are pretty much midgets compared to Americans, even the taller Chinese of the North. It wasn't much trouble to push them out of the way. Even when they were terrified by the shooting and the mob, they saw me as a giant, and they moved when I shoved. One of them, of course, might have used a knife or gun on me, but they didn't, and I didn't have time to think of that till later.

The girl was balled-up on the ground, her legs pulled up and one arm across her face. I pulled her onto her feet, and didn't see any marks on her. Her hair was messed, her face was dirty, her man's shirt was covered with dirt. But no blood.

The crowd was shoving, pulling and pushing us like a current. I grabbed her hand and started to lead her out of it. There wasn't any time to ask if she was okay; she could walk or she couldn't, and I'd find out.

She was walking all right. I ran interference for her. But in a second I felt her pulling hard on my arm. When I turned back to her I was astonished. She had taken a brace like an unwilling child, and her little smudged chin was clenched.

"My camera!" she was saying. "I lost it back there. I've got to go back and get it." She waved in the direction of a frantic, wrestling mob. At the same moment, another shot struck the air in the vicinity, and the yell of the crowd surged louder. I heard a police whistle, and another. Beyond the picket line, the black and white mass of the students seemed to be bending back.

"Do you see the camera?" I yelled above the noise.

She waved the broken leather shoulder strap of the camera and looked helpless. Then at the same moment we both saw the thief with the camera.

He looked like a boy, taller than average for a Chinese, and he was running, hugging the camera, its broken leather strap trailing like a kite tail. He was wearing a grimy American army field jacket and an old pair of pants.

"He's got it," she said. And I hesitated. To try to catch a broken-field runner, probably a professional pickpocket, in the middle of a riot in a hostile city, and take something as valuable as a camera away from him—that would be a dangerous chore.

But I didn't think about it very long. In about three seconds I found myself running again, this time in pursuit of the swift Chinese quarterback.

Strangely enough, I caught him, thanks to the thickness of the crowds and their violent surging movements to save themselves. If they had been less agitated, he might have had a much easier time of getting away.

But he hit a wide, violent spiral nebula of panicky Chinese and couldn't get through or around. I caught him as he tried an end run.

I got hold of his left arm and gave him a spin—he was a tiny little man and he had looked taller because he was so thin—and he flipped over and hit the pavement. He rolled and ended up flat on his back in the wet gutter.

I grabbed the camera and it came away very easily, and I saw that he was grinning, laughing, lying there in the gutter and laughing. Here in the middle of a riot, amid the gunshots and the police whistles and the thudding of billy-clubs, caught in the middle of what was to him grand larceny and tossed flat into the gutter by a giant, and also deprived of booty that could keep him alive for a half-year if sold to a Chinese fence, the pickpocket just lay there and laughed. I laughed too. What can you do with a character like that?

But even in these, my first days in China, I knew enough not to trust the man's good nature. With people all around shoving and clawing each other for their lives, this was no place for leisurely laughter. The little punk might get a bunch together and whip them up against the Yankee Impelialist who had of course been responsible for all this rioting and disturbance.

Right now, as I beat a fast retreat from there, I noticed about ten Chinese who had gathered around me and the little pickpocket and were peeping at me with their bird-eyes, and in doubt whether to laugh or get mad.

I hurried toward the girl, and saw that the black-and-white parade of students had been turned back. The mob of them were moving toward Nanking Road again, and an old high-sided police ambulance was waddling onto the street with its bell ringing. It was heading toward a cluster of people, a sort of doughnut of people with an empty space in the middle. I guessed that would be a crowd staring at an injured man or two, or more. Somewhere in there, forty or fifty pairs of Chinese eyes were no doubt registering what gore looked like on the pavement, and how bizarre human features can be when they are shoved out of line.

As the ambulance jounced closer, two white-helmeted cops jumped out and ran toward the cluster of people. I saw the nodule of people break apart, and left the sight behind as I found the girl.

I gave her the camera and her little round, smudgy face broke into such a sunbeam smile that I knew on the spot any effort would be worth a result like that.

Besides, I felt good about being such a bargain-rate hero. Nothing could have been easier than taking the camera back from the little larcenist.

"Thanks, thanks a lot," she said, still beaming. "I wasn't worried about the camera: it was the pictures, I wanted them."

"It was easy," I said. I grabbed her arm and pulled her up the bridge slope toward the cab. "We better get out of here as fast as we can," I told her.

By the time we got back to the cab, the traffic was clearing down on the Bund, the tangle of cars, trucks, and whirlygig pedicabs was unravelling.

The little cabbie, with a crooked smile; "Okay, mastah-boss." It was the first time I had looked at him closely: I saw that he had a long faint white scar that ran across one cheek and down across his mouth and into his chin. It didn't seem to have affected the contour of his mouth.

And that "Master-boss" bit was his idea of extreme deference. Most of the Chinese servants I came to know used the "master" address, with a tone that approximated our "mister." But this cabbie, when he wanted to add an extra bit of approbation, tacked boss onto the word. He had apparently seen my bit of cut-rate heroism at the expense of the Chinese pickpocket.

Now he jammed the rattletrap into gear and we started down the grade toward the Bund.

"What were you trying to do down there?" I asked the girl, a little irritation setting in as the reaction from the episode. We could both have been kicked to death by the mob; especially after that crazy effort to get the camera back. She could have got me killed over a silly Leica—or was it a Leica? I hadn't even had time to look. Whatever it was, the whole deal had been way off the beam. My breath went out of me in a hurry as I thought what it could have led to.

"I'd like to be a good photographer. I want to do something— important," she answered, generally. She had opened the front of the camera and taken off the lens cover to see if anything was broken.

I gave her my handkerchief. "Better wipe your face, see if you got cut anywhere."

"I didn't," she said positively as she mopped the yellow dust from her forehead. She dredged a comb from a pocket and started to comb her hair. Her hair was short, short curls and whirls, like a boy's hair when it is whacked off with a pair of scissors. But in a second it seemed to fall into place by magic. And quickly she produced a lipstick and tidied up her mouth with a few expert strokes. She could do this faster than any other woman I had seen.

"What did you get pictures of?" I asked her. Her intensity and single-minded ness were beginning to amuse me.

"I got some good shots of the cops hitting people with their clubs." Her mention of it made me feel derelict of my duty. By rights, I should have been busier with the notebook, and not so eager to play Galahad. Especially if I wasn't going to get much thanks for it.

"But," she added seriously, "I missed out on the pictures I really wanted."

"What were they?"

"The ones that are important. That show what the Communists are driving them to—the mechanism. Something showing the paper banners the students carried. I got some from a distance, but I don't think you'll be able to read the lettering. I wanted to catch things like 'Go Home Melikans' and 'Down with Impelialism.'"

She looked down the length of the Bund toward the Nanking Road junction. "It's too late now," she said sadly. "They're all leaving."

"By the way," I asked, "where can I take you? I haven't had a chance to ask you, and unless I tell this driver different, we'll end up at the Cathay Hotel."

"Oh, thanks," she said. "Could you take me by Broadway Mansions? Or I could take the cab after I drop you at the Cathay."

"No, I'll have him swing by Broadway Mansions. Driver: go to Broadway Mansions first."

The little cabbie screwed his head around on his neck, and turned a dismayed face toward us. "Othuh way, mastah," he said, jerking his thumb toward the back of the car.

"That's all right." And then I thought of something important. "I don't know your name yet," I said to the girl. "Mine's Ostermann, Scott Ostermann."

The words seemed to light up that sunbeam face again, and she laughed, a high, surprisingly fragile laugh. "I'm sorry," she said. "I'm Martha Shoop." The concentration on her photographs dropped from her, almost visibly, and she added: "I also meant to say many thanks for saving my—neck—back there in the mob."

I felt better. I felt as if she had suddenly discovered that I existed, and that I might even have been important to her, for a little while anyhow.

On the short drive to Broadway Mansions, she was a model of tact, she asked all the proper questions about me, and I gave her polite answers. I told her I was a beat-up kind of freelance, not a regular news service correspondent, that I travelled for *Beacon* magazine, that I came from New York, that I'd been a correspondent during World War II and in the post-war cycle of bush wars, that I struggled around the world trying to find adventure stories, and usually found them in the midst of political cataclysm, war and tragedy—to which, I said, I should of course be more sensitive.

It was a wonder to me then, as it was afterwards, that she could concentrate so hard on whatever subject she chose. Now she was concentrating on being interested in me, and as usual when she was interested, she went at it intensely, and as usual when she bore down on something, her interest immediately became genuine.

I marveled, too, at the ease with which she got over the unpleasant episode on the Bund. You would have thought it had never happened if those dirty, wrinkled suntans hadn't been there to remind you.

She had heard of the *Beacon*, she had even read my story about pirates in Hong Kong (the tired one I wrote in two days), and she seemed favorably impressed that I wrote for a man's magazine. She seemed to like and respect the fact that I wrote adventure stories— that was a switch in the fair-sex response. Usually, it was one of the "Well, what else is new" order.

She was being so interested that I didn't have a chance to find out much about her. As she left the cab and stepped onto the sidewalk in front of Broadway Mansions, I realized that I didn't even know whether she was married.

I did find out, though, that she was not a professional photographer—not yet; that she came from Pennsylvania, a little town called Oil City, and that she'd gone to a school in New England, at a place called Sargent College, and she had studied phys. ed. I thought of that educational background when she walked away from me in front of Broadway Mansions: she had a stride like a man's almost. Her legs were not long, probably short even as women's legs go, but she took long steps, and many times when I saw her walk after that, I thought she paced like Diana on a hunt, or maybe, much more exactly and less deferentially, like a scoutmaster leading a hike. The walk was so incongruous because she had full hips and narrow, feminine shoulders. I never knew why she walked like that; maybe it stemmed from her phys. ed. days when she wanted so much to be a competent athlete. Maybe—I would say in retrospect—the walk was part of her earnestness. She would have been one hell of a driving, ruthless man if she had been a man. Right now, I was very glad she was so obviously feminine.

When the cabbie slammed the cab into gear and pulled into the traffic of Foochow Road, I realized that I hadn't made any arrangement to see her again, or even discussed the possibility. I didn't know even if she lived at Broadway Mansions, or was just visiting there.

The cabbie helped a little, though. He must have been reading my face, because he grinned that crooked grin and said:

"Mastah, me know lady. She is missy for Melikan sol-yer live in Bloadway Mansion. Take-um many times in taxi."

It was a shock to hear that she was married—or a mistress to an Army man. I wasn't quite sure what he meant, but in either case it was bad news.

I had no right to complain, because I was married too. My marriage seemed to be in the last stages of disintegration at that point, but the legal tie existed. I probably had no right to any romantic interest in Martha Shoop, nor she in me, in that July of 1948, in the middle of the Chinese Civil War. But the attraction was there, this was Shanghai in the year of the Great Collapse, with attendant morality, and I had never pretended to conventional virtue, at least as far as women were concerned—especially since my marriage to Lois had been on the skids.

The driver swung the little rattletrap cab past the colony of soggy matsheds on the river bank of the Bund. I remember the impact this first sight of the Shanghai refugees had on me: the tiny little tent-like houses no more than three feet high, made of brown shipping mats—strewn like bugs along the bank of the Whangpoo, the refugees in brown rags thrown among them, jammed family by family into the little shelters that looked like soggy graham crackers. With the refugees from the Civil War, Shanghai had twice as many people as in normal times, and millions of them were even closer to starvation, thanks to the Communist war.

I had Martha Shoop on my mind. I could still see that bright, blonde face, the wide, healthy arch of teeth that made it so easy for her to smile—but I couldn't fail to notice the things we were passing, the matsheds, the emaciated kids barefoot and ragged, the skeletal old ladies in black, patched rags like the kids.

We swung into Nanking Road and the cabbie was saying: "Here come Cathay Hotel, Mastah." The car squeaked to a stop and he jumped out to assist the porters with the luggage. He fished in his pocket and came back with a bent and soiled calling card, printed in Chinese.

"Name Ling," he said, with a slight inclination from the waist. "Happy to duh-live Mastah Boss anyplace."

The grin on his face still looked genuine. "Big Mastah need good drivah if alltime trying big fight. Like today."

I told him I would call him through the hotel desk, and thanked him. On this, my first day in Shanghai, I had met two good friends. One who I hoped would be a lot more than a friend—and the sooner the quicker.

2

I DIDN'T SEE HER AGAIN UNTIL TWO DAYS LATER, WHEN JOHN Lindahl, the Far East Chief of American News Service, invited me to Broadway Mansions to meet some people in the evening.

The fact that I saw Martha there was my doing. When John called me at the Cathay and asked if I'd like to meet some of the consular and military people who might be helpful, I said that would be wonderful and then I remembered Martha.

"By the way, John," I said, trying to sound casual, "do you know a girl named Shoop, who lives in Broadway Mansions?"

There was a little pause, and then John said with his usual good nature, "Yes, sure, I know her. Mrs. Shoop—" and I wondered if I was imagining that he emphasized the Mrs. "She's married to an Army captain in the MAG. You want me to ask them along tonight?"

"Yes, John, if can do. If he's in the MAG, it might be some good in my search for stories, don't you think?" It sounded pretty lame, so I decided to face the issue. "Besides, I know her. I met her on the Bund the other day, during the riot. A beautiful doll."

"That gal's going to get herself killed some day," he said, his tone of voice about what it would be if he were swearing. "Was she making pix?"

"Yes. And I agree with you about her trying to kill herself. Is she always trying?"

"Most of the time." Again a pause. "Something's eating her, some agitated anti-Communist business. Her husband's just the opposite: a lush. He just wants to get loaded and forget it all."

"If they'll ruin your party, the hell with it. I just wanted to see her again sometime."

I felt the pause again, a hiatus in the conversation. "Okay," he said, "I'll give them a try."

"Swell."

He was hesitating: he had something more on his mind. "He—I mean Shoop—might not be around. Travels to Nanking a lot. You still want me to ask her, if he's not in town?"

"Sure." I had said it without thinking. I wondered then if John might have a crush on the girl or something. He was married too, but his wife hadn't been able to get news service permission to join him yet (might not ever, if the China war kept on getting worse), and I had already discovered that the morals of Broadway Mansions (and Shanghai) were about as straight-laced as those of a rooming house on Bourbon Street, New Orleans.

"Okay," he repeated. "I'll try it. We'll see you about 9:30, right?"

So that night I saw Martha and her husband, and perceived something considerable of their relationship—and also understood why John had acted as he did. There's no sense in belaboring his attitude towards Martha, it was simple: he looked at her from afar, and thought she was beautiful and intense and feminine, as I did, and he wished he could be closer—but he never managed it.

What I discovered about Martha's relations with her husband was a lot more important, it led to a part of my life that made everything before seem insipid. I'll always be grateful for the accident of the moment when I pressed the issue with John a little and induced him to invite Martha Shoop to that party. I guess life is like that: most of the time you just exist, and then there is a time, or times if you are lucky, when the flame burns bright, and in the intensity of the light you see that you are really alive, you feel your life has suddenly been connected to a high-tension line. In retrospect, that was the way it was with her. Martha was the electricity that did that for me. But at that moment, it was pure libido.

That night, sitting in John's bare, bachelor-type apartment, and working up information from the people-it was work, because I was building the new background a correspondent has to have when he hits a strange locale—I kept watching the door and wondering why the Shoops were so late in arriving.

It was a mixed crowd of men—some with their wives, some with other men's wives, some with White Russian mistresses. One was a devastatingly beautiful Eurasian half-caste, devotedly paying attention to a grubby sergeant. Rice might be short in China, but not women. So anything went in Shanghai.

Then they were standing in the hall, the Shoops, being welcomed by Wu, Lindahl's houseboy. As Martha came into the room I was dazzled. When I had seen her down at the Bund, she'd been wearing those rough suntans; the shirt that was too big, the shapeless pants. Now her small, smooth shoulders rose from a dress that shimmered like a jewel, the color of aquamarine. It was the hand loomed silk that comes from Siam, with subtle lights in it that made it luminescent, several shades of blue at once.

But the dress was a nonentity, a thing of no consequence compared to Martha; it was about as important as the dress which Liberty leaves behind as she strides forward, bare-breasted, at the point of attack in Delacroix's painting of French Revolutionary times: Liberty Leading the People.

As Martha and her husband came closer, I noted that her neck curved from her shoulders with the same slight forward inclination as the famous Liberty. Her throat was long and delicately shaped, her small face had the same look of perfection that makes Liberty beautiful, the same slight aquilinity in the small nose, the same wide, straight brow. There was an aggressiveness, a dynamism, built into that beauty—a cleanness, a drive, the look of the leader.

When she moved into the room with John Lindahl guiding her, the waves of her presence vibrated to the edges of the room. And John, being closest to her, caught and reflected some of it, like a minor moon, as if it had become his own light.

Possibly, looking back at the moment from this distance in time, I am remembering Martha as brighter than she was that night. Admittedly, my ordinarily rather impartial newspaperman's perspective was bent, if not warped, when I tried to focus on her. But at least to me, that moment at John Lindahl's, she was one of the most vibrant and breathtaking women I had seen. A sensuous dream hit me—Martha as Liberty, in the semi-nude; I didn't see her husband until he stood right next to me.

"Mrs. Shoop, I guess you've met Scott Ostermann before," John was saying. "Scott, this is Captain Carl Shoop."

"Gladdaknowyuh," Shoop grunted. He had a way of swallowing his words that made him seem surly. I tried to look at him with my best impartial perspective. But the question in my mind, a loaded question, was: "What does this oaf have that gets to her?" She didn't seem to be paying much attention to him—that was a consolation.

It would be truthful to say that he was good-looking, if you like the blue-black type of good looks. His wiry black hair, crew cut, grew down like a pelt to a sharp line about two inches above his dark eyes. His face had the bones to be clean and strong, but it was jowly. Had it once been athletic and aggressive, I wondered?

He was squarely built, with a long, heavy upper body and short legs, the type that accumulates weight easily, and his hands and wrists were thick, with heavy black hair. I should say here that I took an instinctive dislike to him, since he was such a different type from me, and incidentally about four years younger, which would make him twenty-five. But really it wasn't his physical differences or even his lesser years that set me against him; it was mostly plain jealousy. What did this guy have, I asked myself, that he should deserve Miss Aquamarine, Miss Venus of 1948?

But he wasn't knocking himself out to be friendly with me, either. Martha was saying, "Mr. Ostermann is the man who saved me from the trouble down at the Bund."

"Yeah, I know," Shoop said. "He looks like the type." I was startled at the insult, if it *was* an insult. Only the tone identified it as such. I looked at his eyes and was surprised again, to see that they had a vague, out-of-focus stare. Could this guy be half in the bag already? I wondered. I saw Martha's face redden in embarrassment.

Then, before I could say anything, reliable John Lindahl jumped into the social breach. He moved neatly and with the appearance of accident between Carl and me, and said to Martha:

"Martha, can I get you a drink?"

Still red, Martha turned a freezing look at Carl and answered carefully: "No thanks very much, John. I'm not drinking this evening."

John faced Carl good-naturedly. "No use asking if *you* want a drink." He took Shoop's arm. "What I should get for you is a cup of black coffee, but come on, I'll find you some bourbon." Shoop grinned loosely and went along, a willing victim.

And so I had my first chance to talk to Martha Shoop quietly and at length. I took her to a darker corner of the room where there were only two chairs together and she would be out of the line of sight of all the potential wolves at the party, except me.

At first she was still rubbed the wrong way by the little scene with Carl, and she apologized for him. But then, to her credit, she didn't vilify her mate, she dropped the subject, and I shifted us around to more pleasant matters; like how did the pictures she took on the Bund turn out? She said fine, and I said I'd like to see them because maybe I could use them as illustrations for the piece I would do for *Beacon*. That led her to an intense discussion of the present situation of Chiang Kai-shek's government and the way the Commies are using civil war as a cut-rate method of conquest all over the world. As she talked about the Communists her little face grew grim and I could see that what John Lindahl had said about her was true. She seemed a bit screwy about the Communists. To me, at that time, it seemed she had the germ of a good idea, but she was way overboard about it. I could have told you then, with assurance, that the big power-plays revolving around nuclear bomb warfare were the important things. I thought then the Russians were setting civil war bonfires all over the world—but that was diversionary. The big issue was atom war; that's how much I knew about it, in those days before Korea, Suez, Lebanon, Cuba, the Congo, Laos. I didn't know till later on in China why she was so vehement, or how right she was.

At the moment, I just went along with it, and kept her going and was interested. Interested, that is, not only by her views, but by the fascinating degree of concentration she was capable of. All of her small being could gather into a quick blowtorch flame of intensity. I think her manner interested me as much then as the substance, and I would admit that probably the maleness in me was intrigued with the thought that she might be an equally intense lover if the right man for her should come along. In my fantasy, of course, Carl Shoop was hopelessly inept for the role, and I, the outsider who had come so suddenly into her life, and for some reason seemed to attract her, would turn out to be the right man, at least for the time being. I know it was an irresponsible fantasy, inconsiderate of her, of her husband, and of my wife; but in my own justification I must say that the environment didn't encourage morality. The collapsing nation around me, the world's largest nation with a fifth of the world's population, was going down the drain. For the moment, it seemed like a time to gather rosebuds; or perhaps a tulip, clean and boldly formed, would be more like Martha.

"What they don't realize," she was saying, "is that compromise is impossible for a Communist on any permanent basis. To a Communist, compromise is only a temporary advantage while he plans his next aggressive move. We have to play their game and play it better. The only weapon against revolution is counter-revolution. You can never win a war on the defensive."

She was going on like this, and at the same time looking very incongruously feminine in her aquamarine sheath, when the bit of good and bad fortune hit us.

It was bad fortune at that moment, that night, but it was good for Martha and me in the longer run.

I saw it coming when I looked up and saw Carl weaving across the room toward us, his head down, his face dark as a storm cloud. As he came close, I could see that he was what the Malays call *amok*, or *mata-gelap*, meaning "blood-blind." Or in our Western idiom, he was just blind, he was tight as a tick, he had a fighting jab on, and it seemed that I was to be the object of the blood-blindness.

I guess I was close to Martha when he hove in sight, and my hand was resting on the back of her chair, not far from one of her beautiful shoulders. If I had been he, with such a lovely wife, I probably would have been just as jealous, and have done just about what he did— that is, if I were also drunk.

He came up and stood above us, weaving slightly. He fixed me with a baleful glare. I noticed that Martha's face grew pink again, and I read instantly in it that she expected a terrible social catastrophe to strike that moment. And Carl, as a drunk will do while he is waiting for his fuddled mind to give him the next signal, hesitated.

Then he spoke: "Whaddya tryna do m'wife?"

It was going to be one of those "whaddya" conversations that usually end up in an alley. You say to the drunk, "Whaddya mean, tryna do?" He says "Whaddya, wise guy or somethin'?" You counter with some clever line like "Whaddya talking about?" He gets aggressive with "Whaddya want a do—make somethin' of it?" And you go outside where the whole deal may end in recriminations or a broken nose— usually recriminations, with a little shoving around thrown in for good measure. The next morning, you and the other drunk struggle with hangovers (if not broken noses) and remorse.

Right now, I tried to brush it off as a joke. "Pull up a chair, Carl— and you can see what we're tryna do."

But he didn't go the right way. Instead of sitting down, he grew louder:

"I don't like wise guys, I say you're a wise guy."

"Okay, I'm a wise guy. Let's leave it that way and forget it." I was beginning to feel the back of my scalp prickle. And my restraint didn't seem to be paying any dividends; as usual with a drunk, it only seemed to make him more aggressive.

". . . Not gonna forget it. I don't like guys makin' a pass my wife. So she gives the come on—that don't make it all right, wise guy."

His voice was rising. I saw John Lindahl, across the room, turn his head in our direction. I did the wrong thing—although almost anything you do with a drunk on a fighting jag is wrong. I said:

"Not so loud, Carl. I can hear you fine."

That slight sarcasm was just what he needed to set him off.

"You're not gonna shut me up—wise guy. I'll tell the world." His voice was getting loud enough for that, but for the moment he couldn't think exactly what he was going to tell the world. He hesitated.

I got up, because by this time Martha was growing beet-red. "Carl," I said as low as I could, "if you want to talk like this, let's go out in the hall."

"Okay, let's go outside. I'm not chicken."

As I led the way, I saw by Martha's eyes that she felt some terrible tragedy was going to arrive. "Don't worry," I told her as softly as I could. "It'll work out all right." Her look of gratitude was worth all the trouble.

I wasn't so sure that it *would* work out well, though. I must confess that I thought about Carl's solid structure, his wide body, and wondered if he knew how to fight. He had the proper flat nose and square hands for a fighter.

But he too, loaded as he was, had his doubts at that moment. He probably was worrying if *I* knew how to fight. "I'll show you who's chicken," he muttered almost as if to reassure himself. Being almost sober, I noted his insecure tone and felt easier.

We got out of the room before Lindahl could get to us. Fortunately, nobody else seemed to have noticed. I closed the door and turned to face Mr. Belligerence. In the echoing hallway he was still less confident.

I watched him carefully because he might, just might throw a lucky punch.

"A'right," he said, looking around at the wall, "now we're gonna see—" I could see from his stance that he was not a trained fighter— "who's tough."

After that grateful look from Martha I had no intention of fisticuffs. I was just going to let him unwind a bit and try to calm him down, and I'd just try to dodge if he should let anything fly.

Nothing flew. He was still working up his courage when the door came open and John Lindahl burst out, followed by Martha. Both of them were sore. But Shoop hadn't yet sobered enough to realize their feelings. Maybe he didn't even check to see who they were. He seemed to feel that some sort of audience had arrived, and he was encouraged.

"Tryna chicken out, huh? I'll show yuh yuh can't mess around m' wife . . ."

That was as far as he got—about as far as most barroom brawls usually get. Lindahl stepped in and grabbed his arm, they struggled around clumsily.

And Martha's pretty little face, pale when she came out the door, got red all over again.

"Carl," she said, and the word was a blade of ice. "Stop it—or I'll never speak to you again."

There was enough menace in her tone and those precise words to knock off much of Carl's remaining drunkenness. He stopped struggling, dropped his arms, and blinked at her, almost visibly shriveling up in the blast of her cold stare.

"Tell John you're sorry for ruining his party," she ordered, her blue eyes as frigid as a November afternoon.

"Iceberg," he muttered. Then he turned to face Lindahl.

"Sorry," he rumbled. Lindahl was short of breath after the sudden exertion.

"Now—take me home," the small drill sergeant told her husband, before Lindahl could say anything. And she was marching Shoop toward the elevator, her face still pink to the edges.

We watched her push the elevator bell. Lindahl was opening his front door, and saying to me: "Come on, Scott, let's have a drink and forget it."

"Not your fault," I said as we walked back in the noise of the party. "I was the one that asked you to invite him."

He nodded. "Does he always do that?" I asked.

"Practically always."

"How does she stand it?"

"We sometimes wonder. Shoop certainly changed, since they were married. But most everybody does, in Shanghai. Usually, the decay sets in a lot faster."

"You mean, everybody just falls to pieces in Shanghai? Not as much as Shoop, I hope."

"Maybe not, but each in his own way. A guy like Shoop, in the MAG, starts it with booze. There's plenty of that. Then the graft. It's easy with all that foreign-aid money floating around. Then, if Martha freezes him . . ."

"Yeah, I can see she's pretty good at that."

". . . If she freezes him, there are dames for ten cents a dozen everywhere—White Russians, half castes, Chinese, and all hungry."

"Looks as if she hates him."

"She does. You see, she's got strong geo-political views—"

"I can see. What'd he do wrong, politically?"

"A guy in ordnance, in the MAG, can get rich quick. He's got 105-shells and machine gun ammo to sell to the Commies—and plenty of people on Chiang Kai-shek's side to help him do it."

"How come nobody writes about this stuff? How about you?"

Lindahl shrugged. "Like I said, everybody falls apart, in Shanghai. I'm not getting any pay-offs, but if I were on the ball I'd—" he left it unfinished.

"You'd what?"

"I'd get up to the front where everything is happening. But it's real hard to get there. And there's effective censorship, especially on anything political. It's easier, it's pleasant and easier, to stay here. What'll it be, scotch or bourbon?"

"Maybe I'd better have tomato juice."

And that was the end of a routine, stupid drinking brawl. But it was more than that. Maybe, all things considered, it was the most important conversational interchange I'd ever had, because of what it led to, for Martha and me.

3

THE NEXT AFTERNOON ABOUT ONE O'CLOCK SHE CALLED ME. Before she could announce that she was Martha Shoop, as soon as she said "Scott?" I knew it was she. I instantly knew that voice, so clear and high, somehow exactly as I had hoped it would sound on the telephone. Her voice was piping, like a boy's soprano, there was a faint quaver in it which endeared her to me, an unsureness far removed from the frigid tone with which she had addressed her husband on the night before.

"Hello, Martha. How do you feel today?"

"You recognized me!" She was pleased, for a moment, then back to being earnest, serious. "Scott: I called to apologize for last night. I'm sorry about—"

"Forget it, Martha. Those things just happen." I was feeling big-hearted, simply because the girl had called *me*. The reason was beside the point. "I'm sorry that *you* had to get caught in something like that," I went on, feeling that she didn't know what to say next.

She *didn't* know what to say. I realized with a jolt of pleasure: She simply wants to hang on. It crossed my mind that probably she wasn't calling from her home, or maybe Carl had gone on a trip.

I wasn't doing as I'd have others do unto me, I wasn't being considerate of Carl, but I didn't want her to leave the phone, to slip away from me. As early as this in our attachment, some automatic machinery seemed to supply me with all the answers, all the inventions, all the last minute tricks I needed to hold her and keep her interested and keep us together, however unlikely it seemed that our acquaintance could go on.

Now the invention came, maybe a bit lame for the moment, but at least it was functional, it kept her on the wire, and if it hadn't rushed forward in my mind I might never have seen her again. I might have gone up into the back country of China and drifted away from the remembrance of her. Anyhow, there was the idea, supplied by the machine that drove me, and it held on to her:

"Oh, Martha—I'm glad you called. I've been wanting to ask you about—about those pictures you made during the riot the other day. I do think they might be good for the story I'll write on China, for *Beacon*,"

It wasn't true, I was lying as the automatic mechanism told me to, but it didn't matter. As a matter of fact, the story I'd been working toward was up in the back country, not Shanghai. For three days now, I'd been seeing the public relations people at the Kuomintang Press Headquarters and trying to set up a trip to a town which had been in Communist hands and now was recaptured by the Kuomintang troops. I had told them that *Beacon* had no political interest, that I was interested in adventure stories, but that maybe if I could reach a town that had been fought over hard, I might get some stories about the heroic devotion of the Chinese Nationalist (KMT) soldiers. It was a canny idea. I could hear their minds clicking as they saw how this might help to win them sympathy, and further funds, in the U.S. And I was honest: I was interested in an adventure story—something to write off some of the red ink in my account with *Beacon* magazine.

The two towns I'd been hearing about were Suchow, in northern Shantung, and Djin-zuh, way out in Mongolia beyond the Great Wall. Both had been steamrollered by the civil war. Both were far removed from Shanghai or Chiang's capital, Nanking, or from the student riots on the Bund or the big-city strategy of the Communists. But I had forgotten all this on the phone with Martha, and mentioned her pictures of the riots almost without thinking, and I was glad.

"Maybe they're not what you need," she was saying humbly, and at that moment I felt a small shock that seemed like remorse, and immediately justified myself with this thought: who can tell, maybe I *can* work them in somehow or other, and I knew I was lying.

"Well, please let me see them and decide for myself," I heard my voice saying.

"All right," she said. She stopped, and I could almost hear her gathering her breath for the plunge: "When?"

It caught me flat out, but the automaton in me answered before I knew it. "Have you had lunch yet?" I asked her. "I haven't— and we could combine business and pleasure, look at the pictures over the luncheon table at the Cathay, or any place you like." I talked fast, hoping, maybe even knowing that the rush of words would help to convince her; and assuming immediately that her husband was not in town today.

As soon as she had said yes, and we had fixed a time when I would meet her in the lobby of the Cathay, I felt conscience knocking hard at my inner doors. As I picked out an expensive tie, and matched it carefully with my socks, and laid out my best Hong Kong suit,

I cussed myself out for a snako-in-the-grasso, and thought that if another man did this and Martha were married to me, I'd want to beat him to death, and maybe her too. But that would be in West Newton, Mass., or Grand Forks, Iowa—not in Shanghai in civil war. But she had been so quick to agree, she had insisted on coming down to meet me at the hotel rather than being picked up at Broadway Mansions. And she had, I thought, pointedly mentioned that her husband had gone to Nanking. The electric charge of thinking that I would be seeing her alone, and I must admit, fancying that she wanted to be alone with me, submerged the feelings of remorse. This problem, the husband, and my feelings of guilt I could contend with later. I couldn't deny that her readiness—whatever the reason— was giving me at least a 50,000 kilowatt jolt, the thrill of the hunt. The wonderful charge of adventure, the reaching out for a new and dangerous world, was very much with me.

I met her at one o'clock in the lobby. She wore a white silk blouse and a big bright dirndl, and leather sandals, and her smile was as bright as I had remembered it. Now, though, in the dim Cathay lobby, when I came close to her, I saw that she had felt something like the swift shocks of remorse I knew fleetingly. I guessed that in the darkness of the Cathay, the meeting with a strange man seemed to her too like an assignation. There was high tension, a fragility and nervousness about her smile, then and there.

But in the high dining room with the tall windows, and with food to cheer us, our meeting seemed less strained. Especially when she took the pictures out of a briefcase and we began to go over them.

"Very nice," I told her, and the words of praise visibly cheered her. Really they were fair, a couple were well enough composed to be professionally marketable.

But now I gulped down any critical comment I could have made, and told her I thought I could use some of the pix in *Beacon*. I made this much of a concession to honesty: I said that the main story I planned to do in China was probably to be somewhere out in the hinterland; but, I said, the pix that showed the rioting students could probably be tied into the overall story. She believed it, and it could have been true. At least it kept her with me, and her spirits up.

By the time we were finishing the dried-up sole and boiled potato and hard roll and claret, in the British style of the hotel, she was telling me about herself. She asked me about myself, too. I told her a little about World War II and me. But strangely enough, I really wanted to know about her, especially about something she had mentioned, that she had spent a summer in Europe, laboring in a student work camp. It was part of an exchange scholarship deal. I might have guessed something similar because of her humility, her alertness, her durability during times of stress like the mob action on the Bund. She talked about living on bread and potato soup, how hungry she had been, how it was funny now, but not at all comic then.

She slid into how she happened to be in Shanghai: she had come as a *Time-Life* researcher then named Martha Dienst, after a part-time job in the Boston office. She had wanted to travel, anywhere. She was an adventurer, a rare thing in women. She had a restlessness, she wanted to get away from becoming a homebody in Pennsylvania, from getting married and not seeing anything of the world. After college, she could have taught phys. ed. at Oil City, but she could see herself withering away there. She was an adventuress by nature—I didn't know her well enough to know that she was serious when she said it, that she was not just in a mood today. I didn't know. But if she wanted to play Brünnehilde, I would willingly try Siegfried, insufficient as I might be for the part.

We hadn't yet got to her marriage. I wondered if she could be purposely avoiding the subject, and if she wanted to avoid it, that was fine with me. Strangely enough, she hadn't yet touched one of her favorite topics: Communists. I guess, when I reconstruct the situation, that she wanted to be frivolous this day, probably because she was trying to get away from the memory of Carl. And my instinctive automatic pilot, with its normally close gearing to sex and love life, kept me on the beam when she mentioned by chance that swimming was probably her favorite sport. My instinct pounced on the item.

"Well, how about it?" I asked her.

"How about what?"

I knew I had her a little off balance. "It happens that swimming is my favorite sport too. So why don't we?"

"You mean, go swimming?"

"Exactly." I looked at my watch. "It's only about two o'clock—time enough." I bore down on the idea. "It's a hot day, why shouldn't we? There must be a beach around here somewhere."

She seemed a little defensive. "I don't know of any beach."

At this point, I would have wavered, maybe dropped the whole idea. But fortunately, the same compulsive current must have sparked, however slightly, in her. Because she said tentatively:

"There's the Athletic Club pool across the street from Broadway Mansions. Some of the Army people go there."

That little bit of support was enough to keep me going. I didn't like the idea of some steamy indoor pool that smelled of chlorine; and I didn't think she'd want to be seen swimming in this Army hangout with a strange man when her husband was away.

Besides, I had an urge, and suddenly it was a driving urge, to get her out to a sunny, windy—and of course unoccupied—beach, where we could run across the hard-packed sand and battle wild breakers. The imagining was vivid; it would be exactly the right thing to do with Brünnehilde. My imagination simplified everything: the civil war fell away, I omitted the soldiers, the pillboxes, the barbed wire I might have known would be there. I saw Brünnehilde beside me, beautiful, nude, big breasted, running over the beach, her hand in mine. Or, if she was Delacroix's Liberty stripped to the waist, she of beautifully-formed, smooth bosoms, she of delicately shaped long neck and shoulders and Grecian profile, there were no people she was leading in a charge, she was running alone with me. If she was short of breath it was because she was excited, being with me alone on the sand, and there would be more excitement, among the sand dunes I would lay her down laughing and excited, strip off her remaining clothes and find her body perfect, smooth, and of course, willing. I had the male facility for conjuring up uncomplicated sex. It was easy. My automatic monitor drove me to it.

It also supplied the correct words to take advantage of her indecision, I think. Anyhow, they came out this way:

"I know somebody who knows where a perfect beach is—the best." I didn't know, but it suddenly popped into my head that Ling, the little cab driver who had been so faithful during the day of the riot, might have the information.

"I didn't know there was one around Shanghai," she was saying. And I wondered if I caught a note of anxiety in her voice.

"But there is," I told her. "It's a surprise. I'll have to go and make some arrangements."

I got up in a hurry and told her, "Wait—I'll be back in a couple of minutes and it'll be all arranged." As I left the table and hurried to the elevator I was glad to see that she drained her wine glass; she would need her courage, real or synthetic, in the next hour or so.

I got to the lobby fourteen floors below and had the hall porter get in touch with Ling. Fortunately Ling was available, and between him and the hall porter I located a beach which might or might not be a pleasant surprise.

It was on Hangchow Bay, said Ling, to the south of Shanghai, and it could be reached by an old truck route. Ling and the porter were in agreement on these details. They mentioned the same town as being near the beach, and Ling said he had driven the road during his days in the Chinese army. However, Ling said it was white sand, and the porter thought it was rocky. Such was the usual state of geographical information in China.

Within a half hour, I had run to my room to change to bathing trunks with slacks and sport shirt over them; we had swung by Broadway Mansions and I waited in the cab while she made the necessary change.

I remember sitting back in the cab so as not to be too visible to the American passers-by, and I remember too my feeling of unbelief that all this could have happened so fast. I remember too the feeling that I was doing something wrong and enjoyed the wrongdoing, and worrying that something unforeseen might happen, like, say, the sudden appearance of Carl Shoop on the sidewalk beside the car, or maybe a sudden change of heart on Martha's side as she went to the apartment to put on her suit and had a little time to think amid reminders that she was, after all, married.

But she came back with a small airline bag in her hand and got into the car without any excuses or change of mind. And I noticed the same set look about her small jaw and pretty mouth which I had seen before in my brief acquaintanceship. I would have guessed that she had thought the trip over carefully when she was changing, and that she had set her mind and her face to go through with it. And this time, I had no qualms of conscience; it all seemed too good to be spoiled.

4

LING PILOTED OUR RATTLETRAP CAB THROUGH THE TANGLE of streets that was the old Chinese city within Shanghai, we traversed acre after acre of dusty shantytown, and I worried about the girl.

She had grown remarkably silent, and I wanted very much to ask her what she was thinking. But I knew nothing could be more deadly to a new liaison, or any kind of liaison with a female, than this kind of question. Females in my experience either didn't think, or else they resented a man's prying into their thoughts.

But her long silence did worry me. Was she getting cold feet? Would she in a moment tell me that we'd better go on back, that this expedition was silly?

And I had another major worry, too: would it be possible after all, to get to a beach? It could be that the beaches in the Shanghai area would all be mined, posted with machine guns and staked out with barbed wire. Our happy outing could end without getting near the water.

Suddenly she gave me a clue to the current crossing her mind—and it wasn't any misgiving about our outing.

"The civil war!" she was saying, as if it were an indictment. I saw we were passing through a sprawling refugee camp—a few sheds made of wet scrap boards and tarpaper, matshed huts lower than a man's waist, a dense ant-colony of coolies in black ragged clothes spread around a few cooking fires. The camp stretched across an open field right up to a spur of railroad tracks and a decrepit station building. Some of the families were sleeping across the railroad ties, I suppose because the tics were drier than the ground. When a train came, the black ants would scatter quickly.

"The bastards!" she was saying, her small face set hard. "The Communist bastards! And the bastardly racketeers on our side who help them! They don't care about misery and suffering and death. They'll do anything to get what they want.

"That's the Communist strategy: drive the peasants into the cities so they'll be a burden for the Chiang Kai-shek government. Six million people in Shanghai, it's swollen to twice its size."

I could see that I was in the presence of a small storm, and I wanted to be agreeable. I tried a palliating tone. "But haven't the Chinese always had suffering and death for their birthright? If it weren't the Communists, wouldn't it be some war lord or other?"

Now she really flamed: "That's no reason for it to keep on. This is the twentieth century—we're supposed to be leading them out of the Middle Ages, not shoving them deeper in the mud. But nobody will write the truth. Our partners—Chiang and the KMT—are gangsters. We back them because they oppose the Communists, that's all that's required—we back anybody in the world who will keep the status quo—gangsters, racketeers, corrupt nobility, reactionaries."

I said that was true. I'd seen racketeers and kings on our side all over the world—Indo-China, Dutch East Indies, Malaya, the Middle East. "But," I said, "the racketeers and kings are better than the Communists."

"That's not the issue! When I see the fat KMT politicians riding along the Bund in their black Cadillacs, I know they're getting fat from selling American relief rice on the black market. The rice is on the black market and these people who are supposed to have it free haven't got a prayer of raising the money to buy it.

"So every night they die of starvation on the streets, the police truck comes around in the morning and picks up the bodies, and our people, who should be watching what happens to our rice, sit around Broadway Mansions and get drunk."

It was a furious, unfeminine speech, and her eyes snapped with November chill as she said it. And I was relieved: I had thought that maybe it was something really important, like our projected afternoon's love affair, that had been bothering her.

Our love affair was related, I was sure: Probably husband Carl Shoop's drinking, his own involvement in the indifference and corruption, his Chiang Kai-shek gravy train—maybe these were the things behind her fury.

By the time we hit Lung Wha road, and the bumps began to grow more shattering, she simmered down. I asked her gently about her marriage, how she happened to meet and marry Carl Shoop. People have always told me I am a good listener, and whether or not that is a compliment, in this case listening came easily. It was easy to listen, and have an excuse for watching the way she held that clean chin above the curving neck, that slightly querulous smile that came so easily and so dazzlingly. I saw the slight fleck of a beauty spot that set off a perfectly curved nostril, the regular, smooth, even brow that made her seem calm even in the midst of agitation. Of course, I also wondered what the figure would be like.

Under the dirndl and the white silk blouse, the lineaments of the figure seemed trim, promising. The most pleasant item was that later this day we would get to bathing suits, or better, no bathing suits at all, if this swimming ever did come to pass.

"Carl was a good athlete, once." We were reaching the beginning of a rutted, muddy truck road. "You wouldn't have recognized him, if you'd seen him then. He was fit—really fighting fit. And he believed in what he was doing, when he first came here.

"We used to play tennis, and he worked hard all the time. But then the drinking—" She let it go. Of course, she didn't know what I had already discovered about her husband.

"You can't blame a guy for drinking a little bit."

"No," she bit her lip, as if she were holding back some resurgence of temper. Then some of it, a trickle, came out: "We all have our marital problems—I think—maybe I expect too much of the people I know, people that I've—cared for." Her face was tense again. I was afraid she would start to sob. For a moment, the libido slipped away; I wanted to help her—momentarily, anyhow.

"My own marriage," I started, thinking it might get her off that frightful concentration in the blues. "My own marriage—I should say it another way—you fall in love with one person, you find yourself married to another person. He or she has changed."

The blues seemed to be deepening, instead of paling. "Are all marriages unhappy? Surely, they can't all be that unhappy! Is everything failing apart, everywhere? Doesn't anybody care about anything, anywhere? Isn't there anything more than selfishness, money, a racket, pleasure? Is that all people live for?"

The conversation had taken a sinister turn, for my amorous ambitions of that afternoon.

She was plunging on. "No wonder we're losing this war! This war—and the wars we are involved in all over the world."

She stopped, looked at me with suddenly calm, humble eyes. "Forgive me—it's been over a year that I've been trying, trying everything to make him do what a man should—fight for what he believes. I've been trying to make him believe. Perhaps too hard. Perhaps I've tried much too hard to make him—what I would want to be if I were a man." She smiled her quick, bright smile. "I apologize for being so personal."

I was growing very uneasy, and she could sense it, though I was glad she didn't know why. I was sorry for her, as I am sorry for any woman in trouble. But mainly I was uneasy because I could see a good, sensuous afternoon sliding away from me. I was helpless, as in a dream—every word of hers seemed to turn shame on me. I felt guilty of being after some of the selfish pleasure that so distressed her in the world. Futhermore, I was beginning to wonder if this fascinatingly trim Miss Marzipan was going to be utterly unmanageable. Maybe such earnestness, such fantastic concentration and such withering scorn of indulgence would make her impossible. Maybe she was a real iceberg and this was the thing that drove Carl Shoop to whatever lengths he had been driven to. I almost suggested that we give up our trip for today for some quick reason-like the road being too rough.

But suddenly, she seemed to have changed. Suddenly, all her internal torments were shut off. "We'll have a good time—a good swim—that water will feel wonderful." The sunbeam smile was back, all over her face. I felt sensuous fires lighting inside me again, with a sudden rumble, like a furnace. The promise was back there.

I said yes, you shouldn't be too serious, you'd get hump-backed carrying all the world's ills on your shoulders. "You have to get some fun out of life."

"Yes, I must remember that," she said, her head arching back, the wind blowing the light-gold hair. There was a strange, sudden determination in the arch of her chin, her smile was perhaps too fixed and too bright. "We must have fun—we will have fun, like Carl and everyone else, isn't that the main thing?"

I said yes, that was the main thing. Right then, I didn't know what had happened to give her the sudden determination—but I was going to take advantage of it.

The girl was shifting adroitly to questions about me. She was good at questioning, she would have been a good newspaperwoman.

Yes, I told her the stuff about my correspondent background that I thought would be most romantic to her. Carefully omitted was my marriage, the thing crossing my mind persistently, silently; how I too had tried everything to make Lois again into the woman I had first married, or the woman I thought I had married. How all of my attempts seemed to drive her deeper into drink and despair. How she had once been so devastatingly, so poignantly feminine—how she had fallen all apart despite the best specialists in alcoholism, every treatment there was—everything except what I should have tried as treatment: staying home and making like a nine-to-five husband with a family. But I had to go, I had to keep on going— and in my defense, there were some things, big, dark things, wrong with that home life, that family life, as there were with the Shoops at home.

But while the dark currents ran through the back of my mind, I was busy at the front trying to be engaging—and trying, I must confess, to convey how many dangers I had passed in various wars. In

World War II, and after it in the cycle of bush wars, like Malaya, India, Burma, that made such good reading for the men's magazines. I told her about my honorable, decorative, ornamental scars, collected in World War II and in Indo China, and the slight one in Indonesia. I made it clear that the wounds were honorable, not just the results of jeep accidents or falling downstairs during a bombing.

Then we were running into the first check points, squat brown pillboxes like small silos half buried in the earth, with little evil slits of eyes looking at us. The first appeared to be unmanned. But the third had a barricade of rusty wire around it, and I thought I saw a gun barrel in one of the high slits. So did she.

"I see a machine gun in one of those holes," she said. She had sharp as well as beautiful eyes.

"Slow. Slow down, Ling," I told him.

"Yes, mastah." He really didn't have to be reminded. He knew how quickly you could get hurt around soldiers with guns.

As we slowed, two soldiers in green cotton uniforms, wearing sneakers and wrap-around puttees, and green visored caps, popped out of the pillbox and came through a gap in the wire.

They carried rifles with shiny fixed bayonets, and I noticed something inconsequential, as one usually does in a time of stress: their sneakers were blue. They came charging toward us with bayonets lowered.

I got out of the car in a hurry, my KMT press credentials in my hand, and I remembered the thought flashed across my mind that this was a crazy expedition. I might get the girl knocked off as well as my worthless self, just because of an idle sex drive to take her to a beach.

I stuck out my KMT folder toward the extended bayonet of the leading soldier. I saw his face change as he saw the white sunburst stamp of the Chiang government on the folder. The ferocity ebbed out of his features, and he said something staccato to his buddy. The other soldier stopped, and then the leader went ahead to the car and looked in the back where Martha sat.

She had the signals straight. I saw her give something to the soldier through the open window; her passport. The soldier looked at the picture and her face, then handed it back. He asked Ling a question, Ling answered as nervously as an overspeeded gyro, and the soldier waved us on.

Inside the car, I asked Martha: "Do you still want to go on with this?" She looked grim, but she said:

"More than ever." I thought nothing short of a major offensive by the Commies would dent her determination, or maybe, to go on, I thought, a major Communist offensive would make her determination completely unshakable.

From then we had a series of check points to pass—and the road deteriorated until it was barely a donkey track. Pretty soon we had a pillbox routine figured: I was a correspondent, Martha was my photographer, we were on official business. One set of credentials seemed to do; Martha's passport, with the gold lettering and the important-looking stamp, identified her well enough.

If we had encountered any literate Chinese, the story might have been different. If by any chance we had run against one of the propaganda officers assigned to the Nationalist regiments, we would probably have been sent packing to Shanghai. But to the soldier farm boys we saw, the KMT seal was enough. They didn't know it was taboo to allow correspondents in delicate areas like fortifications without suitable KMT escorts.

The trip became a kick, a game as we met the challenge of the successive pillboxes. Once we were nearly drilled when we misunderstood the arm signal of a soldier. We thought he was waving us on, then I looked in the rear-view mirror and saw that he had a tommy gun leveled in our direction. But we stopped in time. The minute the danger had passed, it became a big joke to Martha and me; you would have thought we were drunk, the way we laughed as the jolting road grew more impossible and the road blocks more dangerous. Ling laughed too, not knowing exactly what was so funny. Poor fellow, he would have the job of repairing the old junk of a car, if there was anything left after this trip.

At last, a little after four, we could see a row of tall locust trees ahead, and beyond them the gray lens of a body of water.

"Heah come Hangchow Bay, mastah," Ling announced triumphantly, and as we wheeled through the trees we saw something that was not so funny.

Ahead of us lay a pale white beach, with small dark waves lapping it. And at the far end of the beach, where it curved into a rocky point, a nest of barbed wire and a big pillbox, maybe thirty feet across. Between the wire and the pillbox, three soldiers in green stood watching us silently. Barbed wire had been strung from iron stakes along the far half of the beach, and I would have wagered that at least that part of the sand was mined.

Ling had the same thought as he brought the car to a stop beside the beach. He turned a worried face in my direction and tried to communicate what was probably the most elaborate construction he had tried in English.

"Mastah," he said, grabbing hold of an imaginary machine gun butt. "Lat-tatt-tatt! Sol-yer shootum Mastah." He waved wildly in the direction of the pillbox. He pointed to himself, "Ling—go speak sol-yer. Tell um you—" he paused for the word, it didn't come and he thrashed his arms madly to illustrate the act of swimming. "Ling tellum, okay?"

Martha and I were already smiling, but he was a long way from finishing. He pointed to the beach, and went through the act of digging holes, and putting anti-personnel mines underground, and covering up same. Then he indicated an explosion, by a sunburst movement of his arms: "Pow! Pow!" he declaimed, no doubt remembering the verbiage from an American comic-book inherited from a GI. *"Di-lay-ee!"* he yelled, using the Mandarin word which I later came to know meant "mine." It literally translates "land thunder" in the language. *"Di-lay-ee!* Pow! Pow!" he repeated, "Mastah Missy pow!" It was so ludicrous that even in the middle of his concentration he began to grin, and then we couldn't hold on any longer, we started to laugh.

But he wasn't finished yet. He held up a finger for attention and ploughed on. Now he was mimicking swimming motions again, and he kept saying *"Tsuan! Tsuan!"* and now he was whirling one upright finger round and round as if trying to indicate a phonograph turntable in motion. Then the swimming charade again, and finally an English word came to him in the flash of an idea: "Boah! Boah!" he shouted.

Martha had been studying him and now it came to her too. "Bore! The Bore! He's talking about a current in Hangchow Bay—something like a strong tide."

Ling was delighted. His acting and linguistic talents had scored. "Yes, Missy," he said, waving his hands in triumph. "Tide!"

There was still more to communicate: "Tide! Fast!" he said, going back to his swimming motions—now desperate swimming strokes culminating in a frantic and unsuccessful effort to make headway against the current.

We both burst out laughing, because Ling's acting was so vivid; and also because this was one of those precious moments in life when there is so much danger and trouble that everything is funny. It was a Chinese moment, funny, close to hysteria, and embarrassment, as a Chinese coolie will laugh when he sees a man drowning—or laugh when he is straining his guts under an impossible load.

Maybe in retrospect it is more comic than it was at that moment. I remember that while I was laughing, I was also watching the soldiers who were eyeing us from the emplacement. Now there were four of them. One had come up from the pillbox, and I could see them talking, one of them pointing in our direction. I made a resolve that moment that Ling and I should walk over to them, and while he interpreted, explain that we were going to take a swim, provided the whole project hadn't by this time become too ludicrous to try.

"Do you still want to swim?" I asked Martha, stopping my laughter. Just then the sun came out brightly, and we both looked up.

"Certainly," she said, still smiling. "I wouldn't stop now if they dropped the A-bomb." Now that we were out this far on a limb, she was going through with it if it killed her. It thrilled me to hear her say that. I had a quick, powerful feeling of pride in her.

But all I told her was: "Martha, I'm going over to talk to the soldier on that post, so we won't get shot for Communist frogmen."

She nodded. "Okay, I'll stay here and get ready."

I told Ling: "Ling, you follow me—savvy? We talk-talk soldiers, okay."

He smiled and started with me, but the smile was a nervous one. "Lookout sol-yer don' shootum," he warned. "Ling sol-yer one time, shootum up fast." He indicated the scar on his cheek. I looked at the machine gun nest and saw that two of the men in apple green held bayoneted rifles at the ready. But I knew I had to keep walking toward them and standing straight, meanwhile holding out my KMT credentials.

We fixed it up. Ling was a marvel as interpreter; though it couldn't be said that he spoke English, he nevertheless understood exactly what our problem was and passed it on in acceptable Chinese. The non-com in charge even pointed out where the mines were—and indicated that the *tsuan* shouldn't be too much of a problem right here and now. He was a smiling fellow, once his military mien had been undercut, and he grinned with two stainless steel teeth right in the middle of his mouth as he promised "No lat-tatt-tatt."

And so, in ten minutes, Martha and I, in bathing suits, were walking hand in hand down the cold sand, toward the gray water. And I was feeling warm, because I could see that she *did* have the figure I had hoped for.

5

FOR THE MOMENT, THE MACHINE-GUN NEST, THE BARBED wire and the mines, and the road blocks we would have to pass on the road back to Shanghai, the *tsuan* and the Communists, all were shoved out of my thoughts. Shoved, that is, by the touch of her hand in mine and the sight of her trim, athletic body in the light-blue two-piece suit.

In the sudden bright sun between clouds, her body was as much just right as I could have imagined it: taut, athletic dolphin flesh, her legs firm and muscular, filling the rim of her trunks fore, aft and side. The small shoulders even more glorious than in the evening gown, smooth and flawless in the sun and the more beautiful because in the bathing suit they seemed functional.

Her arms, like the long neck and narrow shoulders, were feminine, but firmness filled the contours—and the bare midriff as taut as shark-muscle in the sea. Now her flesh blushed pink with the afternoon breeze and the exertion of running.

We reached the water, the coldness shocked our feet and she screeched once, but we kept going, her hand holding mine tighter.

I remember the muddy bottom under our feet, the gut-sucking impact of the water as we dived in, the shock of the cold running from the hair roots down to our knees, and the water suddenly a green hood around our faces after it had looked so gray from the beach.

Then we were swimming, the water streaking pleasantly over our bodies and in a few seconds feeling warmer. I looked over at her and saw that swimming *was* one of her good sports. I had expected it. She moved with barely a ripple, arms stroking relaxed and easy, a handsome naiad.

Beyond her, at the pillbox on the point of land, I saw three of the green-uniformed soldiers still watching, the tallest of them waving his arm. That would be the non-com with the stainless-steel teeth.

I waved back and we kept swimming, eighty, a hundred yards out. Then she had to stop, she flipped over on her back and floated, panting for air.

"I'm—out of condition," she gasped.

"I wouldn't say so," I told her. "Compared to most people, you're Bob Mathias."

"Better make it Babe Didrikson, the right sex anyhow," she said between breaths.

"If I hadn't been training at the Singapore Swimming Club and Repulse Bay you'd have pooped me out."

"Most of the Broadway Mansions people—are members of the anti-exercise league," she breathed. "It's good if somebody like you comes along."

"I'm glad I'm good for something," I said.

She studied me, wondering if I was serious. Partly, I was. Then I looked at the shore, and got a shock. The point of land with the pillbox was even with us, we must have drifted an eighth of a mile, and the *tsuan* must be working at this hour with top efficiency.

She noticed it too, at the same time, and alarm came into her eyes.

"The Bore!" she said. "It's taking us!"

I felt the same concern she did, but I didn't want her to see this. By now, the point of land had passed us, and another shore lay beside us, possibly a quarter-mile away. That one, too, might be mined.

We could have tried to swim back to the point of land and the pillbox, but the current was too fast for that. I saw a good alternative: ahead of us, a low-lying island, about as big as a football field, overgrown with scraggy bushes.

"Don't get scared," I told her. "We can haul out on that island and rest up. Sometime the tide'll have to go the other way."

"I'm not scared," she said, her mouth taking on that determined look again. "But what if it gets dark before the tide turns?"

She had a good point, but it was growing a little late to attempt anything else except the island. "Let's try it."

She nodded as if it were an order. But she probably couldn't have disobeyed it if she had wanted to, because in that swift current we were practically on top of the island in three minutes. We had to swim a little to hit the landward end, then we could touch bottom and we were wading in, the current rushing past our legs and making it hard for us to keep our footing. The bottom here was a sandbar, firm and pleasant to the flesh. The water ran clear, we could see our feet through it.

I helped her onto the beach, and we climbed to the top where the bushes began. I watched the sand carefully for the small prongs of anti-personnel mines. None visible.

It was cold in the wind, not much heat in the sun. Goose-flesh marked her arms, in the coldness her face seemed smaller. She tried to set her jaws together, but her teeth began to rattle, and she looked like a small helpless animal with the ague. The streamlined Brünnehilde body was still there, more attractive than ever with the sheen of water on the flesh, her gamin curls soaked with water but the blondness shining through in the pale afternoon sun, and I might have noticed that her figure was full enough in the wet suit. But instead I felt solicitous, as if she were a child in my care.

The island at this point was quite narrow. Beyond the bushes another beach declined to the water, and this strip of sand was marked with large black boulders. The biggest of them sat solemnly like an immobilized heavy tank.

I took her to it, thinking that it would give us shelter from the wind, and it did. We climbed over the barnacles and found ourselves in a calm pocket, a rock-walled patio. In the lee of the rock the air was almost still.

But her chin still trembled with the cold.

"You'll warm up in a minute," I told her.

"S-sure I will."

Then, without saying anything, I put my arm around her and she came to me. I held her close.

"I'll make you warmer," I said stupidly enough. But any inanity would have done. It had happened, that was all that mattered. She put her arm around my bare waist, I felt the warmth of our bodies merging, the two chilled negative entities somehow adding up to a positive new warmth.

She looked up at me and I saw something I hadn't noticed before: there were glints of gold in her blue eyes. In the sunlight the gold flecks glowed like fire. They gave her eyes boldness, an animal vitality.

Her lips were smooth and perfect, an architectural, flawless curve. An electric current flashed through my mind: she wants to. The jolt of energy shot into my arms and legs.

The energy slid into the oblivion of kissing her, the smoothness of her lips and the electricity were one encompassing emotion, going on and on, warmth spreading across my back muscles and chest. My body weighed a ton of warmth. The kiss went deeper and deeper, penetrating the layers of feeling, like flower petals, each layer more sensitive than the last.

Then the blindness stopped, I was looking again into the gold-flecked eyes, seeing the tiny beauty mark on one curved nostril, the lips wide and smooth, the arch of the throat.

"I'm sorry," I said.

She said nothing, but there was a defiant glint in her eyes that said no apology was necessary. I didn't question it, I was glad enough that it was there.

I kissed her again floating through the endless layers, infinite layers of sensitivity, the ascending stairway without an end, the floating in space upside down and in every direction without an attitude except awareness of the fire and the desirable agony ever increasing. It was right and wrong, the blindness and a flash of light at once, hard and soft, rough and smooth in one, reticences and assertions, guilt and virtue, defeat and victory, but I knew that it should go on.

I held her flower-face between my hands and I couldn't read her eyes. I looked away. Across the gray sheet of water a high-sterned fishing junk moved, a couple of miles out to sea. The murmur of the waves on our beach seemed to isolate us from the sea, from the machine gun nest and the mines, the Communists and the mess in China, from my wife and Martha's husband, from the world.

Brazenness was in her fire-flecked eyes and her lips. But whatever the genesis of the mood might be, the mood itself was what counted.

There was a strange moment's questioning in my mind. I was surprised that I hesitated at all. But the bigger part of me had no doubt about what to do. I thought: this is Shanghai, this is a world falling apart—so why worry, why not enjoy it?

I touched her thigh, the tense, cool dolphin flesh. In the sun the water on her body had dried, the fine body hair on her skin was a pale gold sheen like ripening wheat.

"You want to?"

"Yes." She added: "It—will be the first time since I was married. But he does—everybody does—so I will."

I looked away from her. Here it is, I thought. My last scrap of conscience struggling with the sex machine: she is ready, so are you. Here is the holy grail your maleness has been driving you toward, so irresistibly and automatically. Take it. Could it be you are feeling sorry for her?

But really, there was nothing to lose. She was ready, all ready. Conscience may be strong, but not that strong—at least, not mine, not then. "I want it now." But just then I heard the damned insistent sound: the put-put-put of an engine, close by. It grew louder.

We sat up, and that second a gray open skiff, flying the white sunburst of the Nationalist government or her bow, edged round the island. Three sailors in white leggings and round hats stood in the cockpit: also a soldier in green. I thought I recognized the tall figure of the non-com with the stainless-steel teeth.

He waved frantically, and the boat headed straight for the beach. It ground up on the sand, and the soldier jumped off, grinning. He shouted out some unintelligible Chinese words, but his pantomime was clear: back at the pillbox, they had worried about us, the *tsuan* had been stronger than they had thought, they had called the patrol boat. He was joyous about the whole deal.

I helped her climb the side of the boat, feeling naked for both of us—and glad, immensely glad, that we hadn't been caught by the boat a few minutes later. It was bad enough for her to be in the boat in a bathing suit. I sat her on the stern and blocked the peeping eyes of the Chinese with my back, shielding her.

As we chugged in toward the shore, she looked up at me gratefully. The blue eyes were bluer, the flecks of gold seemed less bright. She put her small square hand on mine.

I looked around at the grinning death's heads of two of the sailors and the steel-tooth type, lined up, staring at us. The third sailor fortunately had to steer the boat. One of the sailors had picked up a gun and held it across his chest, a symbol of power and superiority over the two nearly-naked human beings: our fragile interior relationship steamrollered by their easy violence.

"Don't let it get you," I told her, turning back to shield her.

"Not if you're with me."

I knew the peeping, saturnine eyes were boring into my back and whatever of her anatomy they could see around me. I felt ashamed for her—though they were the obscene ones, not we.

"You can't get away from the lousy war," I said.

"I think I was trying. I wanted to try."

I held her hand while the boat curved around the point of land, past the pillbox and toward the iron festoons of barbed wire on the beach.

"Don't give up yet," I said. "I have an idea—Hong Kong." I wasn't going to go into it then, but those smooth shoulders, the curve of that breast, the wet bra clinging to it, the taught dolphin flesh of those thighs—all these had set my furnaces going again, and I could not give it up. "I'll tell you about it later." She didn't ask me, then, but it was a workable plan—take her to Hong Kong or some place away from the war. To hell with the story: I could do it later on.

6

GOING THROUGH THE CHECKPOINTS WASN'T SO TOUGH ON the way back. Most of the same soldiers still stood guard, they remembered us. And it was light enough.

But we still had to stop at every pillbox. It taxed our nerves. A trigger-happy sentry could have finished us off. I did my share of deep-knee bends popping out of the car to be identified. There wasn't much chance to talk.

Then we were through the pillbox belt, the tension lifted, except the muscular tension needed to keep an even seat in that bounding car. And we could talk.

"I'm glad you hesitated, a moment, back there," she said.

"I'm not happy about it," I said, and meant it. Now I was sorry, full of second thoughts: I had bungled all the arrangements, I had missed a chance to sleep with a living Brünnehilde. She had been in my hotel and I hadn't even taken her to my room where it would probably have been easy then. And now, maybe, my chances were dead. Her mood of abandon, whatever temporal reasons had caused it, seemed to be gone, and my mind's eye saw smooth, full hips, curving breast. And the pink tips. Would they be pink, coral or pale purple? I might never know.

"Why did you wait those few seconds?" she asked frankly.

"I don't know—off my rocker, I guess."

"I think you were thinking of me."

I couldn't say anything.

"It reminds me that there are nice people in the world."

"Right now I'm not so happy that I'm nice, if I am."

"I know what you mean."

I surprised myself again. "I'll probably be going out of Shanghai in a couple of days. I can't stay more than a month in China with my kind of assignment. Where would that leave you?"

"What's the difference?" she said decisively, and I was glad that the mood of abandon hadn't left her. "Nobody cares. Everybody's for Number One. Maybe we should live for right now." I moved closer to those smooth lips, and kissed her. The delightful oblivion began to settle over me, but through the hood of sensation I could see that Ling had turned his head and was grinning. She had seen him too.

"Is today a reaction—to what's been happening with Carl?" That question, too, surprised me. I was treating her as if I cared for her, instead of thinking of her as a sex-machine, as any self-respecting male would do.

"Yes," she said matter-of-factly. "That's one reason. But I couldn't, if you weren't—what you are." She smiled. "And while we're being so frank, tell me about your wife."

I told her about Lois: how much I had loved her at first when we had met during World War II, but how that and the other wars afterward had kept us apart: the civil wars in Indo-China, Indonesia,

India, Malaya—how something had kept driving me on to the scene of excitement—looking for adventure stories.

"I guess it was really my fault," I said. "But she had a predisposition to booze. It was in the family—her father was a real lush. It runs in families, too, you know—it hits the ones that are weak. When she was alone, she turned to the booze for company. In the old days, people drank their booze, but they still could do their jobs. Now—well, it's like a sickness."

"Especially in Shanghai." Martha looked understanding and I ploughed on:

"I guess I should have stayed home and taken better care of her. But I couldn't. Or at least, I didn't. I had to go on—something about excitement, I wanted to be where the new excitement was. Maybe— maybe that's the adventurer's curse."

"You wanted to be where the big political news was breaking?"

I went on without thinking about the question. "I wanted the stories that were in high gear, and the big stories were abroad."

"Couldn't you take her along?"

"I tried on some stories. But she—" I realized I was rattling on but the girl listened to every word. "She got back on the booze again, while we were traveling." I said. "Once I asked her what she was trying to escape from, in that bottle. She said: 'I don't know—insufficiency, I guess.'

"I didn't know what she meant. I guess I was the one who was insufficient. I should have been a better husband—stayed home and lived what she said was the gracious life, got some racket so we could live comfortably. I tried it. But that's not what I want—playing it safe, getting along with the right people, staying home. I know one thing, and I apologize: I talk too much."

But she didn't laugh. She was dead earnest. "How about children. Didn't your wife want children?"

"I think they would have made all the difference to her. But we found out she couldn't have any."

I could have told her that it could have been fixed with an operation, but Lois hadn't wanted it. That was the big black mark I held against her. Drinking companions were what she wanted, nothing more complicated than that. But why should I get into that subject? It would sound too much like self-justification.

"You really had your troubles," Martha said.

"Don't we all? You—for instance—had more than I did."

She looked at me levelly. "You know about him?"

"Yes—about the racket—selling the arms."

"You do!" Her eyes were wide, and now they were glinting with those yellow fires. "It took me a year to know—it's horrible to realize that—your husband is a monster.

"I tried, hard. I tried to get him away from those people, the people he drifted in with, Perhaps I was too harsh—perhaps that turned him away from me, and that made it worse. He said I was a drill sergeant, an iceberg."

The points of fire glowed in her eyes. She was a real Valkyrie. "He's soft—no fight in him. Sometimes I could kill him!"

The road was smoother now. It snaked along a fetid canal, where shanty-boats sprawled on the black mud banks. The matshed-covered barges crouched like alley-cats, alive with the usual infestation of black-clad Chinese thick as vermin. The voices shrilled into our window in a packet like sounds of a chicken yard.

A young boy of seven or eight paddled past us in an old wash-tub, floating downstream. The tub bobbled perilously close to submersion. He was a fish-vendor, crying his wares in a sing-song voice.

"The Chinese kids don't have much chance—especially these days," I said, trying to be conversational and calm her down.

The heat of her anger still flared. "That's why," she said. "Can't they look around, can't they see! The selfish racketeers! But they don't look and they don't care—any of them."

She was getting very intense and I tried to get her off it by kidding: "Where'd you get such a violent social conscience?"

She said, "I'm serious. My theory about democracy is: each man or woman should assume that he or she is the *only* voter, the only taxpayer. That's the only way it will work."

"That would make a big difference here—or—or anyplace Americans are."

"Yes—and—and you, as a journalist—should work as if you are the only reporter, and bring people the truth."

"There's a small matter of pleasing the editors," I said jokingly. "I'm supposed to bring them adventure stories."

"Yes, I know," she said, and suddenly looked so crestfallen that I hastened to add:

"But maybe I can bring in a story that's—important—if I can get up to the front." I knew it wasn't true, that I was going to be looking for adventure stories up there; but again I felt sorry for her.

"You're lucky to be able to see—what you've seen of what goes on in the world," she said. Probably in part out of sympathy, mostly out of pure hambone instincts to attract her—the bright plumed male bird doing his automatic dance—I told her some of the stories I'd covered.

She was like a wide-eyed child, listening for any tid-bit of encouragement in her fairy-tale world where she was at once so unbelievably wise and so naive.

I told her about India—the fighting I had seen in Delhi during that civil war, about the Indonesians in Surabaya when they dragged the Dutch out of their clubs and garroted them with spears, about the guerrillas fighting the British in Malaya, and the Annamites throwing bombs at the French in Indo-China. I had covered these stories as adventure yarns, usually writing about Americans involved in them. But I told them as if the Americans were great heroes involved in a great political struggle. When I told the stories, I realized there were a surprising number of Americans who were political heroes: pilots, the young economic and political attachés in the consulates, and some of the MAG soldiers who knocked themselves out to train our worthless military allies, even some correspondents who would stick their necks out for a principle.

She liked it, she kept me going, she loved me for the dangers I had passed or somebody had passed, and eventually, as with a child, her eyes grew heavy and her head nodded on my shoulder. I felt paternal again, or at least avuncular.

Ling, looking back, bestowed a benign smile on me. I acknowledged it with a crook of the finger.

The girl was beautiful in sleep as awake. Her eyelids seemed to fill up half of her small face, her chin line, nose, throat and lips were as perfectly formed as if Praxiteles could have moulded them in flesh. Or perhaps, if Praxiteles could have seen her through my eyes.

We were reaching the concentrations of board and clay shacks marking Lung Wha, at the southern extremity of Shanghai. We had left the truck trail and now rolled over a dirt road which was comparatively a boulevard. In the late sunset light, vivid as blood, I watched a refugee camp move past us, small fires orange like gunfire among the matsheds.

I looked at my sleeping Venus, the curve of that throat, the slow pulse I could see in that smooth skin, the curve of her collarbone, the fullness of her arm flung across the sea. These things set off a bomb of wanting her. More than anything I could think of, I wanted her. I must have spoken aloud because Ling turned and smiled and said:

"Whassay, mastah?"

"Oh, nothing. Uh—you good driver—good boy, Ling. I give you good *cumishaw*."

I put a finger to my lips, but the precaution wasn't necessary. Martha slept as still as Brünnehilde after a battle.

"Bloadway Mansion? Cathay Hoteru?" Ling asked in a whisper.

I looked at her and decided: "Cathay Hoteru."

✳

She didn't object when I guided her through the dark lobby of the Cathay. She was half asleep.

In justification I told myself I hadn't time to find out if her husband would be back at Broadway Mansions tonight. The reasoning part of me knew this for mostly lie. But this time, I thought, I would brazen it out, I would benefit, once, from my mistakes earlier. This time, I would keep conscience in its place. And as for Shoop—the hell with him, it couldn't happen to a more deserving guy.

When I got the key I checked to see if there were any messages: none. She was still a little groggy when we got into the elevator. My plan had been formulated: first a good dinner at the room, with wine, then the rest. Why not? She was in favor of it, too.

"How do you feel?" I asked her in the elevator.

"Sleepy."

"We can have some dinner in the room."

"Good."

As I opened the door to the high, dark room, though, the phone was ringing. I picked it up.

"Ostermann, this is Carl Shoop." It was a blow. I had thought he would be away for a matter of days. And he sounded sober, pleasant.

"Listen, I'm sorry about last night. A little too drunk. I apologize."

"That's all right," I said before I could think.

I felt a pause at the other end of the phone. "Oh, you haven't seen my wife today by any chance, have you?"

A quick decision needed now, and I made it. "Yes, I saw her today, we went for a swim at Hangchow Bay. She took a cab home, should be there any moment now."

"Thanks, see you around." He hung up. No jealous-husband-type questions.

"It was Carl?" Martha had become bold awake in a second. She seemed suddenly pale. "I didn't expect him till the end of this week. Was he sober?"

I nodded. I suddenly knew the miserable feeling of being a cheat, knew that she felt it too, more strongly.

"Where does that leave us?" I asked her, and she smiled bravely.

"It doesn't change anything." But we both knew that things had been changed, even if only temporarily.

"When can I see you?"

"I don't know. We'll have to see." Her tone was listless, almost sullen—probably because she had her imminent meeting with Carl on her mind.

All of a sudden it seemed too much to bear that she would be in the apartment with Shoop tonight, and nights after that. I knew I had not the slightest claim on her, I hadn't even slept with her. It was a ridiculous inversion that a would-be lover should want her not to sleep with her legal husband.

Of course, I couldn't ask her that, but the idea of her being with him or any other man horrified me. I bent over her, and held her small shoulders in my hands so she would have to look at me.

"Martha—I don't want it to end now, here. It can't. I won't let it."

"I don't know," she said. "I don't see how it can work out."

"Don't say that, don't even think it." Her face was still cheerless, clouded. "You don't want to—you don't want—Carl do you?"

"No. I haven't—for a long time."

I kissed her. She resisted for a second, then I kissed her again, and we were off, the rocket in blind space, the fire burning bright, flipping end over end like a pinwheel that grew more unbearably bright with every turn. Then she was pulling away, short of breath.

"It's not like that when you kiss Carl, is it?"

"No."

"I can't give you up." I picked her up abruptly and carried her to the couch and laid her down. She lay quiet, her eyes looking up at me.

I kissed her again and she pulled away. "Scott," she said. "You must be crazy."

"I am—crazy about you."

"I've got to go."

"I won't let you. I want you to remember this."

"We can't do it now. Before, on the island—I must have been—wanting to get even."

"It was more than that."

"No. It wouldn't be good, it wouldn't be right."

"You should worry about right with a husband like him. But it is right. It feels right. It's good."

I kissed her, all of the wanting surging up me, the feeling of wanting that beauty, wanting all the clean and intense perfection I had seen in her today in the sun.

Her lips were opening anemones, they resisted me only for a moment, then we were pinwheeling through endless layers of feeling, spinning, pinwheeling, floating. I didn't want it to stop, it had to go on and not stop, ever. It was complete, it was everything powerful and strong as it had been before, and I didn't want it to be stopped this time, I would not let it be stopped.

And she did not want it to end, either. She helped me to undress her. I held her small shoulders to me. I knew it had not been like this for a long time before: the perfect smooth masses moving together, the blissful pressure of breasts and legs smooth as milk, the small bare waist cool between my hands, the touching of the colored tip of the flesh, a purple tulip shade, the pale purplish shade rigid to the touch, and more rigid, holding rigidity, the muscled legs grasping smoothly, the nipples wine-fire, the feminine flesh soft, the moistness retreating and responding in agony, as I was, and wanting more always, the singing of sensation, the chorus of sensations playing in our ears, higher and lower, softer and louder, rougher and smoother, all at once, continuing imperfect perfection continuing perfectly.

It was what sex should be, the only song, the only reality, the song not ending yet, ever.

"I want to remember, to keep it."

"Yes, to remember."

"To—to always have it."

"Yes, always have it."

"And keep it."

"Keep it."

"Always."

Then it was beyond words, going on, absolutely, beyond believing. And then it was over and I knew it was better than I had ever known it. Some magic made it better, even now that it was over I knew it had never been like this before.

"Could you have wanted more?"

"No, I don't think it—could have been more."

*

I opened the window of this high tower room. It was 8:34, nearly an hour after Shoop's call. I walked back to Martha and sat next to her on the couch.

"I'm glad it happened." She was the unrepentant Valkyrie. I could not have wanted her different.

I was stunned, shocked, but more at peace than I could remember having been, ever. I was shocked because I knew it was one of those things that don't happen often in your life, when mating is just right, when the partners are made for each other, exactly, in the physical way.

She walked to the dresser mirror to put on lipstick. "Scott—do you still think it will work out?"

"Yes."

"Tell me everything will be all right." The Valkyrie was gone—she was the small, defenseless child again.

"It will be. We'll make it that way." But I had my doubts. I knew only that it had been right and perfect, for now, for both of us. I would worry about the rest of it if and when we came to it.

7

I HAD TAKEN HER HOME IN A CAB THAT NIGHT, AND WE HAD deliberated at length what to do. She had insisted I should not go in to face Carl, not tonight. Just, she said, let her explain why she was late: say that she had stopped at the snack bar on the way home—and naturally she wouldn't know that Carl had come back to town. So we decided to leave it that way, and she would get away and call me from somewhere.

That evening was all okay. I climbed into bed and was not troubled as the warm Shanghai night closed in on me. I felt a sublime tiredness, and no guilt, as I knew I shouldn't after having enjoyed the lovemaking session of my life. I was all gone, and being cussedly male, I was not at all concerned then whether I should try to make the attachment a permanent thing.

I didn't even worry about whether she was having trouble with Carl, that night. I remembered how she had frozen him like a stern drill sergeant at Lindahl's party when he got out of control. She could take care of herself.

Besides, Shoop was probably half-blotto by the time she got home. I wasn't concerned. I just fell asleep.

But in the morning, when I went down to breakfast by myself it was different. I brought a book with me to the hotel table, a book Martha had recommended to me, *The Communist Enemy.*

I had bought it at the hotel desk, and I opened it over coffee, but when I looked at the first page of type, I saw something quite different: the tiny nose with the fleck of the beauty spot on the nostril, the curve of the throat in the sun on the island, the taut legs, fresh from the water, the small, smooth shoulders. And the sensations of being with her haunted me—the almost tactile remembering of holding her, the moving, smooth masses—all now just beyond my reach. The feelings of the night clanged in my head, giant steel gongs banging hard in the back of my consciousness— the steel gongs of wanting a certain woman. I had known the gongs before, but never this big, this clangorous, this insistent.

After breakfast I went back up to the room without having read the first paragraph of the book. I told myself it was ridiculous to suffer this much over a woman. I knew I had it bad. This time I told myself: you get a woman-hangover if the woman is good. And the hangover is terrible if she is terrific.

I walked the floor, stopping absently to watch the river traffic on the Whangpoo. I seemed to spend most of my time staring at the phone. But it didn't ring.

Then there was a knock on the door. I practically jumped out of my skin, and a dozen instant imaginings tumbled through my head: it would be Martha, with a small canvas bag in hand and she would be saying she needed me and couldn't stand it, and had to stay with me. Or Shoop would be there, in a drunken rage, or John Lindahl with a message from her that she must see me, or maybe with the nightmare news that she had killed Shoop and was being held for murder, or that he had killed her in a drunken argument, or that in a fit of depression she had killed herself, jumped from the top of Broadway Mansions.

But it was a small Chinese bellboy in uniform, with a cablegram from New York: OSTERMANN CATHAY HOTEL SHANGHAI GODSAKE HURRY CHINA STORY HAIRIER THE BETTER AND QUICKEST YOU OVER-DRAWN TWO THOUSAND LOIS WANTS MORE ADVANCE JOE DODSON.

I knew instantly the meaning of the cablese: Joe Dodson was the understanding, tolerant editor of the *Beacon*, the Magazine for Men—Lois had overdrawn the account to be paid for my stories. Last time I had checked I owed the magazine only two hundred dollars. Now with those hefty liquor bills at Gristede's, and with the vitamin shots from Dr. Trask, the specialist in alcoholism, and the head-shrinker, Dr. Jackson, and the charge accounts from Toots Shor's restaurant and the Stork, and Hattie Carnegie's dresses and the Grand Central florist, the best in town—this was all the old story. So I was behind again—and Dodson wanted stories fast. When he said the hairier the better, that was editorial direction: he wanted action, adventure, plenty of red meat and beefsteak, as he used to say.

The cablegram was a clear fiat for action on my part. it jolted some of the fog from my mind. I would have to get going on work and that, I knew, could be good, and maybe better for both Martha and me.

I went out on Nanking Road, dodging the beggars and pimps, and headed for the KMT press headquarters. Desire for Martha still clanged in waves through my head, the reverberations dazed me still, but a new thought current was running strong, a new questioning and a new resolution: maybe it would be better if Martha didn't see me again, in some ways I was a much worse bet than her husband. At least he was making money—maybe whether it came from a racket didn't make any difference. Maybe I should just get the hell out of Shanghai, leave it and the whole deal, and get to where something was happening, something new, exciting, and productive.

At the bare, unpainted KMT press headquarters which smelled of stale tea and spit, I found Jimmy Yung, third man on the totem pole. Jimmy chewed more gum and spoke slangier English than most Americans—marks of his military training in the U.S. during World War II. Chiang Kai-shek could have used a thousand more like him.

"Hi, Boss," he greeted me. "No dope yet on your trip, from the wheels. Sorry. What's new with you?"

"Not much."

"Boy, you sure look down in the dumps. What's wrong?"

"Nothing printable."

"Okay. We'll try to goose along an okay for the trip. Looks to me like Djin-zuh is going to be the place we can get approved. Maybe a few more days."

"Let me know as soon as you hear," I asked him.

"Check. Wilco."

Djin-zuh was the town way out in Mongolia, right on the front, or rather, in the front. There, I should be able to get hairy enough stories for Dodson. There was action out there, clean action—men in the brotherhood and unselfishness of the front line—far from the fat rackets and the corruption of the rear. If the girl had been any other than Martha, I would have rejoiced about the chance to get that far away from it all. But now the thought of having to leave twisted the knife in the wound.

In the corridor I met John Lindahl. "What you been doing?" he asked. "Haven't seen you for a couple of days."

"You know, the same old stuff." I wished I could tell him what had been happening. At this point, any confidant would have been a help.

"Have you seen Martha Shoop today?" I asked him, grasping at a straw.

"No, not for a few days. Can I give you a lift back to the hotel?"

"Thanks, I need the walk. Be seeing you."

But John wanted to talk. He moved along beside me, as we threaded through the matshed shacks along the Bund, past the ragged coolies pulling long carts of oil drums like beasts of burden, shouting to ease the strain on their guts, while they dragged the dead-weight on long ropes.

"They get a million Chinese dollars a day—one dollar American at the latest exchange rate—if they haul three loads a day," John was saying. "That takes all day, sun to sun—and they have to decide whether to make the third load or not. It's a difficult economic equation: a buck will get them enough rice for a family, but they'll be so worn out and hungry they'll want more rice than they can buy. If they make two loads instead of three, they make sixty-six cents instead of a buck, and they're not so hungry or worn out. But then there still isn't enough rice, at the going price."

He could see I wasn't paying much attention, and he guessed the direction of my thoughts.

"The price of rice is one thing you can't blame on Carl Shoop," he said. "He makes his graft out of arms. The worst villains are the types that turn over our relief rice or the medical supplies to the black-marketeers. Or maybe they're all equally rotten."

I said, yes, that made sense, but it was all too complicated for me, the thing that worried me was finding some blood-and-guts action stories, if I didn't want to go into bankruptcy. John said he would give it some thought—but he guessed I was on the right track heading up to the front to look for some adventure stories.

I thanked him and said I would be bothering him for the names of people who could steer me to stories.

And back at the hotel there were no messages, no phone calls. I couldn't stay in that room. I kept seeing her in the sun on the island and here in the room, the round face and tiny nose and the nostrils arched with very adult emotion, the smooth shoulders with the few flecks of beauty spots.

The feeling of holding her last night, the smooth solidity of her body, the perfect agony, these were weights, pressures, warnings I couldn't bear, sitting there by the damask drapes next to the couch of last night. I had to get out.

I got a pedicab and told the boy: Broadway Mansions. While he bucked into the whirlygig traffic, I wondered why I had said Broadway Mansions. What could I possibly do there? Except be near her, and that, right now would be crazy. I had plenty of time to change the order to the pedicab boy. But the magnet drew me, I couldn't deny the going with it. The pedicab moved to the lower slopes of the Garden Bridge and two push-pushy boys were helping the pedicab driver to get his vehicle up the grade. I paid them their *cumishaw* and we rounded the top of the bridge and still I hadn't changed my instructions. The bulk of Broadway Mansions loomed on our left.

Of course, I could go on up to the restaurant at the top of the building and have a bite. That way I would be in her vicinity and still have a legitimate excuse for being there. I might even see her and hear her say hello, even if we couldn't talk. I was the criminal drawn by a flagellant interest in the atmosphere of the crime.

In the restaurant, I took a small table in a corner and sat over cheese-toast and strong tea for forty-five minutes. I looked at my watch: three-twenty. It had been silly of me to think she might happen in there at this odd hour. But I stayed there, the only customer in the restaurant, with the three white-coated serving boys standing by: the tea and coffee-break hour would be coming up soon. Then, she might be dropping in with a girlfriend. We might have a chance to talk, and I might even get her away alone for a little while—the thought was delicious.

But it got to be three-thirty-five and nothing had happened. Steve Bildo, the *Chicago Daily News* correspondent, came in with two other men to have a hamburger. As I got up to go, Steve waved to me to come over. At that point, I didn't want to talk to anybody, but I owed it to Steve in good-fellowship. He had been a fast friend in Hawai'i and Guam during World War II.

And it dawned on my dazed consciousness, an idea that should have occurred to me long before, that Bildo and his friends might steer me to the kind of story leads I desperately needed.

Steve just wanted to pass the time of day; and it was drudgery to be pleasant, but I have always been glad that I made the stop, that groggy afternoon. One of the two men with Steve was a hulking, pleasant Georgia cracker named Bud Wade. He wore a black patch over one eye and a fixed grin, a cigarette drooping from his wide-spaced, ragged teeth. His remaining eye squinched, probably from the constant grinning; it was light blue intensified by a bushy, dark eyebrow. The other man with them was an Army major in civvies.

Bildo introduced Wade as the hottest pilot in the Far East, and "also the most notorious running dog of Capitalism, according to the Commies—besides being naturally a buccaneer." It seemed that he flew for General Chennault's outfit, the Civil Air Transport.

"Any problems I can help you with, let me know," Wade drawled. And I wished that I could get help from him on the problem which *did* bother me. Being a buccaneer, I thought, he probably would have suggested kidnaping the girl and taking her to Hong Kong— and to hell with everything else—which might not have been a bad idea at that.

But Wade got onto a subject much more productive. He said: "Jimmy Yung tells me you want to go up-country—a mighty good idea. There *is* a war going on up there, contrary to what you might think about it around here.

"You know, this country is cut up into two big islands, the one around Shanghai, that goes out to Nanking on the west and Tientsin up north, and the other island, one way up north—from Peiping over to Kalgan, and all the way to Mukden. That island up north is where the real tough stuff is goin' on. You know, you can't get to it except flyin'. You goin' by CNAC?"

I said that was my plan. CNAC was a Chinese airline well run by Americans. "I hope you can get it cleared with the KMT— they hate the hell out of anybody who jumps on 'em on political stuff."

He fixed me with his one bright, China-blue eye. "A lot of people are dyin' up there," he said, conversationally. "Dyin' for somethin'. Maybe you can see what it is."

I said my beat was men's stories—maybe I could get better ones up there, that was all I was after.

"Yeah, sure," he said. "The KMT wouldn't let you up there if you were doing a political story. It might be critical. Well, if you want leads to some people up there, let me know."

I thanked him, and ducked away because one thing was still clanging harder in my head than any plan to find a story: Martha, and the longing for her. I called the Cathay from Broadway Mansions, checked the hall porter's desk: no messages. If I had been a drinking man, I probably would have gone down to the Garden Bridge officers' club and got loaded. But heavy drinking was one of the escapes cut off by the big World War II wound, the head wound. Perhaps that was a fortunate disability.

I decided to lose myself, if possible, in work. Not a bad idea in view of the fact that my bank balance in New York trembled unsteadily at the two hundred mark and Lois' bills, mostly medical and liquor, were about five times that amount, to say nothing of the two thousand overdraft at *Beacon*.

I walked back to the Cathay, got my scraps of paper together, and began transcribing some of the notes. Thoughts of the last couple of days kept obtruding, and wild schemes for calling Martha's apartment on the chance that Shoop might be out.

Then the phone rang. The shock of the sound bounced me two inches off my chair. I had got up and taken two steps toward it when I stopped myself, and painfully held back while I let it ring. I went back to my chair and ground myself into the transcribing. It was better if I didn't talk to her—not now, not the way things were going.

When I finished that, I must write a letter to Joe Dodson of *Beacon* explaining the great stories I would take up for him, to win still another advance on future articles. There was plenty to do.

When the phone had stopped, I called the hotel operator: "I missed that telephone call. Did she—did the party leave any message?"

"No, sir, no message."

"Was it a man or a woman?"

"A woman, sir." I was helpless, torpedoed.

Should I call Martha now, and the consequences be damned, I wondered. Shoop might pick up the phone, but the chances were maybe fifty-fifty—it was definitely worth the risk.

The gongs were ringing in my head, the waves of wanting Martha vibrating like bands of steel, a machine macerating any reasonableness I could have summoned. I didn't want to be reasonable.

I called her number, the blood pounding in the back of my head like a thunderstorm. Fifty-fifty, I thought, as I heard it ring. Three times, four times, then the click, a voice, a man's voice:

" 'Lo." It was Shoop. My insides hit bottom. At the same time, from that monosyllable I thought I could detect that he had been drinking.

"Hi, this is Ostermann." My voice sounded very unsure. What could I say to the guy? I wondered in a fractious moment.

"Oh, you wanna talk m'wife. Jus' a minute." I was floored, and sure at that moment that he was drunk. I heard his voice faintly as he called her: "Hey—Iceberg! Boy friend."

I don't shock easily, but there was something about that drunken nonchalance that shook me to my shoes. Was he just too far gone to care what happened to her?

In long seconds I heard that high boy-like voice: "Hello, Scott." Her voice was unsure—the unsureness and humbleness that hit me harder than ever now.

"Martha, can you talk?" A properly stupid question for someone as upset as I was. "I mean—did you call me before, tonight?"

"Yes."

"I'm sorry to call you like this. I had to talk to you."

"That's all right."

"I've been missing you, I couldn't stand it much longer."

"Me too." The voice rocked me, I could hardly talk:

"Will you call me tomorrow?"

"All right."

"In the morning?"

"Okay." She added, abruptly: "No, I don't think we should go swimming again there." It was an awkward cover up.

"No," I said, falling in lamely with the game. "That place was too primitive."

"I agree with you: Hangchow Bay is no place for swimming. I told Carl about the mines."

"Call me in the morning." I dropped the pretense. "I—want you."

Pause at the end of the wire. "All right—g'bye."

It was foul, my game of double-dealing, I told myself, while I hung up and sat staring at the phone, as if it were somehow an embodiment of her. But I didn't care if the game was double, I was glad to be in it, it was worth any guilt feeling or embarrassment or crime. And I thought she was glad to be in it too, even though it was harder for her.

I wondered: will that lout beat her up? What kind of trouble is he giving her right now, this minute? Has he tried to sleep with her? She wouldn't, feeling as she does about us, I hope. But he could make things wretched for her, even when he's that drunk. Yet the same old doubts were clamoring still: why should I drag her into something with me, what could I offer her except a profitless involvement with a beat-up, broke, still-too-much-married war correspondent?

8

THE NEXT MORNING WHEN SHE CALLED I HAD BEEN OVER ALL the possibilities, including one that woke me up in the middle of the night and left my nerves shaking: maybe tonight, maybe this minute, he is forcing her—or winning her back.

I couldn't sleep: maybe her adventure with me had been just a day's wildness, one violent reaction against Carl. After all, she must have loved him or at least been infatuated, to marry him in the first place. She had called him a monster, he was a gangster and a lush, but gangsters and lushes have women who adore them, too. Or at least get along with them. I remembered the way she had said only "All right" on the phone in response to my telling her I wanted her; though of course she couldn't talk with Carl sitting right there near her, drunk as he might be. Thank God he *was* drunk last night—and, I hoped, the night before.

That morning I had eaten little breakfast, had roused very little interest in *The Communist Enemy.* I checked the front desk three times to see if there were any cables for me. None. Then, thank God, the phone:

"Scott?"

"Yes. Where are you?"

"In a phone booth at Broadway Mansions."

"When can I see you?"

"I don't know." She sounded awfully guarded.

"Can you talk?"

"Yes."

"Is Carl still around?"

"Yes, but he's at work. I didn't want to call from the apartment, one of the house boys might tell him." Her voice seemed impatient, almost short.

Instinctively, I knew I had to be fast, and firm. "I'll come by in a cab and pick you up in front of Broadway Mansions, in about twenty minutes."

"No, you'd better not. Too many people around."

"All right, make it Garden Bridge, then. I'll pick you up on the Garden Bridge. About ten-thirty."

I didn't give her a chance to object. "Bye." I hung up, but as I jumped into my Hong Kong suit, I felt my heart sinking: she had changed her mind, Carl had got to her with whatever magic he had practiced when he had talked her into marriage, or he had slept with her. But that couldn't be as good as it had been for us— or could it? Maybe I had overvalued the experience, for her. Maybe it hadn't been perfect, for her, as it had for me. Maybe she was as cruel as Brünnehilde, she might be deceiving me; but that, I knew, couldn't be. Little as I knew her, I knew her far better than that.

She was there, considerately enough on the east side of the bridge, the side of the street I would be travelling from the Cathay.

When I had closed her safely in the taxicab, the driver turned to ask for instructions.

"The Cathay Hotel," I told him, and she didn't object. Sitting next to me, she was a blonde angel in a tan seersucker dress as fresh as a halo. But she was also Brünnehilde with *Weltschmerz*, so serious and preoccupied that I felt momentarily like a stranger.

In the mood of the moment, I didn't hold her in my arms as I had wanted to. I put my hand on her arm and we rode silently while the cabbie swept the car around at the Broadway intersection and headed back over the bridge.

"Did he give you a lot of trouble?" I asked her.

"Not too much." She still seemed serious, almost sullen. There was no sign of the sunbeam smile I had doted on. It hurt me to know that she must be dark as a summer storm inside.

I took her hand. "I know you're having trouble. But you're not sorry, are you?"

She didn't answer. *"Are* you?" I repeated.

"I don't know, Scott. Everything seemed so clear when we were at Hangchow. And in your room. But now it's all confused. I wish I knew what was true, what was right."

I shouldn't have committed myself to the word, perhaps, but I said: "Isn't it right to be with the man you love rather than one you don't?"

She didn't answer. "You don't love him, do you?" It was a risky question if I wanted to hold onto her, but I was shooting the works, I wanted her more than anything I could remember and I was going to have her, if I had to mow down her husband, my wife and myself to do it.

"He's weak," she said. "He needs someone to give him strength."

"Why should *you* be elected? You're too good to be dragged down that drain."

"I'm *no* good, Scott. If I were any good, I wouldn't have gone swimming with you—and to your room. I wouldn't be going now. I took the marriage vows . . ."

"Your vows didn't include killing yourself for a drunk, a bum, a racketeer—any more than mine did."

"I don't know, Scott, I don't know."

"You know some people are weak, some are strong. I'm strong enough to know I want you for myself. I don't want you to be wasted on him."

You—I told myself in a moment's contrition—you are making pretty brave noises considering that you don't even know how you're going to pay last year's bills.

But I looked at that small intense face, as intensely unhappy as it could be bright and healthy and happy under opposite circumstances, and the thought overwhelmed me: what's the difference, do anything necessary and hang onto her, she's the right one for you, she's worth anything you have to do, for however long you can have her.

"Look, Martha," I said, following what seemed to me to be an advantage, even though a slight one. "Ever since I got to Shanghai and met you, that first day, things have seemed clear to me.

"Maybe it's something about the town, or maybe it's because of the war and things seem simpler in a war, or maybe it's just you— because I met somebody who's just right for me.

"It was never that way with me before, so much just right. Was it with you?"

"No."

"Just talking about it makes me want you."

That sunbeam smile broke over her gloom, unsure and almost querulous, but it gave me the encouragement I needed.

"The main thing is—that you're the one, the best one. Nothing could get in the way of that. That's what's right. The fact that there are two people in our way, clinging to us like bloodsuckers, shouldn't stop us. We should be together, live together, let the rest take care of itself. You didn't let it stop you when you went to Hangchow with me. You didn't care then, did you?"

"I know—maybe I was wrong. Maybe it was living in Shanghai, seeing people living together, with other men's wives. All that. I never had, before."

"I know you hadn't."

We were pulling up at the front door of the Cathay. What, I wondered, *was* I going to do that would be good for her. Sure, sleeping with her would be good, but what would happen then? After the China story was done, you'd have to shove off for another country. Could you take her with you? You didn't even have any money to offer her—only debts, divorce, unhappiness.

But as I helped her out of the cab, saw those small shoulders and her golden crown moving toward me, I knew I wasn't going to change my mind tonight. That round face, that was a baby and Brünnehilde at once, looked at me and smiled, and I was gone.

"I'll go to Carl and we will talk it over and straighten it out," I said as we walked into the lobby. "We'll force it to happen, we'll make it happen, our way."

I saw the golden glints dance in her eyes. "I think you're right. You're the only one that's worth saving."

"That's my Brünnehilde," I said, half to myself.

I checked at the desk for messages. There was a cablegram. I stuck it unopened into my pocket, and swallowed.

"Aren't you going to open it?" she asked.

"Yes." What kind of bold, bad strong man were you, without courage enough to open a cable, because it might be bad news which could wrench you away from her?

The cable: It was the same old refrain from Joe Dodson at *Beacon*, the Magazine for Men, a response to my cable about going up to the front, to the north: OSTERMANN CATHAY HOTEL SHANGHAI GOOD YOU PROGRESSING WITH TRIP FRONTWARDS STOP PLEASE PROGRESS FASTEST JOE DODSON.

"Bad news," she said, reading my face.

I nodded. "Not too bad," I said. She left it there, not being the nosy type. If I wanted to tell her, I would. She looked like a lost child as I led her toward the room—defenseless, feminine, trusting me.

In the room, she sat on the couch. I took off my coat and suddenly felt as conscience-stricken as I had been on the island at Hangchow. The tall, dark room with the heavy drapes made the moment seem brutal. It descended on us like a weight. She felt it, too.

I sat beside her, and looked into her small face and the eyes now almost black in the dim light.

"Martha," I said. "I have a plan for you and me." And that moment, I did have a plan, a plan of desperation and the moment.

"When I go up into Mongolia to do the story on that town, I'll take you along, as my photographer."

"Would they let you?"

"I think so. After all, you are a photographer, you've had magazine experience, you've been cleared as a security risk."

The dawn came up over her face with a sudden blaze of glory. "Really—would you? There's nothing I'd rather do—nothing in the world—than to see what's happening—out there. Would you? Please?"

"I would. I certainly would."

It was a goofball, harebrained idea, one I had no business suggesting. It was impractical, maybe it was impossible. But for now I knew it was right.

I leaned over her, kissed her and held her. The automatic pilot of love had taken over, better than my reason. I kissed her again and touched her—the touch I wanted more than anything and it was good, life as it should be always, the escalator beginning easily and climbing faster and faster, then spiraling, turning until it was no longer an escalator, it was a plane leaving a white contrail curving, seven planes with contrails and seven, fourteen exploding at once, fourteen times fourteen times fourteen at once.

"It doesn't matter," she said, "doesn't matter, I only care—"

"Only care," I echoed her. "Only care. That's all, only care."

I guess I wasn't caring enough what I was doing to her, to us. It didn't matter; the perfection was beginning to evolve again, the anemones unfolding their petals agonizingly and beautifully, deeper by the minute, and that was all that mattered.

9

I SENT DOWN FOR SOME TEA AND SANDWICHES AT LUNCH time, and we opened the drapes and sat by the window, fourteen stories above the Bund, enjoying the bright sun. She was a creature of the sun, her body modeled by it, the mellow light shaping her bare shoulders and breasts, and round arms, and slick along that long, narrow waist that was as trim as an arrow.

She had wrapped a towel around her waist, as if it were a Tahitian *pareu*, and I was reminded of many lovely Polynesians I had known in the course of Pacific traveling. She had the same pride in her body, I knew by now, and the same wholesome appreciation of sex, the same aversion toward being ashamed of it, as the wonderful Polynesians. She was a pagan at heart, Brünnehilde in the Norse idiom, Pele in the Polynesian—and either, now, was fine, and all I wanted.

To the north, on the river, a coastal liner with clean white flanks and a shiny yellow and black smokestack was turning in the muddy stream, two tugs nudging the bow. Steam jetted from her stack, we heard the bellow of her whistle seconds later. A festoon of wretched Chinese bumboats hovered along one side. They had just been cut loose as the ship got under way.

Martha watched it, the sun modeling that tiny nose with the high-arched nostrils, gleaming on a thousand lights in her hair.

"How would you like to be on that ship with me," I asked. "Heading for, say, Hong Kong or Singapore?"

A child's trusting look. "Do you think we could? What would we live on?"

"On love, I guess, what else?"

She laughed and played with my hair. "I don't think we could shake this place off, Scott. It gets a grip on you. Especially now."

"You mean, with this war on?"

"Yes. We can't leave it. We should go to the fire, instead of running away from it."

I stood up and looked out the window, down at the swarms of small boats moving like waterbugs. The shipping on the Whangpoo was thick—swarms of freighters anchored and at the docks. In midstream, a slick gray U.S. destroyer sliding upstream: things looked prosperous on the harbor water. You wouldn't have known that up-country Nationalist China, the KMT, was on her last legs.

"Will you be able to leave him if I can swing it?"

"Yes," she said simply. "More than that." Her eyes seemed to darken and now I didn't want to probe it. "I want to with all my heart."

Now I was beset by an inclination to chuck the China story, to go back to the well-disciplined British colony of Hong Kong with Martha and find adventure stories there, that would be good enough. Most everybody lives for a maximum of comfort, the easiest way to make a living. Why shouldn't I? Wouldn't that be what the noble Polynesians would do? But that wasn't the way of the kind of pagan Martha was, I found out rapidly.

I said: "I want to think about getting to Hong Kong. I could find a story to work on—the place is full of adventure stories. We could live in the Repulse Bay Hotel, on that wonderful bay. It's like an armchair, the hotel is where the back is, the two points of rock come out like arms on both sides. The water is calm, and clear blue."

"If we go to Hong Kong, how soon could we go?"

"Right away."

"Do you have enough money?"

"Enough to get there. And I'll get an advance on my next story pretty quick." My heart sank when I said it, and the debts swept across my mind like cold winds, but I wasn't going to bother her with these things. They were for me to worry about.

"What will your story be?"

"I don't know, yet."

"But if we go to Hong Kong, you won't be able to do the story on China, will you?"

"No, but that doesn't matter."

"Yes it does. I want you to do it right. You are strong enough to do it right."

"I can't just leave you with him while I go up country—even for a couple of weeks. Besides, it's only an adventure story, a man's story."

"If you go up there where the war is on, it will be a big story—an adventure story maybe, but still an important story. I would try very hard, and make you good pictures."

"My sweet one—I'll find out, this afternoon. We should get you out of here, somewhere, right away."

"Should we, could I, just go, and just leave Carl?"

"I don't know."

"Couldn't I just get accredited as a photographer, and do some work around Peiping, and up at the front with you?"

"You mean you don't want to go to Hong Kong?"

"No. No sense in going to Hong Kong. From what I read, it's like Shanghai, full of refugees and matsheds and hardship. But it's a backwater. You'd be sorry you hadn't been to—where the fighting is."

"You're right about the refugees and the matsheds in Hong Kong," I told her, amazed that she should know. "In a way, going to Hong Kong would be dodging the issue. Give me a kiss."

"I will." She did, and held with it, and my voice was thick when I said:

"Now, take off the towel. Now."

"I will." I pulled the drapes closed.

*

Light still came through the crack of the drapes, though it was fainter, and I could tell from the increasing noise of the whistles on the river that the afternoon was growing old. About four o'clock, usually, the river noises grew frantic as more of the day's work loomed to be done and more people took the ferries across the Whangpoo.

I looked at Angel Face sleeping in the bed next to me. She lay facing me, the coverlet pulled up to her neck, one hand clutching it as if it were insurance that her separation from the world would be complete.

That round face and small head. Now, blissful and quiet, the baby face, the features so perfect, the mouth pouting because she is completely relaxed. What have I done to this infant?

Have I brought out the Brünnehilde in her, have I made her fall in love? Or am I only a kind of infatuation for her, a rebound catch after her husband disintegrated, an affair that could happen only in Shanghai and would fall apart anywhere else?

And to Scott Ostermann is it only infatuation, only the blandishment of perfect face and body and the sunbeam smile? Is it only physical, as with the Polynesians, who have no word for love, except *ha'uti*, which means to play. Maybe it is only play, this fixation with her. No, because you, Ostermann, are objective enough to see that she is not perfect. Even you can see the lapped-over front tooth is not perfection—though it does make her smile bright and easy; and that her jaw is perhaps too prominent, though it gives a winsome little boy determination to the tiny face. Her hands and feet are too stubby, almost ugly—but like her jaw, they make her earnest and capable, they fit her. And her legs, a little too short, though the muscling is fascinating, and her bosom—she is no Jane Russell, but she is ample. Yes, I know she is not perfect but it is always more than that, some quality of light and cleanness and a drive within her—and the strange feeling of wanting to protect her. Fine way to protect her, by hauling her off to Peiping, to battle front, and Mongolia!

But it doesn't matter what else happens, so far this has been right for both of us, just because I feel it and know it is right. And I want her, now and always and again. It was an accident that she should be here and involved in the riot on the Bund, and that I should be there at the time, and Hangchow Bay and this room, the telephone calls and the cables, all these are accidents, but they are somehow correct accidents.

Let us hope, I thought, that correct accidents will help us to hold it and keep it. I would have said more than correct accidents if I had been religious, but it is the accidents and the Communists and what the automatic pilot of the mating instinct tells us to do. That may be accidental but it is right.

I looked at my watch: four-thirteen. I had better wake her, she might want to get home before the guy does.

I didn't care about him. I too wished he might die, quietly, somewhere, somehow. I wouldn't wish death on Lois; only that she might instantly find a good drinking companion, some good time Charlie who had a good racket, who could exist intravenously on society the way good time Charlies usually do, and that they should just disappear from sight, the good time Charlie and Lois, both of them—you dreamer, I said to myself.

"Sunbeam," I said, shaking her gently. "Maybe you'd better wake up."

She stirred, the lashes stirring to half-tide. "Huh, huh? What is it?" She lifted her head, her eyes now wide and alarmed. "Something wrong?"

"Everything's all right," I said, leaning over her. "It's just time to wake up."

"Did Carl call?" She still struggled on the far side of consciousness.

I kissed her cheek. "No, darling—everything is Okay."

She put her arm around my neck and held on. "Scott, what are we going to do?" she asked like a panicky child waking from a nightmare.

"Don't worry. I have an idea for us."

"Tell me everything will be all right."

"Everything will be all right, Baby."

But I didn't know everything was going to be all right, Baby—not even how everything was going to be all right that afternoon, in the next half hour.

Much less did I know whether the idea, the plan to take her up into the dangerous territory as a photographer, would work out. Even if it could be done, it might still be crazy. She could get hurt, she could get killed, out there. While she was dressing, I wondered: would I risk killing her to have her with me? A grievous question. I decided the answer was yes. Was that her answer too?

I said: "If we go out Peiping way, it could be pretty risky. Especially if I do get as far as that town in Mongolia. Even if you don't go out to the town with me, Peiping might fall to the Commies any time."

"I want to go."

"We might be interned in Peiping—or caught in the fighting. The Commies have a lot of power now, pretty good artillery."

"I still want to go."

"Okay—I want you to. And I must say, it shouldn't be hard to get stories out there. It'll be rough and uncomfortable—but there will be stories. Now, how about Carl?"

"How about him?"

"You want me to go home with you and talk to him?"

"I don't know. You tell me what to do."

"What time does he get home?"

"Later. He usually stops to have seven or eight fast ones somewhere before he gets home. He comes home senseless, usually— *if* he comes home."

"Call now and see if he's home yet, will you?"

She did, she was surprised. "Mastah go Nanking again," she relayed from the houseboy to me.

"Good, that's very good," I said. "That gives me another day, probably, to set up the Peiping trip. Maybe we can be all set by the time he gets back—I hope." Frantically I was going through the list of the people who could help: Lindahl, Jimmy Yung, maybe even Bud Wade. And at the same time I melted inside with one central, overwhelming fact. She could stay with me tonight.

"Better call the apartment and tell the houseboy you'll be staying at the Cathay tonight," I said.

"I will."

"Are you sure you wouldn't rather try for Hong Kong? We could make it."

"I'm sure I wouldn't."

"We could climb the Peak, and swim at Repulse Bay, and eat at the Parisian Grill."

"I know. And we would also trip over the refugees sleeping on the sidewalks, and see the shantytowns, and be reminded of China. I'd be happier here, with you. And I want you to do your job right, too, to be where things are happening—and to write what is true about the war."

"That's my girl."

I was ashamed, as once before, that she seemed to have so much more confidence in me than I did.

10

IN THE MORNING, EARLY, I WENT AFTER JIMMY YUNG AT THE KMT Press Headquarters.

"Hi, Boss," he greeted me, bright and gum-chewing as usual. "I was just going to call you."

"What's up?"

"Good news. The Wheels have approved your junket to Djin-zuh. We set up an interpreter to make a meet with you in Peiping Friday."

"You mean this Friday? Day after tomorrow?"

The flashing smile. "I tell you, man, the inscrutable Orientals are fast workers. Furthermore, we booked a seat for you on tomorrow's CNAC flight to Peiping—used our influence, that is, to get you in ahead of the backlog. Is that rapid enough?"

"Breathtaking," I said. He didn't have any idea how breathtaking it was for me, with the sudden issue of kidnapping Martha on my mind. Might as well have at it, right away.

"Jimmy," I began, "while you're getting your A for all these efforts, I want to ask you about one more thing."

"Shoot."

"I want to get a photographer accredited to work with me. You know, pictures of the Chinese military heroes and all that."

"You mean KMT heroes, of course. It'll take a few days, though, to get him cleared, you know. Is he in Shanghai?"

"It's a she. But she *is* in Shanghai."

"Hmm." Now he glanced at me like a mysterious Oriental. Then the American smile: "Who is this Asiatic Margaret Bourke-White?"

I thought I read him pretty well at this point. "She's really a wonderful photographer," I lied a little, though it was literally true: she was wonderful and she was a photographer. "Matter of fact, I've already arranged to buy some of the pictures she's made around Shanghai."

"But what's her name?"

"Shoop, Martha Shoop."

"Shoop. Is she related to the Captain Shoop at the MAG?"

"His wife."

"Hmm." In other locales, the fact that she was married would have reassured him. In Shanghai it was cause for suspicion. Jimmy temporized. "Well, offhand it seems it would be okay if she worked around Shanghai or maybe even Peiping. But I don't have to tell you that Djin-zuh is a hot seat. The Commies are all around it. You know you'll be risking your neck to get in and out."

"I know. Maybe she could get accreditation for Peiping, anyhow, make some pix around there that would fit with the story. Or maybe she could go as far as Kalgan. Kalgan is in the clear, isn't it?"

"It's like Peiping, relatively it's in the clear. You couldn't exactly call Peiping in the clear with the Reds thirty-three miles away, on the south."

"I mean, the railroad is clear from Peiping to Kalgan, isn't it?"

"Yeah, sort of. The Commies have a cute little way of going in and blowing up the tracks at crucial moments, like when there's a train on them. It's not like Peiping, where you can fly in or out any time with almost no risk."

"Well, if I get together her papers, you'll put 'em in the works, won't you?"

"Natch."

"And will you nudge the project along a little for me?"

"I'll give it the college try." I could tell I'd better not push it too much more, right now.

"Thanks, Jimmy, I'll remember you in my will."

The wide, white smile. "Yeah, you better take care of that detail."

I didn't want to load him up with too many favors. I could have asked him to try for a seat on tomorrow's CNAC Peiping plane for my Brünnehilde. But that might be too much, and it would also tip my spontaneous plan to have her wait for her accreditation up there rather than here.

One name stuck in my mind, Bud Wade, the CAT pilot I had met at Broadway Mansions. He had offered to help if I had trouble, and he seemed like the type who might do it.

I found the man with the black patch and the drawl in a dark office way up in one of the Bund skyscrapers. "Hi, boy," he greeted me, smiling as usual around the dangling cigarette. "You got trouble already?"

"Not bad trouble."

"Just sorta mild, like say you picked up one of them there social diseases from a White Russian, you gave it to another and her Chinese husband's gonna turn you in for a Communist spy."

"Nothing like that."

"Well, spill it."

"I need a seat on the CNAC flight to Peiping tomorrow."

His bushy eyebrow rose. "That all? No trouble at all. One seat?"

"Yeah, I already have my own seat. It's for a woman photographer."

"Sure, I figured there was a she-male in the pictures somewheres."

"She's going to make some of the pictures for the story I'm doing for *Beacon*. You know the Man's Magazine." He bored into me with the China-blue eye. I felt myself coloring again.

"She's a photographer, honest-to-God? You got her cleared with the KMT press people?"

"I'm trying."

"Sure, sure, well, that's a new angle, anyhow."

I knew I had to level with him. "It's Martha Shoop, the wife of an Army captain—"

"Yeah, I know him, Carl. A rear-echelon type, getting nice and fat on the service of supply. He's no friend of mine, otherwise I wouldn't—"

"I know you wouldn't. I was hoping he wasn't a friend of yours." The grin widened. "And just off the record," I added, "this is no White Russian-type affair."

"Okay." The smile was warmer now. He got up, stretched, and walked over to a big map on the wall. "It may be none of my business, but where are you figuring on staying up there?"

I felt I could trust him completely, that he wouldn't mention it if I asked him not to. I said: "I plan to take her to Peiping, then out to Kalgan, if we can get there. I'll probably leave her at Kalgan and go out to a little town called Djin-zuh, one of the towns that have changed hands a few times in that vicinity. Can pick up some stories about the fighting there."

"Sure, I know it. Miserable little hick town. But should be plenty fascinatin'—I envy you the trip." He squinted at the map and swung around to face me. "I know that lady, I've met her. Sure you wanna take her out that far?"

"She wants it."

"Okay, say no more, Joe. I'll get the place for you, and leave word for you at your hotel. The Cathay, right?"

I nodded and got up. "Thanks, Bud, I appreciate it."

"Think nothin' of it." I shook his hand. "I may be out that way sometime, be meetin' up with you. Sometimes we air-lift stuff into that territory for the Gimo when his soldier boys are gettin' in trouble locally; maybe we accidentally kind of kick out a bomb or two on the Commies, where it'll do some good. But Uncle Sam wouldn't like it if you told that story."

He walked to the door with me and gave me a card engraved with Chinese characters. "That's Shin-yu," he explained. "He's in Kalgan. Very savvy. He can help you, he knows everything." Wade had written on the back of the card: "This is a friend of ours, Scott Ostermann. Help him if he needs it."

At that moment I would have done almost any favor for Bud Wade. He reminded me of the can-do type I had known in World War II and assorted other wars afterward—Indo-China, Indonesia, Malaya—the Grade A soldier at the front, at the workaday, rifle-company level: the man who would give you his shirt on a moment's notice if you were on the right side—or kill you just as easily if you weren't. A type that tended to disappear rapidly with the coming of peace, but was especially needed in this time of the bush war. I hoped that he was being especially friendly with me because he sensed I was simpatico with his breed, and maybe valued it more than the less destructive, less daring and more selfish creature of peace.

"Some time I hope I can do as much for you," I said.

"Just you write the truth up there, what you see, that's all. And burn a joss stick for me, sometimes." The grin broadened again.

The card of introduction reminded me that such things are immensely important preparation for a trip in Asia. I hurried to Broadway Mansions and got similar introductory letters and cards to people in Peiping from John Lindahl and Steve Bildo. When I got back to the hotel Martha had gone, leaving a note:

"Darling Scott—I've gone to the apartment to get my things ready. Will go with you any time." I read it several times because those simple words were so lacking in reservation. I phoned her, taking a chance that Carl might have come back.

But he hadn't. "It really knocked me to find you'd gone when I got back to the room," I told her. "Most of the time I was out I was thinking how good it would be when I saw you again. But the note made it better."

"I feel the same way," she said, with that little quaver of distress that pulled me in pieces. Then, more businesslike: "How about the accreditation?"

"I think we'll make it."

"Good."

"Don't worry," I said. "Everything will work out all right."

"That's what I wanted to hear."

"When can I come over?"

"As soon as you can get here."

Then I remembered I hadn't told her the big news. "Can you go to Peiping tomorrow morning?"

"Tomorrow!"

"Yes, by CNAC." Suddenly, the enormity of what I was asking her to do rose like a geyser over me: to throw up the marriage completely, to leave her friends in Shanghai, to give up an easy life in a cosmopolitan big city for the danger and discomfort of the frontier; to trade a fat, if crooked income to live with a man who could offer little but uncertainty, and probably a lot worse than that.

"You haven't changed your mind?" I had to say it straight out.

I held my breath until she answered. "I said I'd go with you any time."

"That's good, Baby." But as I hung up and started for the elevator, I wondered if it was good. Good, that is, for her. It was good for me, that was certain. I felt that moment that if she *didn't* go, I might as well cut my throat, there wasn't much else worth surviving for. But aside from the fact that this was Shanghai in the middle of a military and political earthquake, wasn't I wrecking her life for a couple of weeks' pleasure? Or maybe that was too dramatic a frame for the issue. People lived for the moment in Shanghai. And the future would come up with the answers. I knew one thing right then; I had no intention of giving her up after the Peiping trip. Somehow, I'd work it out—that is, if we made the trip, and survived it.

✳

Now I realized, as Ling wheeled his cab up in front of Broadway Mansions, this whole deal was going to come out in the open. And it was better that way.

This time I could walk right up to her apartment—and if Shoop should be there, have it all out with him.

And if he wasn't? Would I just sneak her away like a thief in the night and wait until later to face him, or write him a note from Peiping like a miserable little clerk to tell him what I had done?

But all the misgivings washed away at the thought of seeing her as I walked into the bare, dilapidated lobby of Broadway Mansions and headed for the elevator that would take me to her.

And she was there, at the door, when I rang, the sunbeam smile was there for me, but I could tell at once that there was still a current of nervousness and uneasiness behind it. It made me feel awkward as I put my arms around her; and she held her head so that I couldn't kiss her.

"The servants," she said. "I don't want them to—"

"Of course, Baby, of course." I dropped my arms and looked at her cloudy face. In the next room I glimpsed a house boy in a white coat peeking around a comer. "Did you pack your things?" I asked.

"Yes." She indicated a medium-sized suitcase and a camera case at the side of the room.

"Is that all?"

"We won't need too much."

"No, but a sleeping bag—it might be rough living up there. I'll get one this afternoon. I have to go down and pick up the tickets, I can do it then."

"You haven't got the tickets yet?"

"No, but Bud Wade made the reservation ..." Then I realized that she might be hoping I *hadn't* got the tickets. "You're not sorry, are you, Baby?"

"Of course not," she said shortly, and that was a bad sign.

But I knew instinctively not to push the subject any further right that moment. "Let's go, then." I picked up the suitcase and put my hand on the door knob, to open it.

"Wait," she said. "Just a minute. I'll need my coat." She went to the closet and opened the door.

I looked around the apartment, registering it for the first time. There were some thick heavy silk drapes, handsome custom-made damascened furniture, big red and gold lacquer chests, vases, an ancient T'ang horse statue that must have been worth a fortune, an expensive rug. I could see all around me signs of affluence, Shoop's *cumishaw* from his racketeer buddies.

She came with her trench coat over her arm, and saw me taking in the luxurious interior. She saw what was on my mind.

"You'll feel better when we get some lunch," I told her. "I know how you must feel."

She nodded, but in the big blue eyes I read that she wondered if I did know how she felt.

"Did you leave a note?" I asked.

"Yes."

"What did you tell him?"

"That I was leaving him."

"Was that all?"

"Yes."

This was a lot harder than I had thought it would be. She was leaving a plush, luxurious existence for a big, dangerous question mark.

"I'll come back tonight and have it out with Carl," I said, trying to reassure her. "Will he be back from Nanking?"

"I think so," she bit her lip. "Do you think it's a good idea? Couldn't we just—go away?"

"Martha . . . poor baby," I patted her shoulder as I put down the bag and pushed the call button. "You won't have to be in it at all. You can stay at the hotel and I'll come up here and see him."

"But what if he makes trouble? He could, you know."

I couldn't help laughing. "If I didn't know you better, Baby, I'd say you were spooked. Where's the famous courage I saw on that first day, at the beach?"

I couldn't have said anything more effective if I had calculated it. I saw her little chin jut. "You're right. We're going to see it together, aren't we?"

"Yes." And then, a second thought: "See what, Martha?"

"The war."

"That's right." Now, suddenly, the sunbeam smile was back again. As we waited for the elevator, the sureness came back to her. "And I'm going to get away from all this—corruption. And we are going to get a story that tells the truth—the truth about the war, the war where the war is really being fought—aren't we?"

I said "Yes—we are." But her sublime confidence undermined my own. She had a fantastic faculty for simplifying, and concentrating. I knew the story couldn't be that simple but in a time like this she made it seem to be.

She saw that I had been feeling some doubts, we had almost exchanged moods. "I know you're looking for adventure stories, Scott," she said, the wide-set blue eyes level. "But if you weren't interested in getting good ones, you wouldn't be going up to the war zone. You'd get them sitting around the bar in Shanghai."

My mood of depression seemed to be deepening. "That's because my job is writing eye-witnessers. So I have to be somewhere—where there's action. It doesn't show any special virtue."

"But you said you always wanted to be where the big exciting stories were."

I had to admit that she was right, that I'd had a drive toward the big excitement, the action—although my persistence had been wearing out much too soon recently, as in the Hong Kong water police and piracy story, too much of which had been gathered in the bar at the Peninsula Hotel, too little out on the patrol boats.

"We're going to a town that's been conquered by both sides at different times, aren't we?" she asked. "Didn't the Communists hold Djin-zuh for a year?"

"They had it twice—once for eight months, another time for a couple of months. The Nationalists have it now, but the Commies are getting pretty close again. With the troops from the town, I should be able to see some of the fighting up there in the hills."

"Yes," she picked it up excitedly, "and we should have a wonderful chance to see what happens to a town when the Communists take over. What they did to the people when they were in control. Everything that happens, just as if we were behind the Communist lines. But with relative freedom to write about it."

I could see the bright yellow glints flashing in her eyes, a mammoth excitement had got to Brünnehilde and she had clearly been turning her researcher's brain to the trip. But I was thinking: This trip is too big and too wonderful to get sidetracked into a political story *Beacon* will never buy.

"That's too political for my market," I said somewhat shortly.

"Adventure stories can tell political stories, coo," she said, with such confidence that I felt myself believing it too.

The elevator came and she walked proudly, unashamedly into it, as if she dared the Chinese elevator operator to stare at her. He did, and so did I: Brünnehilde had a brain, as well as a Valkyrie presence which, I thought, would make any man proud, or maybe, get him into plenty of trouble.

11

A GOOD LUNCH AT THE METROPOLE BROUGHT US CLOSER. Over coffee, she said:

"I'm sorry I was so grumpy before."

"That's all right. You had, and have, a lot on your mind."

"I can't help it, that's the way I get when I'm worried."

"Maybe you can tell me about it, now that you feel a little better."

"I will."

As we were going up to my room, she told me: "When I went to Broadway Mansions this morning, everything went wrong. There must have been some kind of student rally downtown. I didn't see it. But at Nanking Road two Chinese men ran up to the car. They were all upset, and I didn't know who they were. I thought they knew me, they pointed to me and cursed and spat on the window. I thought they might be anti-Imperialists, or I thought maybe they were coolie-boys that worked for Carl, and knew me.

"We were stuck in traffic and couldn't move. The two men— they were really only boys—kept beating on the window and I was afraid they would break it. I felt trapped.

"The cabbie opened the window and yelled at them. They yelled back something about Imperialists and I was so relieved. I didn't mind that, I was used to it, but if they had been friends of Carl's, I don't know what I could have done."

"Poor baby. Did they give you any more trouble?"

"No, the traffic cleared up."

"Was that all that happened?"

"No. When I got to Broadway Mansions Vivian Black jumped on me and—"

"Vivian Black?"

"Yes, Colonel Black's wife. She followed me into the apartment and talked all the time about what tough luck Carl was having. Of course, she doesn't know about Carl's racketeering involvement— the money he's making. Very few people do. Vivian kept saying I should help my husband in his troubles. I didn't know if she was talking about you—she's a busy-body and always prying into everybody's affairs. I felt all trapped again. And it made me think maybe I was doing Carl all wrong."

"What, after all your trying—the boozing, the dames, and the graft he gets from the racketeers—his friends that sell arms to the Commies?"

"I know, but I couldn't seem to think straight. Then I went down to the lobby to get a paper and saw John Lindahl, and he seemed peculiar too. He kept talking about his wife, what a good wife she was to him, how he wanted me to meet her when she got here from California. I couldn't understand what he was driving at—"

"Maybe nothing, Baby. Maybe you were just jumpy about you and me, and you were too sensitive to everything people were saying to you. You were reading meanings—"

"I know." Talking about her troubles only seemed to bring them back to her, rather than lightening the burden.

"Don't worry about it, Baby. Tomorrow we'll be out of here." There was one small detail I hadn't mentioned. Even if the plane took off on schedule tomorrow, we would have to fend until then with Carl. When he got home and saw her note, he might fly into a rage and decide to come around here with a pistol and try to finish off one or both of us. His reaction could range all the way from that to sodden indifference. In his current mood of desperation, anything could happen. And I would be prepared for anything. I wasn't really worried about it. A lot of people had tried to kill me before—much better men than Shoop had tried in various violent situations. The main thing was to keep him off Martha's neck.

I wasn't sure what I should do if Shoop didn't try to reach me. I didn't particularly want a confrontation scene, where the lover faces the husband and various theatrics occur. Shoop, the bastard, didn't fit that mold. Neither did I, as the lover.

Yet I knew what to do, and that it was right. I had planned, this afternoon, to leave Martha at the room and run around on my various crucial errands, like picking up the tickets, and checking with Jimmy Yung to see if he could send the accreditation to Peiping, and getting a sleeping bag for Martha. But now I knew I should go into the room with her and stay with her for a while. And I tried to gear up my neutrons, deutrons and positrons by setting my will—and if I had been religious I would have done the religious equivalent, I would have prayed—that when I would hold her now the mating would be perfect again, and our nervousness this day might not upset it. Because this was the reminder of what we had. Maybe it was all we had, but it was a lot. It was a lot more than a punch in the nose.

There was one good thing. I looked at her distressed small sunbeam-face, with the unseemly furrows between her light eyes and at her long neck that seemed translucent above the white blouse, and that moment she was all I wanted, ever, and that moment was good enough forever and I wanted her with everything I had. I looked in her eyes obliquely, where the light from the tall window of the hall struck through them, and I saw the fire of my own feeling flashing there, I knew she felt as I did.

I opened the door for her and went to the curtains, which had been set against the bright eastern sun of the early morning, to pull them back. When I turned back to her she was taking off her white blouse, and one shoulder strap of her brassiere had fallen. I saw the smooth shoulder and the flecks of beauty spots where the smallness of her shoulders curved beautifully into her long neck. I went to kiss her and felt the warmth rising in my back and flooding over into my chest, and my breath coming short, my hands shaking, and I knew everything would be all right, I could somehow make it right, and I would.

*

My God, I thought, looking half asleep at my watch, it's four o'clock, and I woke up fast, conscious of a great gratitude that the lovemaking, the Polynesian *ha'uti* or play, hadn't missed. It was perfection, maximum encouragement and confirmation, the two bodies matching so at the time both of us knew it was perfect. Now, afterwards, though the sense of involvement, responsibility, complications flooded over me, I could face those things with concentration. After the encouragement of that perfect sex, I could see those things clearly and willingly, as if they were the only important things. Perfect sex, with the right woman, made you feel like working. Until now, I had never thought that there was such a thing as the right woman for time after time.

Now, even right after perfect sex, when a man usually thinks another woman might be exciting later on, I looked at that long, smooth narrow waist, those deep-curved white hips pressed against the bed as she lay on her back, like a child completely relaxed, her arms flung above her head, the small features composed, and I knew that when I came back, I wouldn't want any other woman. Every contour might not be perfect, every line might not be within the ten-thousandth of an inch that means the difference between passable good looks and beauty, but to me, this moment and therefore much more later on, she was what the Polynesian bucks looked for—*hina 'aro*, the woman you want to come back to, or literally, the wanted one.

Martha was still sleeping. I left as rapidly as I could, taking care to lock the door from the outside, ran through my errands quickly, even managed to get a sleeping bag for Martha at White-away Laidlaw's store. Jimmy Yung hadn't promised anything about Martha's credentials—he had been evasive—but he had at least promised we would be met at the Peiping Airport by somebody from Chiang's public relations office. Somewhere in the late afternoon I'd managed to call the desk and have Martha's suitcase sent up to her from the checkroom and when I got to the hotel room she was waiting for me in a Hawaiian type *muumuu* I will always remember.

It was gold, with some sort of faint floral pattern, and it had been taken in at the waist by some expert seamstress so that it fitted as closely as her own skin. She stood up, smiling, and turned to show it to me, and she was a lovely thing of gold from top to toe.

She was all composed and rested, she had showered, she was as fresh as the stem of a flower. Wanting her came back to me with a rush. I kissed her and held her.

"You'd better get a bath," she said. "You're soaking wet. Take a bath then come and tell me how everything went."

"It went well," I said, like a husband coming home from business. And tonight, her being there in her gold robe seemed to make that place suddenly home.

She called down for room service while I took a shower. She didn't hesitate, because the Chinese were not bothered by women's being in men's rooms, and in fact seemed to think it normal.

And by the time I was out and shaved and in a fresh robe, the room boy was there at the door with dinner. Still there had been no visit or phone call from Shoop.

It was an early dinner, and after it there was still light on the Whangpoo. A white river boat turned on water that was slick with sunset red, the rows of windows like candles on a cake. Pinpoints of white, and a green running light, marked an American destroyer.

"Good thing the Reds don't have any aircraft," I said as we sat on the couch and watched the boats passing on the slick water. I should have thought before I said it, because it brought a surging reminder that tomorrow we would be off for Peiping. And also, to me, the resolution to call Shoop. When we left, we should leave a clean track behind us.

I went to the phone and she was reading my thought. "He's not home," she said.

"How do you know?"

"If he were, he'd have called before this—that is, if he cared, and I don't think he has the courage to care."

It struck me suddenly that all this time she had known this, that the phone might ring and it would be Carl; but she had been holding the thought under strict control, as I had. She was better than I was, but she was a lot like me, and I was glad for that.

I picked up the phone and told the operator: "Please don't ring us if anyone calls. Tell them we are not here and ask for their number."

"Yes, sir."

I moved back to my golden girl. The purple sky cast shadows in her gown, it became metallic purple where the gown was moulded into curves.

I sat next to her and stripped off her gown and held her, the smooth shoulders filling my hands, the hips like a perfect, complete world moving under me, her body trim as a tiger's while it turned in the deepening darkness. We didn't bother to turn on the lights.

✻

Afterward, we lay in the dark, watching the lights moving on the river, and it was as if this were our honeymoon. She asked me about the girls I had known before her, and I would tell her about some of them, but not the one girl I had known before who had been nearly perfect mating—nor my wife. Then, when I had been only twenty-one, and before I had seen other peoples, like the Polynesians, the Balinese and the Annamites, who know the true value of sex, I hadn't appreciated it. Now I did.

She asked me very little about Lois. Once she said: "Is it good— sleeping with your wife?"

"It was in the beginning—but not now. It was never like—you and me."

That was enough about Lois to satisfy her. I said: "Most girls want to talk about marriage. You don't."

She nodded. "I was badly enough burned by marriage. So were you."

I was lying with my head propped up on the couch pillow, watching the lights of a ferryboat. We heard the sound of the steam whistle, floating up from the Bund, echoing along the river flats and among the European-type buildings of the waterfront.

"You remind me of the freest women in the world as far as I know, the Polynesians," I said. "They're so free they want to be damn sure they like to sleep with their man before they make it anything like permanent.

"That's what I was telling myself before, that you're the kind of woman I want to come back to—even just after it happens. In Polynesian terms, you're my *hina 'aro, my* desire."

"If I am, I am satisfied."

"I think you are a Polynesian, though you're more like a Valkyrie by racial extraction."

"Well, the Valkyrie were pagans too, like the Polynesians."

But her mind seemed to be on something else. "All those lights in the river," she said. "All those ships, loaded with millions of dollars worth of arms and supplies—but most of it won't go where it will do any good against the Communists. It'll be profit to some fat KMT racketeers. And I don't think the Americans care whether it is delivered or not. They don't care about it because they don't know. There are no good correspondents to tell them what's happening, here in China or in any other of the civil wars the Communists have started. The correspondents don't care, like all the rest of the Americans—with some few exceptions."

I could see she was starting her favorite theme, and right now I felt inclined toward other subjects of conversation.

"Tell me about Carl—about that racket he has."

I saw hate flick across her face, because Carl was identified with the corruption and cynicism and ignorance she had just been speaking about. She didn't hesitate:

"Many of them are doing it, and it's so easy, a lot easier than struggling to make sure the work is done right. You just turn over whatever it is—arms or rice or trucks—to the right Chinese, and you don't check to see if it's the right one, really, or whether it's going where it should. So you get your commission, your *cumishaw*, in one form or another, under the table, and you close your eyes and have a ball, it's easy. So very often the guns get to the Communists—and the rice doesn't get to the people, it's a profit to a KMT racketeer."

I said: "It's' too bad I'm not doing a political story."

"It doesn't matter. It's more important to write about the war where it's happening, at the front, where people can see it in unmistakable terms. Just write the truth up there—about what happens or doesn't happen. The reasons will be clear. It's a simple thing—just tell the truth."

"Is that an order?" I thought for a moment I could see the stern drillmaster Shoop seemed to find in her.

She laughed. "I'm sorry. I—get carried away. I'm afraid I get carried away too much—in making love with you, too."

"It's in your character to get carried away. I think, if you'd been a man, you'd have been president. But I'm damned glad you were born with all those curves in all the right places. I'm willing to do without you as president."

"How many did you have before?" she demanded abruptly. "I mean, girls. No, I withdraw the question," she added quickly. "I don't want to know."

"I wasn't going to tell you anyhow."

What was it in lovers that made them want to know about the lovers before—masochism, jealousy? Or just the reassurance that it hadn't been quite like this before?

And why did lovers want to tell about the ones before? She told me without any prodding about the Boston University student who had been the first one. He had been a medical student, he had been wiser and more experienced, he had given her a big pep talk about how people needed it and it was not serious, and I hated him and said I would like to punch him in the nose.

And there had been only two others before Shoop. One was an older man who worked for *Time*, and he had been married and refused to mention the word love, and he had treated her with what seemed a flippant casualness, and I hated him too.

Then there had been a Dutchman, in Europe, and he had seemed more worthy of her, and gentler, but he had been attractive and I felt jealousy, not hate, toward him. As for Shoop, he had been rough, quick and drunk, and she had not slept with him for a couple of months. I did not press her to talk about him—I didn't want to know any more. I knew one thing: Of her various lovers, I disliked him most.

And so we talked on into the cool night, looking out at the black river slick with lights, and it was almost like a wedding night for us. Probably it was the fact that she had brought her suitcase and her golden gown, and that we had eaten dinner in our dressing gowns, and that we had our own private castle above the harbor.

She told me a little more about herself: things that seemed most critical and vital in all the world to me, and I knew from this that I must be hooked. She told me about her vexatious childhood. Her family had been broken—she had stayed with her father, an editor on a small country paper, a man who loved books, certainly was considered bookish in his community—a man who had fought a running battle with the booze. He had urged her to read good books, but had been sadly lacking in the wherewithal for her education. But she had been a bright student, with the necessary scholarships.

"I knew you were smart as well as sexy, Baby. You know, Brünnehilde was both."

Then I remembered suddenly that I had planned to see Carl tonight. I looked at my watch and it said eleven-thirty.

"Wait, Baby." I went to the phone and a sleepy operator answered.

"No, sir, there were no calls."

"Okay." I was about to hang up when it occurred to me that he might have got home and somehow not got the word. "Operator, please try this number." I gave her his number and braced myself for the sound of his voice. What would I say to him? I looked over and saw that Sunbeam had turned on the light, and that she, too, was leaning forward intently.

We waited, and then I told her, "No answer. He's not answering."

She sighed. "I'm glad. I'm glad you tried."

I hung up the phone. "I'm coming over but I don't want to hear about Carl," I said. "And I don't want to talk much."

She laughed, teasing me. "What will we do then?"

"Lots of things. Very good things. The best you've ever had, and lots of them."

"You seem to be made to do them to me. You look right and you are right, and I want more things done by you. Now."

"Do you really mean that, Baby? Is it really important, or are you doing it because I think it's important? Is the war against the Communists more important?"

"Both are important," she said. "Both are of maximum importance. I believe both of them call for maximum effort. More than that: what Nietzsche used to call 'an overgoing and a downgoing'—the kind of mammoth effort he expected of his Superman."

I laughed: "Just because you might be Brünnehilde, I can't qualify as Siegfried."

She was smiling too. "You do well enough for me."

12

I HAD TO GET UP ABOUT FIVE TO GET MY PACKING DONE FOR the Peiping trip. I moved carefully so as not to wake her.

Rain drummed against the window pane, the sky was smoky with clouds. Only a faint mother-of-pearl light came into the room, barely enough to see by. There was no sign of the rose and pale green tints of pre-dawn.

Across the room in the dark for once the girl was faceless and shapeless, only a mound of bedclothes. I felt alone, though I could hear her breathing.

I had finished packing the first suitcase when the pain began, the numbness, the throbbings in the lower part of the right arm. I knew that echo of World War II in the Pacific—Iwo Jima by name, a Japanese mortar shell, well aimed in 1945. The strange, faint wind, a kind of aura of uncertainty and a hint of panic, seemed to be settling over all the objects in the room. The arm pain was only an indirect effect of the World War II brain injury—a motor area residual, the doctors called it.

I knew it for the echo of the old wound, the bad one. My mother had always told me that if I wanted to be a wanderer, I would collect scars in the process; like a nation that wanders in foreign fields. I could have told her that. This was the worst of my scars. In a moment, if the aura ran in the usual form, the images in my eyes would not make sense, as if each eye had an image that wouldn't synchronize with the other.

It was beginning to happen now. These things hadn't been happening so often in the last year or two, but I was pretty tired now, and it happened often in the times of tiredness.

You musn't give in to it, I told myself. I said it aloud and gave thanks that I could, because when it got bad I couldn't say words, I would get them backward or get the wrong sounds.

I stood rather than sat, because one reason I was sure I hadn't had more trouble with the injury was that I had tried against it. In one of the military hospitals where I'd been I knew a captain who had almost the same injury, and he had fallen down several times in a big swoon, cold conked in what the doctors called a *grand mal*. One of the doctors had joked with me in the cold-blooded way doctors have and had said I couldn't afford to have a *grand mal* because I wasn't covered by government disability insurance.

"Light to moderate brain damage, periods of total disability," one of the medical savants had written on one of the many reports I had seen. But almost all of the time, the thing didn't bother me, and if the girl had been awake and watching she couldn't have told anything was happening. It was one of the secrets between only me and me. My employers at *Beacon* and elsewhere and my friends and the girl wouldn't have appreciated knowing about it.

"Knowing about it," I said aloud, and still said it perfectly. Maybe this was going to be an easy one. Don't feel sorry for yourself,

I thought, and it'll be easier. After all, it was only a head injury, whether it was caused by crossing the street against a traffic light or by an enemy shell. Except, of course, that you get a medal for the latter and free medical care and usually a pension, whereas if you get run over by a car you pay your own medical bills and are cussed out as a damn fool besides. The wounds of the cold war are more like the latter.

The aura was passing, not a bad one at all, maybe the thinking about it as an ordinary traffic accident and yourself as a damn fool helped.

Vision was straightening out now. I looked out on the Bund where the rain had stopped and the gray sky was lightening. Down on the strip of earth between the street and the water of the Whangpoo, orange fires flickered, as if on the dark ground someone had punched holes and you could see hellfire below. They were only the cooking fires of the coolies in the matshed colony where the lucky ones had a scrap or two of meat to throw on top of their rice bowls before they faced the world for the day.

I walked over to the bed and looked down at my heavily-sleeping beauty. She slept in what seemed to be her favorite position, the fetal posture, on her side with her legs pulled up protectively. I marveled again at how beautiful she was—in the mounting light of the morning the wide curves of her heavy eyelids filling half her face, her little nose and cheeks still dainty and smooth, though gravity tried to pull them out of shape.

She was defenseless and fresh and beautiful as a child, and my heart went down to her with tenderness and something like pity.

Pity, I thought, was a fine word for me to use when I was taking her into what a lot of people would call catastrophe, offering her nothing except a shot-up war correspondent trying to readjust to peace—and married to boot and unsuccessfully at that.

What would be the end of it if you did have trouble, with your abominable head injury, or with the Reds, or with your wife or with the sottish husband? Supposing you got knocked off up there at Djin-zuh, you that always wanted to be the brave correspondent, risking shot and shell for the Great Truth. You, the Ham What Am—it's easy to risk your neck if life doesn't mean much, but how about her life? Didn't her life mean anything? It did, it meant everything because her life was fixed with yours, inextricably the same, and not to be cut off except as you would amputate an arm or leg. Because of her, life was alive now and it had been dead, or half-dead anyhow, you and she were life now.

Suppose you go up there, Mr. Ham What Am, and get hurt, which is more likely than being killed in this kind of life called war—what about her, where does that put her? What if by that time she is pregnant? She had said it couldn't happen now, this week, but how about next week and the next, and after that? Okay, if it happens and she is pregnant, I am strong enough to fend for both of us, if I am not in a lousy cot somewhere with bullets in the gut, or a foot swollen black with gangrene.

Do you have the guts to appear chicken?—and insist that you take her to Hong Kong instead of out to the miserable back country and the Reds?

In the gray clouds over the Bund, I could see the light edge of the sun rising, silver like the moon. My watch said nearly six-fifteen. If I were going to change my plans I must wake her. There would be a lot to fix.

I shook her gently by the shoulder. "Baby, wake up, Baby."

"Huh, what, huh?" she asked with her eyes still clamped shut. Then she put up her arm around my neck and hung on. "Are you all right, Scott, is everything all right?" The wide eyes came open, fear that was like glaring hostility in the blue.

I kissed her gently. "Everything's okay, Martha. But you'd better get up."

"Okay." But the eyes closed again quickly and I shook her once more.

"Okay," she said, sitting straight up with the covers clutched around her.

"You might as well get washed up and waked up, Baby, because we've got to talk before we go."

"Nothing's wrong, is it?"

"No, Baby, nothing's wrong."

When she came out of the bathroom all tidied up, her hair a crown of spun gold in the brightening morning, and wearing her golden gown, she was as fresh as a kid scrubbed hard in the tub and dried hard with a big warm towel, her face and her ears shiny clean, and her movement wafted the scent of a talcum that she liked. Not perfume and not sweet, but it was music to me, as if sunshine on a wheat field could have a scent and make music.

"Come and sit next to me, because we have to talk."

Dread came over her face, a kid about to be given a talking to, as she walked toward me. "You haven't decided to leave me?"

I couldn't bear that. I got up and held her hard and tight. "No, no, Baby. Nothing at all like that. Quite the contrary."

"That's good." She was smiling now, her brightest smile that always seemed shy because she had a way of lowering her head when she was most delighted.

I sat her next to me on the couch. "Martha, I think we should cancel the trip to Peiping, and just go to Hong Kong. We'll go on from there. I can figure some story from there that'll satisfy *Beacon*. This isn't the only story around by a long shot."

She looked as if I had just pulled all the stiffening from her round face. "But why change your mind? Isn't that a good story up there?"

I nodded. I had to agree. "But I wasn't thinking enough about— you and me. We—" I was trying to choose my words carefully. "We could get badly hurt out there, and . . . supposing I should get hurt, where would that leave you?"

She was trying to read the extra signals I wasn't sending out verbally. She couldn't find them. She smiled. "If that's all there is, there's no reason to change our plans."

"I know, but—my just saying we could get hurt doesn't tell anything—about what it's like to get hurt. If it hasn't happened, it's hard to imagine how bad it can be, and mostly, how long, how many years and centuries, your pain and the misery seem to go on. Those days and weeks take forever to pass."

The smile was there with full brilliance, and also the composure, the calm and assurance of womanhood that everything has got to turn out all right ultimately. She kissed me as if this time I were the child. Her lips were smooth and cool, better than food for me. I turned away. Her power over me was too palpable.

"Look, Martha—don't think about what I want to do. All I want is what's best for you. If we look at it with any perspective, if we look back on right now from the perspective of next year, we'll see that it's best to shuck this war, go somewhere else, it'll be forgotten and there will be other things people will be interested in. Plenty of other adventure stories they'll buy."

Her chin was firming. She said, "You're sounding like everybody else: take the easy way, never mind what happens to the world, to the kind of world you stand for when you are at your best. Live for yourself, take it easy. Never mind the struggle you're rightfully part of. I've admired you, Scott, for the things you have done, things you've seen for yourself and written about. Instead of taking somebody else's word for it. Your courage."

There was something sinister about the way she put admire in the past tense. And I just plain didn't have the courage to pretend that I wanted to dodge the trip to the front. I wanted desperately that she should respect me. Also, I must confess I knew just an edge of exasperation. Here I was trying to think of the very best thing for her and she was bucking me with everything she had.

"You mean you'd really rather go up to Peiping and all that mess than stay in the Repulse Bay Hotel in Hong Kong?"

"Repulse Bay would be dull."

"Even with the swimming?"

"Even with the swimming."

She kissed me again. "Dearest one, I want you to do what you should do, what some of the others don't have courage enough to do. I want to be proud of you and I want to be with you. Don't worry about my future. I'll be happy if you and I can be doing something important."

It was quite a long speech for her. She was very earnest, her eyes showed it, and the arch of her nostrils sharpened as always when she wanted something very much.

"And," she added, "I want to do as well with pictures as you do with a story. We could be a team. We can, can't we?"

"Baby," I told her, feeling myself softening toward her, "I just don't want you, when we're in some bad trouble up there, to be sorry, to regret that you ever decided to go."

"I'd never blame you for it," she said. "That's a promise."

"All right, and that's a deal. If you're sure it's what you want."

"I'm tired of being cut off from it here, not being really in it or out of it." The flecks of gold fire sparkled in her eyes. "I want to see for myself, too."

She ploughed on. "Here in Shanghai, I've seen some of the things I've read about. Don't forget I was a researcher. I've seen the Vanguard that Lenin wrote about—the students who are being trained to lead the revolution, propagandized into thinking it's nationalistic, patriotic. Then the flip-flop—they find they're working for Russia. And once they're in it, there's no escape— they're in jail for life in a police state. I've seen that propaganda war here, in Shanghai. But not the shooting war, out there. I want to."

She was the Valkyrie now, her eyes flashing sparks. And I was proud of her; and probably elated that she seemed to think I was worthy of her, too. I walked to the window, where the pale rim of the sun was cleaving a hole in the overcast.

"I'm glad you changed my mind," I said. "Every correspondent should have somebody like you around."

She came over and leaned her head against my chest. She is mucho woman, I thought, mucho more than a little scoutmaster, and I am sorry that I ever thought that of her, even for a moment.

I put my arm around her, and holding her I thought of something that should have occurred to me long before.

"Wait, I have something for you." I went to my big bag and flipped it open. I had a ring, a family heirloom that I never wore because I didn't like to wear rings. But it would be just right for her, just right for this morning and this moment.

The ring was soft gold, a native ring that an uncle had brought back from Togoland or British West Africa, somewhere in the middle of the Dark Continent. He had been a chemist in a British mine there, and the ring, a wide band, carried some hieroglyphic legend all around it.

I put it on her second finger and strangely enough, it fitted very well, and it seemed to go very well with the squareness and capability of her hands.

"It's a family heirloom," I told her. "I'm sorry, but it's from the British imperial domain. From Africa, probably that's Swahili writing on it, and probably it says 'Death To The White Man,' or maybe only 'Use Murine Eye Drops.' But to me it's an unworthy ring for Brünnehilde—who after all should have Rheingold, at least."

She glowed when she looked at it, the shy head-down smile that was the brightest of all.

She said: 'The British may be bastards in the Empire—but they're trying to do better—and they're lily white compared to the Communists."

I picked up the phone. "Operator, this is Scott Ostermann. Any messages for me during the night? Any phone calls?"

"Just a minute, sir," the girl said. "No sir, no messages."

I asked her to try Shoop's number. The house boy answered. "Mastah not here. Mebbe back Thursday." Thursday was day after tomorrow. Martha's note would have to do the job.

13

PEIPING WAS PASSING UNDER OUR WING. WE BOTH FELT
the electric charge of seeing a great old city for the first time.
Also the isolation of reaching an island, for Peiping was on the
edge of an island, an island of Nationalist territory surrounded by
Communists. For hours we had been flying high over land held by
the Communists. We couldn't have traversed it on the ground, but
in our plush DC-4 it was easy. There had even been lunch served by
the Chinese stewardess.

But the impressive thing to me had been that Martha was such
a good traveling companion: she demanded no more than a man,
no special treatment. And she knew the ground, she was a good
researcher. When we passed over the sprawling brown mouths of
the Yellow River or Hwang Ho, the Big Muddy of China, she pointed
upstream where, she said, Kaifeng, the great trading center of
central China, was under siege right now by Communist forces
coming down from the north. Farther along, partly under a cloud,
she indicated Weihsien, now in Communist hands. She said that

Bud Wade had flown a light plane in and landed in a street there to rescue a couple of trapped KMT generals, while the Communists were beating on the gates. I made a mental note to ask Wade about that story, when and if we met again.

"I'm glad my photographer is such a trained researcher, too," I said, and it made her happy—happier than she would have been if I'd told her another notable fact, that she was the subject of admiring glances from the other passengers.

The little brown wisp of a Chinese businessman who sat ahead of us had hauled himself up on his seatback to point out landmarks in the dusty city that crawled below us. The little man with the western-style suit and collar that was too big for him indicated a big walled enclosure. Even from this distance, those earth-colored walls looked high and thick. Beyond them, we could see high red buildings with pagoda roofs. There seemed to be many ridges of lower walls inside the bigger one.

"Bei-shing," he said, pronouncing it in a way I had never heard before, "is city of many warr-es. Everything is crosed in the warres."

"City of many walls," I translated to myself. "Enclosed in the walls." I remembered how one Chinese in the PRO office had struggled with the *l* and *r* proposition. He was essaying the name of *Collier's* magazine; it took me a long time to catch it. He called it *Korea*, exactly like the country.

"Melikan say it 'Fo-bidden city,' " he went on. "Capital of Manchus. Pink one with green loof. Some of old city standing, made by Genghis Khan—eight hundled yeah ago. Big rump up theah is Coal-a Hilluh. Last Ming empelola hang himself by rocust tree on Coal-a Hilluh."

Martha and I nodded politely, choking back laughter that would have come much too easily. The little man was proud of himself for his English.

"Thank you," I managed to say. "You speak very well the English." I didn't dare look at Martha or we both would have broken down.

"Oh no sah," he said, smiling happily, "my English very snafu." We couldn't help laughing at that, but he wanted us to, then.

"I take it you have some friends in the American army."

"Snafu, not to say Batfu and Fubar," he went on, for once with perfect enunciation.

"I don't know those," Martha said.

"Some time I'll explain them," I promised, knowing I never would mention those words unless she pressed me for them.

The warning lights at the front of the cabin went on, telling us in Chinese characters and in English to fasten our seat belts. The stewardess said something in Chinese and translated: "Please fasten your seat belts. No smoking please. We will be landing at Peiping Airport in ten minutes."

It was a small airport, with barn-like wooden hangars that seemed old fashioned. As we taxied in, whipping up clouds of tan-colored dust, I saw a large crowd of spectators by the gate. Somewhere among that crowd of people in summer clothes would be somebody from the PRO office, maybe a deputation. Jimmy Yung would see to that, he was thorough as well as efficient.

Before we got to the police booth for our security check, two men from the PRO office had made themselves known.

They came straight to me, ignoring Martha. One was a short, fat man, in his middle twenties. He wore American Army suntans, spotted and wrinkled, the shirt open at the collar. His face shone with sweat, but he moved very quickly, lightly on his feet for a man of such girth.

The older man looked much taller, although he wasn't. He simply was thin. He must have been fifty-five or sixty, and he wore a pinstriped Western-style suit, a heavy worsted in a sad state of disrepair. His rumpled white shirt had a collar that was too big so that you looked down and saw the golden shine of his collar button inside, and the collar tabs flew at wild angles like wings never pressed into shape. He wore a khaki army tie that seemed full of lumps and extra twists, as if a student of Western customs had been practicing with it. Halfway down on his nose sat round tortoise-shell spectacles, and the misalignment of the glasses seemed to set his eyes almost comically crooked.

The plump one spoke first, in good English. "Mr. Ostermann? We are from the information ministry. Mr. Jimmy Yung from Shanghai contacted us. I am Min Lau and this is G. Duncan Wong."

"Glad to meet you," I said, and turned quickly toward Martha. "And this is Martha Shoop." I had said the name before I could think about it, and I knew right away the question of her name was going to be a tricky one. Should I have introduced her as Mrs. Ostermann, since they obviously hadn't been told she would be with me? I had done it, though, it was right. "I guess Jimmy didn't tell you that my photographer would be with me, Mrs. Shoop." I could feel that I had stepped on Martha's toes, but probably most any way I said it would have been wrong.

The older man was bowing ceremoniously to Martha, a courtly smile fixed on his lined face. "Beautiful lady, we are charmed to make your acquaintance."

The man in khakis shot an impatient look toward the Old One. "No," said the fat man, "Jimmy Yung didn't mention it." He shook my hand and Duncan Wong, again assuming the vertical, maintained his unctuous smile. He turned to me to deliver what was evidently a welcome speech he had planned some time in advance:

"My heart is in America because you have come to visit us—and the beautiful Mrs. Shoop," he added hastily.

"Mrs. Shoop is an expert photographer and her pictures will probably be a lot better than my story." I was struggling, trying to make up for some of the awkwardness I knew she felt.

"Assuredly," said Duncan Wong, "both will be excellent."

"We had better get the formalities over at the terminal," said Min. "The police, baggage, that stuff." Being a Nationalist or KMT island in a Communist sea of land, this airport would have a checkpoint for all passengers.

As we moved toward the terminal building I asked Min if it would be trouble to find a hotel room for Mrs. Shoop. I had decided to play it that way, as long as I had introduced her as somebody else's wife.

"There is no problem," Min said. "There are plenty of rooms in the first class hotels." I had the feeling that both Min and Wong would be friendly and cooperative.

But Martha was being very quiet, and I was hoping that the turn of circumstance hadn't hurt her too much. "Martha, we will have to see the Forbidden City before we leave Peiping," I said.

She only nodded, and Wong offered, "Yes, it is beautiful. You must also see the Temple of Heaven and the Summer Palace of the Empress."

I tried again. "How close are the Communist forces to Peiping?"

"About thirty miles on the south," Min said quickly, and Martha's eyes brightened. "But our territory still stretches five hundred miles to the east."

"Can you get through to Kalgan by train?" she asked. She knew what she wanted to concentrate on and it wasn't architecture.

"Usually, you can get through," said Min.

"Good," Martha said, and I could see her busy mind working out plans for a quick escape from this zone of embarrassment, especially to what she might romantically call the front.

Considerately enough, Min and Duncan Wong took us to the hotel straightway, rather than subjecting us immediately to their office and myriad polite introductions.

"We are able to understand that the travelers are fatigued," said the Old One without, however, being so corny as to quote Confucius on the subject.

I suggested, "Why don't we all go to the hotel and we can have tea together before we go on to the information office?" For once I had grasped the moment, although the occasion was minor.

"An excellent suggestion." Wong bowed.

So we shuddered and rattled our way to the Wagon-Lits Hotel in an old Ford sedan with one door tied by a piece of frazzled rope, and we sat in the grand living room of the suite they had reserved for me, after Martha had been installed in a separate establishment.

The room was tall, with tall windows and the usual damask drapes and plush *fin-de-siècle* furniture, a hangover from the old Imperial days when the Europeans built and ran China's big cities. The windows gave on the trees and low walls of the old Legation Quarter. The trees seemed an olive-green color, the gray walls lighter than gray, probably because the coating of dust neutralized every shade.

"How do you propose to go to Djin-zuh—you and Mrs. Snoop?" Min asked abruptly when the steaming glasses of green tea were set out for us. I saw the courtly Wong shoot a sharp look at him, critical of his gaucherie.

"I talked to Jimmy Yung about it," I said. "He seemed to think we wouldn't have any trouble getting to Kalgan. From there we'd have to improvise." I didn't want to say that we'd talked about the plan I had been considering, of leaving Martha in Kalgan while I went on to the last and most dangerous lap.

"I think Mrs. Shoop might have trouble going to Djin-zuh from Kalgan." Min was ignoring the critical look of his compatriot.

Again my Sunbeam was visibly clouding. "The main thing is to get her accredited first," I temporized. "Jimmy said he would send up word on that as soon as it came through."

"She can go to Kalgan without accreditation," Min said helpfully enough. "We shall have more difficulty from thereon, as the danger increases. We shall have to set up a truck convoy to get through beyond Kalgan to Djin-zuh. Perhaps thirty or forty soldiers. The Communist guerrillas would probably come down and do some killing, otherwise."

"I know," I said, still feeling Martha's hurt that she wasn't being included in this crucial part of the story.

"It would not be wise to expose the beautiful lady to the misfortunes of war," Wong offered, trying to be tactful.

"Well," I jumped in as quickly as I could, "first we should meet the other people at the Information Office here in Peiping, shouldn't we?"

Wong bowed. "By all means, we must."

I was still trying to derail the subject of Djin-zuh and reassure Martha. "Are you and Mr. Wong going to make the trip to Kalgan with us?" I asked Min.

"Yes, both," he said. "And the trip to Djin-zuh with you also, Mr. Ostermann."

"How soon could we get a train to Kalgan?"

"At any time. But perhaps it would be better to have the message from Jimmy Yung about the accreditation, first."

I thought I could feel the current that was probably crossing Martha's mind at that moment. Was it just because she was a woman that they didn't want to let her go, their prejudice against letting a woman into a very dangerous area? I didn't think so.

She was clever and well-informed, but this was her first trip into the field, and she had much to learn. In some of these things, my considerable background in war corresponding, the field stuff was a help.

"Baby," I told her when Min and Wong had left us at the hotel, "you know, this is their method of censorship in this KMT press set-up. They don't censor your copy directly, they just exercise control over where you go. But don't worry, they're giving me a break because they know *Beacon* is nonpolitical. You know, they've checked over some of my stories to make sure that they're adventure stories about big heroes. They figure I'll find some good heroes up here and they're probably right. So there shouldn't be any real holdup in your accreditation."

She still seemed crushed. "Things always seem so complicated when you get around to doing them," she said.

"You seem to have a way, usually, of cutting right through to the simple hearts of things," I said, thinking that it seemed to be true back at Shanghai, but wondering if she could do it in this new, strange territory.

But she responded not at all to the compliment. That tell-tale furrow of desperate concentration marked the wide, fair brow: I knew that look usually yielded decisive action on her part, wrong or right.

The visit to the ramshackle PRO office didn't help to raise her spirits at all. Tong Lau, the number one man, was polite but noncommittal. He kept saying it would take time to arrange these things, one must be patient with the Chinese way, it wasn't so dynamic as the American—all this as if nothing had been prepared at all. It seemed to me he was stalling until word could come through from the Shanghai office. His good-by to us was that he would have Wong or Min contact us "the moment anything is achieved."

Back at the hotel, with the hot desert breeze stirring the heavy drapes, Martha and I sat over a drink in my room and tried to puzzle it out.

"Don't let it get you, Baby," I consoled her. "Trying to get going with any new PRO set-up is always a drag. It probably doesn't have anything to do with you or your being alone. It just takes them a while to get used to any new arrivals. Then they get to know you and start unbending."

"I think there's something behind it," she said fixedly. "Do you think Carl could have sent a message or anything like that?"

"I doubt it. After all, we just left Shanghai this morning. He didn't call us at the Cathay. Besides, the Chinese are ultracivilized, they wouldn't have any objection to the fact that you and I are—together."

"Yes, but after all, Carl is with the MAG. If he complained, they wouldn't want to offend the American Army people."

"What would he complain about? If you want to be a photographer and go on an assignment in North China, that's legal, isn't it?"

"It's legal if the accreditation comes through. But suppose Carl tried to stop the accreditation? Suppose it never came through, and they just held us here until—"

"Baby, don't be so down-beat. Suppose Carl came up here—" She gave a kind of shudder. "Suppose, though, that he did, I'd talk to him just the way I would have if he'd been in Shanghai, just the way we tried to."

Now she really did shudder. "Scott, I'm so afraid if you do—talk to him—something awful will happen. He gets so drunk—so crazy."

I couldn't help laughing. "Look at our situation: here we are way the hell and gone up in North China, with the Communists thirty miles away. We're going up where it'll be a lot hotter. We might get knocked off, or hurt, or caught by the Communists, or all three, and you're worrying about a fist fight or maybe even a knife fight your husband and I might have. Look what happened last time he wanted to have a fist fight—nothing. And he was damn mad."

She walked over toward the window, the rectangle of sunbaked sky. "I still wish we could leave right away—go to Kalgan."

"Maybe we can. Min said there was nothing to stop us."

"Except, they wouldn't go with us until we get it straightened out. And we do need an interpreter."

I got up and walked to her and put my arm around her. "Baby, I know there's something we—I can do to speed it up: right now. I'm going to send a radiogram to Yung and not take a chance that the PRO people here will do anything about it today.

"Besides, there are a couple of newspaper people in Peiping that we should see. I have notes to them from John Lindahl. They should be pretty much in the know, they should have some ideas about what to do."

But she seemed so irrevocably in the dumps: "I don't think we should see Lindahl's friends, what good could they do?"

"People, friends, Baby. What makes the world move. Whatever you want to do, you have to do it through people."

She clung to me. "Scott, you're not going to go to Djin-zuh without me, are you?"

It was direct and I had to answer it. "Baby, I want you to go everywhere I go." I meant it, the thought of being without her was like death to me. I kissed her, my little summer storm cloud looked so dark, shadowy, fragile. Her white silk blouse had pulled out of her skirt in the back, and I touched her warm bare skin with my hand, my hand spanned her small waist, my finger-tips knowing the fine body hair like gold mist smooth on her skin. The heel of my hand found the long hollow of her back and held her, and I picked her up and carried her into the bedroom and put her on the big mahogany bed. Then I drew the blinds. My funny valentine, my Valkyrie, my little Kraut, I thought, turning back to where her hair shone against the mahogany bedstead, even in the dim light. Like most women I had known, she wanted to escape; but her idea of escape was to go to the front, where, she seemed to think, things would be simpler. Right then, I didn't care, as long as we would be together.

14

HAROLD VAN REMO, THE ANS BUREAU CHIEF IN PEIPING, wasn't much help with our problem, when we trekked out to his house that evening. But at least he and his crazy White Russian wife or mistress shed light on one important issue. They couldn't have cared less whether we were married, or married to other people, or what our sexual status was. Harold and his mate Marya seemed to have the free-wheeling attitudes of most of the people we had met in Shanghai—only more so.

It seemed an eternity before we could get to dinner. Marya, a black-haired five-by-five, kept delaying it in favor of more vodka martinis.

"Go back," she shouted each time the house-boy peeked in to remind her that dinner was ready. "Keep the dinner warm. We are occupied with more important matters. Light another fire and burn the dinner."

On these occasions, Van Remo, a big, easy-going Oregonian, would smile tolerantly. And I felt double hunger pangs, half of them for Martha.

Another couple had come for dinner, a mild British correspondent for Reuters and his Irish wife. He was less inclined to get drunk in a hurry, and willing to offer advice about our trip to Djin-zuh.

"I'd tell them you simply want to go to Kalgan," he said. "That you want to give up the trip to Djin-zuh, and won't have need of any interpreters. Then they'll scurry about and worry, and send your two little conducting officers with you to Kalgan. As you say, they won't stop you from going to Kalgan, if you want to go—but they'll want to keep an eye on you, their method of censorship, you know. So you'll have your two China boys with you in Kalgan, and you can improvise from there."

"Politics bore me," Marya interrupted in her harsh, loud voice. She slapped me on the back. "It is only dancing that matters. Come, Peter the Great, we will dance." She pulled my arm, but before I could get up, she squatted and began kicking her muscular legs in a Russian dance, slipped and tumbled on her rear end.

"China fell," she said, scrambling to her feet.

"Russia did, anyhow," Van Remo corrected.

"*Dway-bu-shi*" remarked the Englishman. "Face-not-up."

Later on, when we had at last finished a handsome dinner of Peking duck—which she largely ignored in favor of the vodka—she slipped into a kind of crying jag.

"When I was three years old, the Reds have chased me six thousand miles to China. Thirty years later, they still chase me. This time, they are getting closer, they will catch us, they will be most bad, most cruel."

Nobody but Martha and me seemed to be listening, the others were fairly soggy.

"You can get out by plane, right up to the last minute," I said, thinking how she reminded me of Lois.

"Will be most bad, most cruel," she repeated like a broken record. She fixed on us a stare which didn't quite focus.

"But you, two blonde babies in gold, go now when able. Back to America and your milkshake vanilla. Tarzan, do not try being big hero for your lover. Take her opposite direction from Kalgan."

The sentence hung on dead air for a moment, and then Martha said: "It's late, Scott. We should be leaving."

"Yes, damn near midnight—and we've got to get up early. You'll excuse us, Mrs. Van Remo?"

She looked away without changing expression. "Good night. Good night, Peter the Great. Go back to Shanghai and your hot dog and your milkshake. Do not worry so much about the world. It has got along for many centuries without America. Please leave it to the experts."

We walked back to the hotel, under the sharp, clear desert sky. I took a deep breath, relishing the coolness.

"The air tastes good, after that."

She was seething: "That horrible old bag. The kind of bastardly reactionary we must contend with, all over the world. All they care about is their own miserable skins."

"I thought you'd be jealous."

"Of her? She did seem to want to paw you all the time." We walked on quietly, along a high gray wall. Her heels clicked on the sidewalk. "Scott?"

"Yes, Baby."

"Was she like Lois?"

"Something. But I'll have to concede Lois is a lot better looking."

"I should hope so. I wouldn't want to share you with such an awful woman."

"I'm not dividing my effort."

Silence, only the clicking of the heels. I went on, thinking I followed the current of her mind: "I'm going to write to Lois tonight, when we get back to the hotel, and ask her for a divorce."

But I hadn't hit a responsive chord. She walked on, her face set and serious, her clean chin-line beautiful in the starlight. "No—just so I have the 'come back' of the 'wanting' or whatever the Polynesians call it—for you."

"You do—and I will write her."

"No, I'd rather—leave it."

"But I will. I'll write Lois tonight. I should have done it long ago."

"I just want to get to Kalgan."

"I'll write the letter anyhow."

I did it, working at the ornate desk in the sitting room till after one a.m., while she slept in the big bed. The letter was not easy- good moments with Lois lived in me, as well as the bad. Once I had loved her, and grown to her, tendrils still joined us, much distaste as we might now have for each other. Trying to hack them was agony, the frayed nerves were steel, my reason was a poor tool to cut them. I tried not to think of the individual moments but they kept crowding me—all turning bitter at the thought. The letter sounded banal, hackneyed: she and I had grown apart, we were never happy together any more, we had enjoyed some good moments and our marriage had meant a lot to us at one time, but everything had been scrambled, the bastardly wars and my traveling—why should we go on being thorns in each other's sides?

I would provide for her until she could find someone who would be a better husband for her. Someone who could make a good living in business and be happy with regular hours and the kind of existence she liked to call gracious living. And, I thought, a safety from and forgetfulness of the things Martha thought were our obligation—a leadership toward a free democratic form of government for the world, a free press, a free economic shake. I didn't share her idealism. Maybe too many bloody noses had left too many scars with me. But Martha was a lot closer to what I wanted than Lois.

I didn't mention Martha in the letter. That would have been sure death to our plans for divorce. Fury, insane cussedness, murderous sabotage, would have sprung from Lois like a sky-full of arrows. I would wait until the divorce was done—then Lois would accept the new regime.

I signed and sealed the letter, then finding myself bolt awake, nerve ends all rubbed into awareness, I decided to put in some time transcribing my recent notes.

Usually I took the scraps of paper and the small disorderly notebooks and copied what seemed to be important items in a big daybook. That way I had things arranged chronologically, a kind of diary system that seemed to lend a modicum of order to my notes.

But instead of dutifully writing my diary, I stared at the page, and there I saw a repulsive vision: Shoop, sober for once, sitting in a chair in his ornate apartment, addressing himself to me. He was being very polite and circumspect, and maybe that was one reason why the vision was repulsive. I much preferred him as the black-dyed villain he was. But since he was so apparently courteous, I felt obliged to plead my case with him.

"Why do you want to take her up there to the end of nowhere?" he was asking me. He indicated that plush apartment. "I got ten servants—they do everything for her. She doesn't ever have to worry about anything. She has everything."

"Except what she needs and wants," I said it as I thought it, "a man who can be a credit to her—not for providing money, but for living with her the kind of life she deserves—a vital life, a life full of the kind of challenge she wants."

He puffed a cigar and looked at me curiously. Since this was a dream, he seemed to know everything. "You?" he said, unbelieving. "You—a beat-up war correspondent with too many scars. You, a writer of beefsteak adventure stories. You—who would rather gather your adventure stories in the bar at Hong Kong."

"That's not true—just not true—just the one story."

"That was your most recent one, wasn't it?"

"Yes, but—this time I'm heading for the front."

"And taking her with you—on false pretenses, pretending it will be the kind of political story she wants to do, the truth and all that."

"It *will* be true—and that's the main thing she wants—that it should be at the front, and true."

"Who's to say you are better for her than me. You know she's naive. She goes for you because you're a war correspondent. A better type for her is one that will provide for her—will humor her."

He was making this cussedly well-informed dream vision into a nightmare—but after all, he was Shoop, a devil's voice. He was all she hated in the world.

I looked at my watch. The time was nearly half-past two, my eyelids had been closed, and I felt a presence at my right elbow.

Martha stood there, in her gold gown. She bent to kiss me, her lips cool, the sweet flesh moving. She patted my head gently as if I were an infant.

"My poor baby is so tired," she said, soothing me. "I've been watching for the last ten minutes—you were concentrating so hard."

I pulled her onto my lap and held her, and in a second she had transposed from mother to child. "I want to be worthy of you, Scott. I want to make pictures as good as your magazine articles."

"That wouldn't be hard."

"That's not true," she said vehemently. "You've written some very good articles for *Beacon*."

"I didn't know you'd read any."

"I went down to the second-hand magazine store in Shanghai and bought some back copies."

"Beefsteak adventure," I said. "That's more than Lois ever did. She preferred a still-lower literary form—whodunits—to my writing efforts."

"It's going to be different with us. I'm going to read everything you write, and make fine pictures for you. I'm going to shoot everything, beginning tomorrow."

She was so earnest I couldn't help laughing. "Not everything, I hope. We'd run out of film in a couple of days. Incidentally, I'll bet you don't have enough film and flash bulbs. How much film?"

"Six of 35 and three of 120," she said.

I squelched a chuckle. "All right, Baby, we'll find a few dozen more in Peiping somewhere tomorrow. For somebody who once worked for *Time-Life*, you are very frugal with film."

"I'll practice hard and work very hard."

"Brünnehilde, I promise you: we'll get to Kalgan, maybe even to Djin-zuh. And soon."

She was only confirming what the devil-voice of Shoop had been planting in my brain, that she was naive—that I was going to be a big disappointment to her, and so was that life which she thought would be so simple, at the front.

Almost as if she knew my thought, she suddenly unfastened the gold *muumuu* in the back, moved her shoulders slightly, so that the gown fell from one shoulder, then the other. In the faint light, her moving breasts were a melody, a dazzling counterpoint of masses moving as she urged the gown downward to her slick waist.

She stood up, bringing one beautiful breast close to my cheek. With my face, I touched the rigidity of that pale lavender tip, ready for me.

I heard my voice, far away, almost a growl, "And I thought you were naive."

"No," she said, moving her breast gently. "Not naive when it comes to important things—like this."

"Isn't the war more important?" I asked, really asking if she loved me because I was taking her to the war.

"They're equally important—and you are the only one who can bring them both to me."

I stripped the golden gown the rest of the way off, thinking how perfect those round, deep hips were and also: I am lucky to have such a woman beside me, even if only for a short time. And I said: "You know, I'm a happy man—and it's your fault."

15

IN THE MORNING I HAD A RADIOGRAM FROM JIMMY YUNG: MRS. SHOOPS ACCREDITATION DELAYED SORRY MAY BE SOME TIME STOP WILL CONTACT YOU. It didn't sound good. But at least it didn't seem to be Shoop's work. If he had wanted to stop it, it probably would have been denied, point-blank.

There was also an urgent rate radio message from Joe Dodson at *Beacon*: NORTH CHINA STORY SOUNDS GOOD BUT DONT SPEND TOO MUCH TIME ON IT STOP IF BOGS DOWN TRY ONE MORE ACCESSIBLE FULL STOP OKAY ADVANCE FOR LOIS BUT MUST HAVE STORIES FASTER TO COVER ADVANCES.

Added up, the two radiograms spelled one conclusion to me: we'd better get moving to Kalgan. I took Martha with me and went down to beard Tong Lau in his Information Ministry office. It was clear what Martha wanted to do: to get out of here and go as far away from Shoop, and Shanghai, as possible.

The dapper little man offered us tea and an attentive ear, as I told him we were thinking about just going on to Kalgan and waiting there for Martha's accreditation. I decided to try what the Reuters correspondent had suggested: tell Tong we would go as far as Kalgan, and wait there until the accreditation of photographer could be straightened out; then we could make the next step.

His face stiffened. "Is not your personal trip to Djin-zuh the main item on our agenda, Mr. Ostermann—regardless of whether Mrs. Shoop—the photographer—can be cleared to go with you?"

I could see that they were still resisting the idea of letting a woman go up there. This pointed up one important idea to me: the trip to Djin-zuh, from Kalgan on, must be plenty risky.

I could see the whole structure of my story tottering, and I confess I felt a momentary regret that I had encumbered the whole project by bringing a female into the picture. But after all, the female was my Brünnehilde.

"The article will need pictures," I said, coming up with a quick, instinctive answer that fortunately turned out just right. "And I don't make them. I always hire a photographer on a story. Of course, in this case she happens to be the wrong sex—that's a complication."

He laughed. "Yes, and sometimes I forget the differences between our two countries. With us, the little good-for-nothing sex isn't given such important work. The female has lesser privilege."

"I appreciate all the effort you've put into this so far," I said, feeling that I had him a bit off balance. "And I'm sure it'll work into a fine article."

"Yes. And when did you want to leave for Kalgan?"

"As soon as possible. Today—tomorrow?"

"I'm afraid today would be impossible. Min and Wong will have to make their preparations."

"Would they be going with us to Kalgan—even though the trip to Djin-zuh is postponed?"

"Uh, yes." He smiled. "You'll need an interpreter even in Kalgan, you know." The Reuters correspondent had been right about the conducting officer bit. Wong and Min would watch over us, as well as doing our translating. They would be censoring our material at the source.

"Fine," I said. "Shall I buy the tickets for tomorrow?"

"No. I'll have Min pick them up—if the train runs tomorrow. You can reimburse him later."

"We'll stay by the hotel and wait for word from you, then. Thanks very much."

He turned to Martha, bowing slightly. "Gracious lady, I hope that my remarks about the more beautiful sex haven't caused offense."

She was at a loss in this kind of florid conversation. "Not at all," she said plainly enough.

"I find it difficult to believe that one so beautiful can also be so talented."

She fidgeted, anxious to be going. "Thank you."

In the cab, going to the hotel, she was still uneasy. "Do you think he meant anything—special—by that remark about my being talented?"

"No, darling—if you mean the fact that you and I are obviously living together."

"It is so obvious?"

"It would be obvious to them even if it weren't true. They're used to polygamy."

"You mean, concubinage."

"I never think of you as a concubine," I told her firmly.

"Oh Scott—I want so much to get—out of here."

"Don't worry, Baby. We'll work it out."

*

We couldn't hang around the hotel that afternoon. It was too likely that some unpleasant message would come from Shanghai, or New York, from Shoop or *Beacon* or Lois or Jimmy Yung. If word came from the Peiping Information Office about tomorrow's trip, if there was to be a trip to Kalgan, the hotel operator would keep it for us.

"Come on," I told Martha, "we're going out and get some sunshine—and some film, and you can practice your photography."

"Where are we going?"

"Fo-bidden City," I said. "Big rump call Coal-hilluh, where empelah hang himself on rocust tree. Maybe see some Communists, too."

"I want to see the Communists."

She put on her flats, took her Leica in hand, and we set out to see the sights of Peiping, as if we were a couple of tourists, these were normal times, and the Communists were not thirty miles away.

We meandered through the dusty, imposing walks and gates of the old Imperial City—which, said Martha, were as frightening and imposing as the approach to Henry Luce's office at *Time* magazine. We walked through the marble party boat of the Dowager Empress, fixed in a pond. The once-white marble had grown somewhat grayish, and the pond stagnantly green. Chiang Kai-shek had moved his capital south to Nanking, and left the old Imperial capital of the Manchus unkempt, and accordingly, Martha told me, he had changed the name of the place from Peking, which means Northern Capital, to Peiping, meaning Northern Peace.

"I like the word Peking much better than Bei-ping or Bei-shing," she said, giving it the local pronunciation.

"So do I," I said, and I was reminded of what I had thought about her last night—that I was lucky to have such a woman—such a woman and such a lover, too, by my side.

We took pedicabs to the disk-shaped Temple of Heaven, and the adjoining Altar of Heaven, and retained a little ragamuffin guide in knickers and an old torn undershirt. Martha and I made pictures of each other and him while the guide explained about everything in the temple and altar being arranged in nines, nine phoenixes and nine dragons, nine marble knobs and nine times nine squares of marble, eighty-one being the most sacred number. We paid our entrance fees to the various buildings like the few scattered Chinese tourists we saw. We remarked over the fact that our tour was cheap —that all it cost us for all admissions and tips was a mere three million dollars in the devaluated Chinese currency, which would be two American dollars.

It was corny, it was touristy, but it was fun. We were reminded how corny we had been about it when later in the day we walked through the shantytown of the thieves' market, the hundreds of shacks stacked against each other, the grimy peasant people like moving bundles of old clothes, the sick smell of sewage. This was more like the Peiping we had expected, because Peiping was a refugee city too, like Shanghai—though of lesser magnitude.

The mobs of wretchedly poor in the thieves' market somehow managed to keep their sense of humor. These were the immensely civilized (while also often barbarous) Chinese. We laughed when the little urchins ran up giggling, to measure their height against mine, and yell *"Gao! Gao!"* meaning tall, as if this were the most amusing thing they had ever discovered. And Martha flew into a Valkyrie rage as we noted the piles of big silvery cans that would be UNNRA supplies, U. S. Army stuff with tiny black lettering that said beef and gravy, peaches in syrup, powdered eggs. There were crates of C and B rations, jeep and truck parts piled on one of the little fly stands. "I'll bet you could buy 30-06 ammunition, Garand rifles and 81 mm. mortar shells if you knew where to look in this market," I suggested unwisely.

Martha's face was suddenly grim. "I was thinking about Carl—how much of this stuff got here because he got drunk some night; or how much of the furniture in our apartment came from those payoffs."

"Kick him out of your mind, Baby."

"I will. And I will do a good job on my pictures for your story."

"I know you will, Baby."

On the way back to the hotel we found a photographic shop, and to reinforce her determination, I bought her three dozen rolls of 35 film, and two dozen of 120—and that seemed to cheer her up considerably.

At the hotel we found a message from Tong Lau: the trip was on for tomorrow morning. Min and Wong would pick us up at eight. Fortunately, there were no other messages. It was a night to rejoice.

16

MIN AND WONG PICKED US UP ON TIME, WITH THE SAME RAM shackle government car that had met us on the first day at the airport. The signs of graft which so infuriated Martha in Shanghai, the black Cadillacs, were not easily visible here in Peiping—closer to the military power of the Communists. And Min wore what appeared to be the same greasy suntans, not noticeably dirtier— but of course it would have taken a lot more dirt to be noticeable. Wong had abandoned his pin stripe in favor of suntans, these not as spotted as Min's, but equally wrinkled. He still wore the khaki tie with the impossible knots. Martha in her neat khakis made them both seem disgracefully unmilitary.

At the bleak, countrified station that needed paint, we joined the mob waiting for the train—mostly ragged civilians, with a scattering of soldiers in apple green uniforms and blue sneakers. Most of them didn't seem to have any rifles.

"Going on furlough," Min explained. "They travel free on the China trains."

But there were some soldiers on duty. When the train came chuffing in, I noticed near the end of it an armored car. At the top of the car, pillbox-like domes had been added, with gun slits. One of the steel hatches had been opened, and the green tunic and peaked cloth cap of a soldier stuck up. I knew there would be more inside.

"Do they have much trouble with the Communists—on this line?" Martha was asking, but it was excitement, not fear that made her eyes shine.

"Not very often," said Min, almost growling it.

"Never fear, madame," Duncan Wong added solicitously. "You see we are well protected." Both of them misread her interest, not knowing the Valkyrie in her.

We found seats in one of the European-type coaches, and a boy came through to bring us tea. He set out numbered China mugs on the window-stand between our facing wooden seats. He poured fragrant, subtle jasmine from a huge steaming beaker.

Men and women in rough tunics and pants were jostling for the seats. A soldier settled himself and his barracks bag across the aisle from us, slurped tea and hocked and spat on the floor, then delicately smoothed it into the boards with his rubber sole. All through the car rose the customary morning sounds of slurping, throat-clearing and spitting. And, of course, the train was late.

Once on our way, we rapidly rolled through the farmland in the Peiping vicinity, then into drier country that looked like Southern California, with bare hills like huge, sleeping animals. It was dry-farming country, with sparse fields of wheat, and poor adobe shacks dotting the hills.

There were towns, marked by wide-open, sun-baked platforms, sometimes partially covered by narrow roofs. The adobe shacks clustered close near the station. Before and after every town, evil-looking little pillboxes stood guard, watching us with their slitted eyes.

At a few points along the line, we passed troops in dusty green uniforms, strewn in foxholes just beyond the railroad embankment. I pitied the men in the dry, hot sun and the dust. They had no shelter, though some wore goggles to keep the dust out of their eyes.

"Sol'yers are more numerous where there is a bigger town, or geography harder to defend," Duncan Wong explained. "Such places as the Communists are wont to raid.

"See how quiet they are in their hardship," he said with enthusiasm. "Manhood at its best is quiet—if I may quote from Master Kung."

Master Kung would be Confucius, the name Kung Fu-tzu rendered into English.

I nodded politely, thinking how very few Chinese in my experience were manhood at its best, by the standard of quietness. In Hong Kong, Indonesia, Singapore, every place I had seen them they were the noisiest, most ebullient people I knew, even in abject poverty and near-starvation.

Min held down a snort of distaste at the Old One's venture into poetry. Wong was clearly impractical and square, in his view—like someone quoting Thomas Jefferson in the States.

"The next station should be Nan Ko," said Min abruptly, almost embarrassed. "A big one. We gain an extra engine for the climb up to the Great Wall."

When we clicked into the whistle-stop station with its bare concrete platform, we saw our first concentration of troops. The troop train, a long line of cattle cars jammed with soldiers, stood beside the ribbon of concrete, on the track across from ours.

In the cars the mass of troops stirred like sections of a dusty cane field in a wind. As we came abreast of them, we saw there was not enough room for most of them to sit down, they could do nothing but stand.

"Probably are troops being relieved from action," Min guessed. We saw he was right when we pulled up abreast of a cattle-car marked by fewer men standing. From the higher elevation of our car, we could see men lying on the floor, and the dirty white splashes of bandage: wounded. There were about twenty, and they were extremity wounds—arms, legs. Most war wounds are extremities.

Our train had to wait for our extra engine, so we got down from the car and Martha made some pictures and I encouraged her. Even if they didn't tie in directly to the story, they would be useful to the magazine. Min interpreted while I talked to the closest non-com. Min seemed honest enough in his translation, if somewhat brusque.

"He says most of the casualties are accidents. Some from a mine that blew up. The regiment has been on guard duty near Tsinan."

I checked with a soldier who had lost the lower part of his leg. The stump was tied with what appeared to be a dirty towel. He seemed glad to talk to me, probably because in bending over him I blocked off the sun which had been shining in his eyes.

"Ask him, please, what caused the wound?" I said to Min.

Min conveyed it in Mandarin, but the soldier looked blank, then answered in a few short, choppy words.

"He says he's from Fukien and doesn't understand Mandarin," Min translated. The soldier grinned, fished a pencil from his pocket, made motions toward my notebook, and when I gave it to him, he printed in laborious English: "Jump down by uncareful on bomb."

I noted that Duncan Wong was talking to an officer, a captain, by the stars on his shoulders. This gave me a good chance to check one of the interpreters against the other.

"The honorable *lien jung* says very little action stirring farther out rail line. Only guerrilla action. Raids are occurring on line. The soldiers have been fortifying the area about Tsinan. He suggests we may have trouble with guerrillas farther out line. A cheerful suggestion."

Wong was philosophical again. "They are guerrilla bandits until they become stronger than we. Then we become guerrilla bandits." Min glared at the old man, and I felt encouraged: with this system of checks and balances, in translation, I should be able to get the truth.

On the other track the conductors were blowing whistles and the cars jerked, the couplings shuddered while an engine banged into the rear of the train. I knew we'd be leaving in a minute but as a conscientious newsman I should check one more thing. I turned back to Min, who now was talking to the non-com.

"Min—could you ask him, please, who is the senior medical officer of the battalion?"

Min relayed the question, and the soldier looked surprised and pointed to himself. He answered a short sentence: "For whole regiment." Min rendered it.

"Why did you want to know?" Min asked, with sudden suspicion.

"Just curious." Actually I wanted to check on a story I had been told by a medical officer in the MAG, back in Shanghai, that lowly medical orderlies, corporals and sergeants, supplied all the medical attention for battalions and sometimes regiments out in the Front areas. The Chinese Army doctors, the officers, paid their *cumishaw* to the proper superior, stayed back in so-called civilization. I made a note and thought: it's good to be working again, at first hand. And it felt good to be digging at the heart of a dramatic story, a hot story, the story of the China war. I knew I could thank that little Valkyrie for the strength that got me this far.

Back at the train they were blowing more whistles and shouting. "It is time to go," Min announced, and started for the nearest car.

Martha was still making shots around the wounded. "C'mon, Baby."

"Just one more," she said, snapping the Fukienese amputee I had talked to.

As we hurried for the train, she asked me: "Do you think I was working well?"

"Yes." I had been so occupied with getting my notes in the short available time that I hadn't noticed how she was working. "How many pictures did you make?"

"Thirty."

"Good, Baby. You know from your experience at *Time-Life:* film is the cheapest item on a story, shoot plenty. Didn't the *Life* guys used to say that? I want you to overshoot always, rather than undershoot."

"Yes," she said seriously, "what we remembered about Mr. Nietzsche's philosophy—an overgoing instead of an undergoing. And I appreciate your telling me."

I had to tell her what I had been thinking. She deserved it. "Yes, I was just thinking that you have plenty of power—power in both ways."

"In both ways?"

"As a lover—and in your mind."

She smiled that wide beam of sun. "That's very nice. And I hope I have power as a photographer, too."

"I know you will."

Duncan Wong was standing courteously by the steps to the train vestibule. He helped her aboard, and later, when we had taken our places and the train was moving again, he said something which if it had been calculated, couldn't have delighted her more: "Our lady in man's uniform is talented as well as beautiful."

I watched Martha, wanting to touch her, stopping myself so as not to embarrass her. The little activity, and perhaps Duncan Wong's compliment, had given her fresh color. She was perfection, a wondrous organism when she smiled and was interested in what the two men said. And they liked her: she seemed shy and modest, virtues they revered in women. I thought of tonight, when I would have her in some bed, in Kalgan, for myself, and I would know her as she is, the Valkyrie, with plenty of power in both ways.

We chugged up the grade toward the Great Wall, ticking off the whistle stops and falling steadily behind schedule. We lunched on the buns called *saw-ping* and *bao-tze* sold by flystand vendors at the stations. Min gave us the PRO-paganda line: how the uncertain, wavering policy of the United States in their efforts to assist China had been the main cause of Nationalist defeats—and maybe he was right.

We hit a steeper grade, ran out of single track, went up a part of the route in reverse, saw the Great Wall of China, a fairly sizable ridge of earth and crumbling stones snaking over the brown hills. Then we came into our first signs of fighting.

The train clattered into a small town called Wu-tu. Next to the railroad platform stood a large, wrecked clay-and-stone building, maybe once the administrative building of the station. One corner, including the roof, had been ripped off, and the round beams of the roof were fire-blackened. A round hole, like that of a shell or a mortar, cut raggedly across the remnants of the wall.

In the distance, beyond some adobe huts, a curved line of fresh foxholes had been dug. A few men in Nationalist uniform were scattered among them.

Beyond the curved scar of the foxholes, I could make out another line of fresh-turned but empty holes which made an arc facing the nearer ones.

"Is this war damage?" Martha was asking Min. I could see the bright fire-flecks of excitement in her sky-blue eyes.

"I believe so," Min said. "But you see, we still hold the position."

"It is give and take," said the Old One, aware that he was getting a dirty look from Min. "The concept of *yang* and *yin*. They take, we give; and then the converse."

The conversation planted one impression in my mind: Min was a neophyte in war, scared of it and unfamiliar, and he lacked the round perspective you see in an old soldier. To him it was all flat, a collection of unsorted facts. He couldn't see the shape of it. But Duncan Wong could.

As our train slowed to a stop, a rank of soldiers, about a platoon in strength, came into view in a square near the station. They were porting their arms for inspection by a non-com. The non-com barked a command, and they started to march, chanting a monotonous song. The non-com swung on his heel, and double-timed to the head of the column, leading them toward a large pillbox at the edge of the town. A round hole had been made in the wall of the pillbox, big enough for a man to walk through, as by a high velocity shell. Nothing had been done to repair it, as yet.

"This must have been a pretty recent raid?" I directed my rhetorical question toward Min.

"Five days ago it ended," he said shortly.

Duncan Wong was still being mischievous. "One knows the doctrine of the strong-point, the *Schwerpunkt,* a favorite doctrine of Generalissimo Chiang," he said, his near-black eyes bright behind the crooked glasses. "The *punkt* in this case was not *schwer* enough. Much of the *schwer* is in the will of the men to fight. If they knew what some of us older ones have learned—those of us who have not also learned to be corrupt."

"Let's hope Kalgan will be *schwer* enough," I suggested, trying to fall in with the spirit of the talk.

"No doubt about that," Min was solemn. "Kalgan is more than a strong point. It is a major city, a major objective for the Communists. We have heavy forces deployed there." He was speaking as if it were an official communique.

In the next town as well there had been recent fighting. The bridge before the station had been blasted, one of the stone supports broken off. We rode over shaky fresh timbers put up to heal the breech. The pillbox guarding the steep hill beyond the bridge had been seared, as if by a flamethrower; about half of the squat, truncated cone was black. And again we saw the sinister sign: advancing circles of enemy foxholes, empty but fresh-dug, creeping down the slope above the pillbox. Two Nationalist soldiers squatted beside a cooking fire just outside the pillbox, the only human beings visible.

"This place isn't very *schwer*, either," Martha said to me. "Seems to have a garrison of two." Those were her last words before the blast.

I remember that I had stood up and said something about getting some fresh *bao-tze* at the next station. Then something pitched me violently on my back, against the seats across the aisle, away from Martha, and the ground came up against the window beside her, and slowly, as if in slow motion, I saw the glass break and shatter into streaks like rain. Darkness came in a cloud, things flying, dirt and gravel.

Tearing and shuddering sounds ripped into my ears, a dozen auto crashes at once, and I was falling back on top of Martha and Wong and Min, someone else I didn't know, a Chinese in a black padded tunic, sliding next to me. Other bodies tumbling with me. I saw Min on his back toward the window with his arm up to shield his eyes. Dust like smoke, showers of gravel still flew in where the glass had been. Wooden benches were breaking, the boards splintering, an elbow of black steel flew out and I blinked.

I collided with a mess of other bodies which felt surprisingly soft. Then, everything suddenly stopped. I heard something dripping, that was all. Swirling light dust filled the air.

I twisted around, tried to free myself of some other bodies who were struggling too. I looked around frantically for Martha, couldn't see her, managed to get up.

Then the human noises started: someone alternately gasping and squeaking in panic as if his breath were dying out, another man's voice a moan, a woman screamed and kept screaming.

Then a familiar sound, mostly covering the human crying: small arms, a heavy machine gun. *Bap-bap-bap-bap*, slow, distinct shots. It sounded like an American BAR, the heavy, measured pace. Then a quick waterfall, a cacophony of rifle shots. A heavy crunch that would be a mortar shell—one explosion. The train had been dynamited, it was being attacked. Would the machine gun be from the armored car? Must be a Communist mortar.

I got up, seeing two strange Chinese scrambling to their feet, apparently unhurt. They wore rough black tunics, quilted.

The car lay on its side, that was what had happened, the torn window frame in a pile of baggage, wicker baskets had spilled, barracks bags and ditty bags broken, clothing and food scattered, splintered pieces of wood. People still sprawled among the debris. Light came from the windows, which were the ceiling. The floor of the car was the side now, the wooden benches stuck out of the side. They hadn't broken loose.

My reporter's mind automatically sorted out the bits and pieces, holding back the fast heartbeat, the panic that was instinctively there. And then it hit me, hard and frantically: *Where was she? Where had she gone?* It didn't matter about any of the rest of it— about Min, or Wong, or the China War, or the cycle of civil wars, about the Vanguard or the Reserve, or Mao Tse-tung. None of it mattered—they could all bleed to death and so could all these people on the train and so could I, but she was the one that counted, and she was gone.

That moment I knew she meant more to me than I'd ever felt before—more than sex, more than excitement, more than any new hot story or new challenge had ever been or would be.

I would fall if I didn't find her. I would rip the tangle apart and find her, rip apart the people, the debris, until I found her. Panicky. Min had disappeared somewhere. And Wong. Maybe, I thought, this was the wrong place, maybe I'd slid down the car, these were all strangers. It was a nightmare. Where? I saw a soldier, without his cap. Blood had spattered across his green uniform, seeming very red. He looked familiar. He was getting up from among the broken benches. Foolishly, he was looking for his cap. I staggered among the human debris of the overturned car, pushing my way, wildly. My mind had one thing on it: find Martha. Nothing else mattered.

Bap-bap-bap. The slow machine gun. Then, the faster pace of a burp gun, probably Communist: *Brrddtt! Brrddtt!* Single rifle shots in a cascade, sounding distant.

A Chinese moved almost under my feet, his gray tunic dark and slick with blood. The wreckage of a face moaned faintly.

I was in the wrong place, I knew it now. I saw Min standing in the debris farther down the car, his face blank. Didn't seem hurt. The Old One leaned on him, his glasses gone, his face streaked with blood. *Where is Martha?* My own blood seemed to pound out the words.

Now all the passengers seemed suddenly to be on their feet among the wreckage of the car. Distant firing. I heard the distant gasp and squeak of the injured person I had heard before. A scream, maybe a woman. It could be Martha!

My leg was aching, coldly. Broken? No, it would support me, it would move. I felt my face, no blood. Where was Martha? I yelled to Min, my own voice sounded distant: "Where is she?" He didn't answer. He could have been deafened by the noise of the firing, his own quivering fright.

Then I saw her: Martha, Martha—she was getting up, standing, she could stand. Red on her face. Blood! Were her features hurt? Her face, her body hurt? Body and face, more to me than mine. Closer to me. Let nothing have happened! nothing have happened!

Why did I let her do it?—the instant indictment ripped through my mind. I had warned her against it, told her it might happen. I should have insisted, made her see it my way, because she wouldn't know about it. You can never know what it is, the war, until it's happened once before, or more. And she didn't know.

I pulled my way through the clot of people and got to her. It was blood, over her face and neck, staining her blouse. I tried feverishly to mop it with my handkerchief. I gulped; blood had never made me feel faint before, now it did. My vision mottled like light-struck film.

"I'm all right." Her voice was coming distantly. I could barely hear it. "I think—they're glass cuts."

There were three small cuts on her cheek and chin, one large gash across the side of her neck, a deep one that ran blood steadily, but didn't spurt; it had missed the carotid artery, thank God. Seemed to be no cuts on her body—blood spattered from the face cuts. I tied my handkerchief double around the neck cut, maybe it would slow the bleeding.

Her face was drained of blood. She swayed and I held her. "They're glass cuts but they're clean—no glass in them." My voice still sounded distant, almost comic.

Somebody banged into us, jostled us, ran by, a demented Chinese showing his teeth and yelling, "Yahh-a-yahh-a." He ran to the end of the car and scrambled up on a pile of luggage and debris like a goat and disappeared through a shattered window at the top of the car.

"Are you hurt—otherwise?" I yelled at Martha, shouting because the machine guns were rattling and they seemed closer, and another avalanche of small arms fire was falling.

"Don't—think so."

Then I saw Min, bending over something, somebody. Duncan Wong had gone. I realized it must be Wong down among the bundles of luggage, the debris. Dead?

Four or five crazy Chinese bumped against us, rushing for the end of the car where the other one had exited. One of them was the soldier who had lost his hat. Another was frail, a running skeleton. Somehow his shirt had been torn off and his face and body were streaked with something black, maybe grease. But it was nothing—Martha was alive. Now to get her out of here!

If there's a fire they'll trample each other to death. Better get Martha out first. The Commies might set the train on fire.

Leave the rest—except her cameras. Grab them quick—before the looters. And the film.

Around us the Chinese were on hands and knees, rooting in the debris like pigs, some hurt or scared, some probably looking for their baggage, some of the more self-possessed no doubt already looting. The same man was crying somewhere close: aah—eeah, aah-eeeeah, gasp and squeak. A steady moaning, like sighing, somewhere, one man, but the sound seemed to fill the air. A female voice wailing at the far end of the car. I could hear better. A chorus of fast-firing machine guns ripped the air—but they sounded farther away.

I pulled Martha by the hand and found my way through the mob toward Min. Duncan Wong lay on his back, with his head propped on a barracks bag. His face was smudged with blood, blood had spattered on the bag. Could just be glass-cuts, small ones, plenty of those everywhere in the mob.

His forehead, free of blood, was waxy. His eyelids closed, peaceful. Min, kneeling beside the Old One, wiped the face with a smudgy handkerchief. No injury visible on the face.

"What is it?" I asked Min.

"I think—his heart." He put his ear against the rumpled cotton shirt. "I can't hear."

"Let me try." I pointed to Martha. "Watch out for her." I bent over the Old One, and as I did, his eyes opened. They were vacant without his glasses. His face seemed relaxed. It startled me that his features seemed beautiful.

"—*wah—yee gah chuggah*" he said faintly, raising one hand.

"What's he say?" I asked Min.

"Nothing important. It means—give me one of these."

"Maybe a heart pill. Did he have any?"

Chinese were jostling by us. They nearly knocked Min down as he stood between them and Martha.

Min shook his head. "I don't know." Nearby the heavy machine gun chugged again.

"We'd better get him out of here," I said to Min. "Ourselves too. They might set fire to the train."

He nodded. "We can carry—" He stopped, we looked at Wong. Wong's chest heaved once, deep, then deflated as if punctured. "Aahphratt." Half animal sound, almost comical, it jerked through his throat and nose. His eyes were frozen open. I held my ear against his shirt. No sound. No pulse. No heroic last words. That was the way it was in life, a collection of accidents—some fortunate, some bad. Later on, they would invent last words for him, if he were famous. What counted was what he had done in life—the chances he had taken for what he believed in. From knowing him slightly I knew he had believed, had taken the chances. I closed the lids.

"Dead," I told Min. A fine man had gone—a good Chinese, one of the ones who tried. I pulled the quilt over the Old One's face. "We better go." I was reminded of my father's death: another philosopher, like Wong, who could see the essences in men—what was strong and good in them, and their weaknesses, too.

I checked the bandage on Martha's throat as we moved. It was soaked with blood but the bleeding seemed to be slowing. She was quiet, not complaining; she didn't show fright.

I was kicking myself for getting her into this. I could hear the distant heavy beating of the BAR, there was a lot of small arms stuff flying around out there. I was going to have to haul her through it, quick, get her somewhere away from this focus of Communist attention. They were trying to wipe out the train and the troops on it. If I could get her into the fields, it would be safer. I promised myself one thing—if we got out to Kalgan, I'd make sure she got out of this war zone. Maybe I'd take her to Hong Kong—why not? I could write the story of this Communist battle, that would be good enough for *Beacon*. That is, if we got to Kalgan or Peiping with it, if we survived.

"We can go up through the last window," I suggested. "Where the others went."

"Okay." Min seemed dazed.

We struggled in the current of people stampeding to get out. I remembered my notes, the cameras. I dropped on my hands and knees where I thought I saw my barracks bag.

"Wait a minute," I yelled to Min over the uproar. "Need something." Martha sensed in a second what I was up to, and bent to help. "Don't," I ordered her, "the bleeding."

I scrambled through the mess of Chinese quilting—clothes and blankets, looking for my musette bag. It turned up, in it the big notebook. Martha's camera case should be someplace close. I found a flimsy green canvas bag I recognized as the Old One's. "Duncan

Wong's bag," I said. Without a word, Min took it, holding the sprung sides together desperately.

My hands were shaking as I clawed through the wreckage. I was suddenly aware of a lack of something crucially important: the sounds of firing. In the lull the animal cries of the injured seemed to swell louder. And a frantic, shrill shouting and yelling rose in a squall, as when you open the door of a henhouse and the sound hits you.

Somebody was down on all fours next to me, Martha. In there pitching, turning over the debris. Min still stood there dumbly holding the broken canvas bag together, his plump body jostled by the people passing. He turned a weird, wild stare on us: "Better hurry," he said dully. "They talk about fire—something on fire. Better get out."

Is he going to run? I wondered. He looks as if he's about had it. Seeing Wong's broken suitcase had pushed Min over the edge, maybe. Then Martha and I both put our hands on the camera bag at the same time. Feverishly, she opened it.

"They—look okay," she said.

"All right," I told her as if she were any photographer covering my assignment. "Get one out and make some pictures." My brusqueness surprised me. She obeyed without a word, took out the Leica.

"The fire! Got to get out," Min was saying. Someone bumped him—the green canvas bag slipped from his grasp and everything spilled out. He stood there staring at it.

"We'll get out." I tried to reassure him, and hardly believed myself. My hands *were* shaking, my breath was tight in my chest. Scared. Because of Martha. I almost laughed: helluva gentleman, blaming being scared on his attachment for a lady. But it was probably true, I had never felt I had so much to lose before.

"Others going through into next car," Min was saying. "By which way shall we go?"

Besides scrambling up on the debris to climb out the window at the top of the car, some of the mob were pushing through a tangle of wreckage, torn steel beams and smashed lumber in the direction of the next coach. I thought I could see light through the mess. It could be that the next car had broken away in the wreck—might be a gap between the cars, a clear exit to the ground.

Climbing out of the window at the top of our coach was a bad risk. Up there, you would be a pretty target for grazing fire, stick up like fingers—you'd still have to get down too, quite a jump.

"Next car," I told Min. He started moving that very fraction of a second.

I checked Martha's bad cut, lifting the bandage gingerly; it looked okay, bleeding seemed to have stopped, maybe it wasn't a very deep cut after all. But seeing her sweet flesh marked, the ugly red edge of the cut ripping the skin, set my stomach teetering. I tied the bandage back in place as quickly as I could. I was ashamed for my shaking hands. I thought I had grown immune to shoot-em-ups, in five wars. I knew then what she meant to me now because blood had never affected me like this before.

Then we were following Min, buffeting our way through the mob towards the wreckage at the end of the coach, trying to get around the men and women who struggled to get out of the window at the top, getting past them, then hitting the mob at the end of the car.

I hauled Martha behind me, and momentarily remembered that it had been the same that first day I met her in Shanghai. But now my worry seemed ten thousand times greater. We had become part of each other; I was part of something I wanted to keep.

Right ahead of us, three men in dirty dark clothes struggled violently, they gasped and shouted and tried to slug each other. An opening in the wreckage ahead seemed to be what they were fighting for, the chance to get through first. The tallest man, with a bloody cloth tied around his head, kept hammering at the lower objects, his hands clenched to form a kind of club. The lower mass was tangled arms and legs, like Laocoön and the serpent. A round, shaved head came out of the mess and butted someone's belly hard. I heard the grunt, then the struggling mass was falling toward us.

Min somehow skinned past them, scaled a heap of timber, steel and broken glass like a goat, and disappeared toward the end of the car. But the struggling men hit me, pushing me back toward Martha. I fell, striking some hard object with my back, and was momentarily glad I hadn't hit Martha.

A smelly body rolled over me and wrenched me around. I could see Martha's brown pantleg and rough walking shoe beside me. I fell over flat and saw her standing straight up above.

"Go ahead, go ahead," I yelled to her. "While it's clear." Then a heavy, greasy garment that smelled strong of peanut oil covered my face. My wind was choked, I saw pinpricks of light, like stars on a black night. I flung around and tried to twist away from the body that smelled of peanut oil.

I could breathe but I still saw stars, evil sparks of light on the rough black. Then the struggling mass on top had suddenly lightened. I gave a heave and rolled clear, saw a pair of Chinese feet in felt slippers crawling away from me, more Chinese feet running by, then I scrambled up and saw the tall Chinese with the bandaged head disappearing by the route Min had followed.

Martha was standing beside me, she had stayed with me. In her hand she gripped a stick that looked like a broken slat from one of the chairbacks.

"I—waited," she said, in that moment she dropped the stick and I saw that the Chinese with the shaved head was getting to his feet a couple of feet away, holding his head with both hands. I almost laughed: looked as if my Brünnehilde had beaned him!

I retrieved my notebook from a mess of spilled luggage. "Come on." I grabbed her hand and we skinned over the pile of junk at the end of the coach. There *was* an opening; bright light shone through.

We came to the door frame, it was wood, the wood had been smashed and the pieces stuck out at angles. But you could squeeze through. Beyond the upended frame the next car stood maybe thirty feet away, still erect on the track.

A wide column of smoke leaned over us from a car somewhere at the back of the train. The smoke bubbled from tall, greasy orange flames. Was it the armored car afire, I wondered? The smoke smelled like creosote, it was thick, dirty, gray-brown.

Min stood by the doorway, hesitating. "Shooting back here!" he shouted, his eyes wild. Evidently the whole first part of the train had been derailed, the Commies were now attacking the rear.

Passengers were huddled along the edge of the railroad cut, several hundred strewn like lumps of dirt. They had run from the fire, but from the devil to the deep blue—they'd given up the shelter of the railroad car for a position nakedly exposed to enfilade. Scattered through the dark mass of people were green KMT uniforms like grass cuttings strewn among dung heaps. The position was impossible because the brown side of the railroad cut rose steeply, like the side of a trough. Toward the front of the train, I could see a wide tan pillbox high in the cut, a nest of barbed wire strung in front of it. No shooting from it, but it was probably manned. I thought: if only we could get to the pillbox—

"Nose—your nose," Martha was saying, horror in her eyes. I touched it with my fingers and they came away bloody.

"Just got a bang," I told her. But it did feel stiff and swollen. I must have hit it during the scuffle in the car. But the bone and cartilage felt straight, to my fingers.

"Is it broken?" Martha's face was still aghast, as if *she* had been bashed harder than I.

"No, Baby. It's all right."

"Promise?" It was her way of saying, "Are you sure?"

"Yes."

I told Min: "We'd better try to make that Nationalist pillbox."

This seemed a good time to try, no firing going on. A Chinese Nationalist soldier ran past us close, heading in the direction of the pillbox. He carried an American carbine and he was running hard. Not just a soldier on leave, he could have come from the armored car or from some local garrison guarding the railroad.

"Let's follow him." I took Martha's hand and helped her through the door frame and we jumped down to the ground. Min followed, and we pelted along beside the overturned car, beside the ventilating ridge which had been the top, now was the side. People were lined up along what was now the top of the car. Three or four jumped and the rest hesitated. It must have been a ten foot leap.

Up toward the head of the train we could see more cars lying on their sides, and a streamer of silver smoke beyond them, that must be the engine. The Commies must have knocked the whole forward part of the train off the track, including the locomotive. A neat job. Must have taken plenty of guts to plant the charges and the blocks right under the nose of the Nationalist pillbox: guts and skill. We were running in a line with Martha in between Min and me. That was good because any sniper fire from either end of the cut would be more apt to catch him or me than her; we were the bread of the sandwich and she was the valuable filling.

I hoped that Martha's bad cut was holding together despite the running, and I tried to will that the clotting should be okay. I knew we must run as far as we could on this dash, though our lungs were bursting: any moment the small arms firing might break out again. It might sweep the railroad cut where we were.

We thudded past a crowd of fifty or sixty passengers huddled in the ditch below the railroad embankment; many of them women in ragged black and gray clothes, some holding kids, the white of bandages swashed through the dark. The people crouched there as exposed and forlorn as the line of tar flung up by a wave on an ocean beach. A couple of the women were shouting, their yelling scratched the dead air. The blood of the innocents, I knew, was inconsequential to the Communists. This was only a raid on our forces, hampering our communications. The end justified any means ... at once, the Communist strength and weakness.

Ahead of us, maybe three football fields away, the big, dust-colored pillbox sat quiet, no sign of movement around it. And I worried: maybe it was unmanned—in which case it wouldn't be much protection when, and if, we got there.

But, I thought, the direction was right. Judging from the sounds of firing we had heard from inside our overturned coach, the fighting so far had been around the rear end of the train. Which would make sense: the Commies would want to stay away from the pillbox and chop up the armored car and the troops in it.

I twisted around as I ran and checked on Martha. She was running bravely, chin up, legs pumping, mouth gasping for air. But she wasn't falling behind. Beyond her, Min's roly-poly figure kept its place. His face was beet-red, but he wasn't slackening.

If, I thought, we could make another fifty, a hundred yards more before we stopped, or the guns opened up again! About a hundred yards ahead the track curved gently, and there, around the bend, we might be a little out of the direct line of fire from the rear—if we hugged the ditch and the railroad embankment. We could stop there and then maybe make the final move toward the protection of the pillbox.

My legs and chest ached with the running. And then it started again, before we could get to the bend: the firing. *Brrrddt! Brrddtt!* They were Commie burp guns. But the sound seemed to come from way behind the train, quite a distance off.

I glanced back over my shoulder again just as the slow-paced BARs talked once more: *Bap-bap-bap-bap.* Those would be Nationalists probably, though often the Commies fought with arms they had captured.

From this angle I could suddenly see the side of the armored car. The plain windowless steel flank gleamed in the sun. And I felt a sudden boost in morale: the car was upright on the tracks, it was not on fire. The smoke I'd seen back there was coming from an ordinary passenger coach. In that flash of vision I spotted threads of gray smoke, gunfire, trailing from one of the turrets at the top of the armored car. The Nationalists were still in there fighting.

Another cascade of small-arms firing burst from the rear of the train. The Commies would still be trying to take out the armored car, probably.

Then, a heavy toned machine gun firing from the other direction, from the head of the train somewhere. Maybe the pillbox. But the wide, tan face showed no expression of firing; no smoke from the slits. It was quiet, impassive.

"Fifty yards more!" I yelled back to Martha and Min. "We can stop just—around the bend." The heavy machine gun up ahead didn't seem to be firing in our direction. No bullets snapping, not even a fuzzy ricochet.

Then, suddenly, a crashing sound: *carrummpp!* That would be a mortar, probably Communist. From somewhere behind us: loud, but mortars were loud even a couple of hundred yards away. *Carrummpp!* Another shuddering crash from the same direction.

Forty—thirty-five yards to go. Breath short and heart thumping like a big Polynesian drum.

Looking back, I saw the two black mortar bursts sprouting from the ground, like genies, there by the armored car. It was a shock: evidence the Commies must be raiding in some force. Probably they'd be at least a company, to have mortars with them. And maybe they were much heavier—a battalion, a regiment This could be a big-scale attempt to grab and hold this section of railroad. Or if artillery started screaming in, we'd know it could be still a lot bigger, might even be a full Army attempt to take another flank on Peiping.

We and our laboring hearts were pounding toward the curve of the railroad cut: fifteen yards, ten yards, seven. We rounded the bend and slid into the ditch, panting, Martha landing next to me. That moment, I checked her bandage; the cut looked okay, it wasn't as bad as I'd thought in the first shock.

We could see along the curve of the track toward the armored car. The car was still in sight. In that moment a black explosion squashed on top of it, splashing dirty balloons of the smoke straight out, like fat fists. Then the explosion: *carrummpp!*

The smoke disappeared fast, leaving the car apparently untouched. But you could never tell: could be plenty of soldiers cut up inside the car, by the blast and fragments.

Then, in a flash like orange lightning, fire tongued a jet of black smoke from underneath the armored car. A crashing explosion rattled our ears. The car heaved up heavily, seemed to sit for a moment motionless on top of the greasy smoke cloud, then settled back toward the track, into the smoke, and slowly rumbled onto its side, bounced and settled. The earth under us shook. What would it be—artillery? Or had the Commies dynamited it? Either way, it was a catastrophe for a bunch of Nationalist soldiers.

I saw that Martha had her Leica out and was shooting, although she still panted as if her lungs were gone.

"Good girl!" I told her.

Min was talking to me, his eyes wild, his mouth wide open for air. "Shall we—run for the—pillbox?"

"In a minute."

The hulk of the armored car, lying in the smoke, seemed to be burning, streaks of flame lanced through the smoke. Then there were bright, small bulbs of flame flashing sharply, something exploding in there, maybe ammunition. Black stuff, angles of metal, were ramming into the air above the fire. A woman screamed somewhere near us.

Figures of men seemed to be running amid the fire of the armored car, but they moved too fast to be running, they were being catapulted by the explosion. One black dot kept moving, the other went down, gone in the smoke. We heard the blasts of the explosions, the popping of small arms ammo going off in the wreckage. A big metal part of the car seemed to have come loose, the blob of a man was climbing out of a gap in what seemed to have been the side of the car. The man's dark body flared into a yellow flame.

Behind and to the right of the armored car three or four more dots moved, running, then fell out of sight. How did they get blown so far from the car? I wondered, and then it dawned on me these must be Communists, the raiders moving in behind the blast. I opened the big notebook and made a couple of observations, my hand trembling a little with only normal battlefield fear now, and the sweat streaking the blue lines on the paper. I felt a tremendous relief: I had got Martha away from the hottest fighting. So far, so good. But still, anything could happen in this area. I had to get her farther away. I almost laughed when I saw that she had fixed a long tele-photo lens on her camera and was making pictures. Good nerves she had!

"At what time shall we go?" Min asked nervously, and the formal phrasing at this juncture was ludicrous.

"Pretty quick." If Min had known those dots moving in behind were Communists, he probably wouldn't have waited a second.

The blobs sprang up again, running beyond the smoke, and disappeared again into the earth. They were moving well, exposing themselves for only a few seconds at a time, then flopping out of sight.

I was sure now that they were Communists: the dots reflected a light brown color, not the light green of the Nationalist uniforms. Martha was seeing the same thing through her telephoto finder. She glanced at me with eyes wide and inquisitive, and I nodded, and she went back to her finder, still snapping away.

Brrappp! Brrraap! We heard the light tones of the submachine guns going. And some sharp separate rifle shots. Maybe the Reds were mopping up among the wreckage of the armored car.

Then green dots sprang into sight this side of the burning armored car. They moved this way: the guard troops bugging out before the Communist drive.

More burp gun fire, more rifles cracking. And a ricochet furred the air over our heads. I decided we had better bug out too before the Nationalist troops reached us. In a few minutes, then, the Commies would probably be overrunning this very ditch.

"Ready?" I asked Martha. I didn't have to ask Min.

Martha snapped one more shot and nodded, her chin set. Brünnehilde was the right name for her. I looked back at the smoke of the armored car, saw some of the brown dots moving in it. Then a *thud-thud-thud*, a *thud-thud* coming from somewhere near the head of the train, a heavy machine gun, probably Nationalist, and the brown blips disappeared.

It *was* a Nationalist gun firing and the Commies were taking cover. Maybe the firing had come from the pillbox; the pillbox was covering the retreat of the armored car crew.

It cheered me, the firing from the pillbox. It was, after all, manned —and if the gunners kept up their enfilade fire, it would slow, maybe stop, the Reds. The raid was far from over, but it seemed evident by now that it was a raid, not an army movement that would try to hold the terrain. But you could never be sure, in a war action. This could be only the first stage of a bigger attack.

Then it hit me that we three, wearing suntans, might be mistaken for Communists as we moved up toward the pillbox. Our clothes were about the same color as the Commie uniforms. Fortunately, I was also wearing an olive-green field jacket which looked different. I should make sure they saw that when we worked our way toward the pillbox. I could stand up once in a while and wave my arms. They might see the color of my hair and Martha's hair—that should help. They'd also see our height, compared to Min. Of course, all the waving would make us a nice target for the Reds, too, if they happened to have infiltrated in our direction. It would be chancy, but this kind of small-arms stuff always is.

"Better take off your hat," I told Martha. And without a word she whipped off the brown fatigue cap she was wearing. She didn't ask my reason, but I explained: "The people in the pillbox—I want them to see our blond hair."

She nodded. Min was sitting on nervous springs, ready to jump like a bunny. I wanted him to lead the way, so I could run last, and be a big piece of bread between Martha and the Commies. Min would somewhat protect our precious sandwich filling from fire from the pillbox. But I was afraid he'd make a record, nonstop dash toward the pillbox, maybe breaking ten seconds with his adrenalin flowing so nicely.

"Min—better run only fifty-sixty feet at a time, then hit the ditch— take it slow. Otherwise we might get shot up by either side, or both."

"Okay." Now I was sure this was his first time. Even on that short word, his voice shook.

"Let's go!" We were up and running, again, holding close to the ditch, the image of the overturned train coaches bouncing on our right, the high side of the coaches lined with people hesitating about jumping, some breaking loose like raindrops from eaves, and falling. Some of the drops were green, soldiers among the crowd.

So far, no firing in our direction. A heavy machine gun banged from the pillbox, I saw the orange flashlight of the muzzle blinking at one of the wide slits. It kept firing and I twisted as I ran and looked behind, saw the smoke-zips of the tracers arching down into the smoke near the wreckage of the armored car. The firing lay high above our heads. If they wanted to depress their fire toward us, it would be a pronounced movement and we would see it—that would be short comfort before we caught it.

We were close enough to the pillbox now so that we had to look up a sharp grade toward it. We would have to climb a steep embankment to get to it.

Would the approach be mined? The forbidding idea jumped across my thought like an electric arc. I was gambling that they would signal to us a way through the wire and the mines they might have laid in front of the box.

"Let's stop now, Min!" I had to call him to it, he might have otherwise run all the way to the pillbox. He hit the dirt in the ditch, Martha beside him. I stood next to them, feeling hellish conspicuous—but I wanted to be, to attract their attention in the pillbox. I waved my arms wildly, hoping my hair and the dark green color of the field jacket would show.

"*May-gwaw-run, May-gwaw-run!*" I yelled something like the Mandarin word for American. More credit to Min, he heaved himself up onto his fat haunches and bellowed something in panting Chinese. I heard the words *Gwo-min-dang*, roughly meaning Nationalist, and the proper pronunciation of *may-gwaw-run.*

I held the standing position for a minute more, feeling any second I might draw a burst from the Commies back by the roar of the train, knowing, though, that they were probably five hundred yards away, pretty tough range for light weapons—and the Nationalist pillbox, only seventy or so yards from us, could be a lot more dangerous.

I heard somebody shouting in Chinese, the sound seemed to come from the blank face of the pillbox, from somewhere behind the motionless tan facade.

"They—say—come closer—twenty yards and halt," Min rendered.

"Let's go." This time I went first, since it seemed more important they should see me, I probably looked more American than Martha because there was more of me—and, of course, there was the green field jacket to prove something or other. I hoped now that my guess about the Communists was right—that they didn't have the plan of taking out the pillbox as well as the train. If I was wrong, we might get in there just in time to get blown up.

I dashed the twenty yards or so up the slope, and stopped there, standing up, knowing they were watching us through the slits. "You and Martha better get down," I told Min. But neither of them did, they stood beside me, maybe not knowing just how much of a chance they were taking.

We stood in the sloping tan earth of the embankment, and Min shouted some more in Mandarin. In the loose, sandy earth under the slits where no doubt a couple of heavy machine guns covered us, I felt as impermanent and insecure as I ever had in my life. But Min was coming through well, with the Mandarin language identification. Without his help, we probably wouldn't have lasted long under the guns of the pillbox.

Along the base of the pillbox we could see a thicket of barbed wire, a belt maybe eight feet deep, as dense as a briar patch. But at the left end it seemed to be clear—I imagined I could make out a narrow path.

Bap-bap-bap-bap-bap! A gun spoke just above us, the noise so close to the muzzle was deafening. The three of us hit the ground in an instantaneous reflex, and in that second I saw the orange flash of the muzzle brighten an opening in the middle of the pillbox. In that moment my heart jumped high in my chest—but I knew in another second that they were firing down the railroad cut, in the direction of the armored car, not at us. They would have killed us with one burst, at that range, if we'd been their target.

The gun flashed again, and another ripped out a burst from some nearby slit. I could see now that this pillbox was really a small fort, maybe fifty or sixty feet across, bending around the slope. I could make out a dozen wide slits, though from this low angle I couldn't see into them. I saw smoke trailing, a thin wisp, from one of the apertures.

Then silence. One of the inexplicable sudden silences of a skirmish, that might mean a thousand things, good or bad. But in the silence, now, a voice was calling out in Chinese, a loud, angry voice electric with violence, coming from the pillbox above us.

Min raised his head. "He says—tell the tall American to come up to the right edge of the barb wire—that would be our left—and stop there."

"Okay." I gulped, got up and started walking as steadily and quickly as I could toward the left end of the wire. I fished out my Kuomintang correspondent's folder with the white KMT seal on it, and held it straight out in my hand. Now I could see a path, close to the edge of the wire, and a sort of half-door, evidently made of steel, at the left end of the pillbox. It looked like a plate of armor taken from an old tank, it was rusty and so it blended in well with the tan adobe, and I could see the lumps of rivets in it. Suddenly it banged open and I saw a dark shade and in the shade, the barrel of a tommy gun covering me.

The barrel moved toward me, a green-clad soldier emerged behind it. He was small, he moved at a crouch, his lips drawn back so he would look dangerous. But he didn't have to prove the point to me.

He barked something in staccato Chinese, and I held out my KMT folder and said *"May-gwaw-run"* the way Min had pronounced it. He snatched the card, and glanced down at it while he held the gun on me.

That minute the machine gun at the center of the pillbox blasted away; I had to grip my nerves to hold back the automatic reaction of hitting the ground. The gun was firing into the draw where the Reds would be. The sentry with the tommy gun jumped too, and I was momentarily afraid he'd squeeze his trigger in a quick reflex. My senses were honed sharp—I smelled the burned powder from the machine-gun burst; it seemed overwhelmingly strong.

Holding my KMT folder in his fist, the sentry motioned toward Martha and Min, indicating they should come forward. They did, Min holding out his credentials like a sacrificial offering. The soldier prodded at him with the gun and barked something.

"He says—get in the door—and hurry," Min translated, and he did as requested, with a leap.

I helped Martha into the dank shade where Min had disappeared, saw another soldier crouching there in the darkness, covering us with a carbine. The smell of lime—a clean dugout— came to us like a wall. The armor door clanged as the sentry with the tommy gun hurried in behind us, darkening our vision so we could see almost nothing.

Somewhere very near a machine gun shattered the air, a deafening sound. The empty cartridges tinkled on some hard surface after the burst. I reached out in the darkness to touch Martha's hand.

Our eyes rapidly accommodated to the dark; I could see daylight in long oblongs spaced across the front of the pillbox, narrow picture-frames for silhouetted soldiers' heads. The walls of the gun slits were thick, maybe two feet thick, and the pillbox must have been made of reinforced concrete. This *punkt* was very *schwer.* I had picked a secure place for my Sunbeam—provided the Reds didn't have artillery, or too many men. In such cases, the strong point in war was worse than useless—a trap.

In that moment the impact of what I had done in the last few minutes shook through me: I could easily have got Martha killed, moving up to that pillbox. I had made a quick choice to try to save her; it would still prove to be right or wrong, decisively, probably in the next hour or two.

A Chinese face cut in close to me in the rapidly growing light. A handsome man's face, a hard, crew-cut head, a wide smile.

I could see the three stars on his green collar tab, a captain, likely the commanding officer of this post. On second look, that wide white smile was not as happy as it seemed; I saw the tight lines around the ends of the lips.

He held my KMT folder in his hand, looked down at the picture, and matched it with my face.

"Okay," he said quickly, folding up the card. "You Mistah Ostuhman. Who others are?"

Someone gave him Min's identification folder, and he glanced at it and nodded. "Hah, hah—yes, yes." Min's face appeared close to us and rolled out a string of Chinese. Min gestured toward Martha and me, explaining lengthily.

"Hah, hah." The Captain cut in, bobbing his round head again.

A gun blasted again inside the pillbox: *blap-blap-blap. Blap-blap.* The Captain was talking but the words were inundated by the firing.

His grin seemed wider. "Okay," he said to me. "Big honor is having Melikan visitors in fort—during batteruh." He nodded toward the front wall of the pillbox. "Not interfere in firing. Otherwise complete welcom-uh."

He handed me my credentials and hesitated a moment, apparently wanting to say something more, then suddenly ripped out a string of Chinese—something about *kung chan dang* which I already knew meant Communist. It was repeated several times, with vehemence. He charged into a long speech, and when he finished, his wide-set eyes seemed to flash with anger.

Min translated rapidly, with something of the same staccato effect as the Chinese: "Captain says Communists took over town he live in Chahar. They promised to give better wages to the workers and give the peasants more land. All sounded very good— but everybody could see only good party members got the good jobs; and they were the only ones who got land. And a man had to think exactly a certain way. They put you in prison if you didn't, or they killed you."

It was momentarily quiet in the pillbox—the Captain could hardly wait to go on. He charged ahead as vehemently as before. Min translated expertly:

"His cousin was exchange student at California University, he came back to Chahar before the Communist took town. He said in America you don't have to think certain way, or work certain job. Captain and cousin got away from town, joined Nationalist Army in Kalgan. He would have to go in draft—but he believed in war against Communists."

The Captain shouted something like a battle cry, with the word *kung chan dang* in it, twice, and a definite exclamation point in it. Then he turned away abruptly, and Min translated.

"He says death to the Communists—kill the Communists!"

Martha had been hanging on every word. Now her eyes found mine, as if to say: Here it is—what I promised would happen at the front. When she was around, things did seem to happen clearly, simply—as if her being there somehow made everything come sharp.

The Captain had moved quickly to the center firing slit where two men had been operating a heavy machine gun. He squinted through the slit, said something in Mandarin to the crew. He tapped them on the shoulders lightly and smiled, as if to say well done. The Captain moved to another slit, crouched beside the gunner and peered through. He pointed down toward the railroad cut and waved his hands to indicate lowering of the point of aim. He seemed completely un-selfconscious again, as if he had no American outsiders near him. He moved on to a third firing slit and jogged up the gunners, with the same enthusiasm, the same smile.

Our eyes were accommodated to the darkness now. The inside of the pillbox was lined with bunks, two decks high. A desk with a field phone stood against one section of the back wall, a soldier was talking into the receiver. Maybe two dozen shadowy shapes of soldiers moved around behind the firing slits. One group, near a slit, were belting cartridges. Next to them was an opening in the earth wall, a tunnel half as tall as a man, apparently connecting with another pillbox. That moment a soldier in Nationalist cap appeared in the opening and hurried toward the captain, snapped a salute and handed him a message paper. This would seem to be a real fortification—and well led and well run—a cheering thought.

Then three guns were firing at once and the noise seemed to deafen thought with the thudding and yammering. I moved up behind the central gun-slit, into the smell of the burned powder, and looked over the shoulder of the gunner. The crew paid no attention to me.

From this angle, the gun-slit seemed surprisingly wide and open, felt almost exposed. I could see the small shape of the train below us in the cut, the engine and four cars tipped on their sides like a kid's toy train pushed off the track in a fit of temper; the dark line of the passengers strewn along the ditch, the uneven clumps of people still clustered along the tops of the overturned cars, beside the line of windows where glass flecked reflected light. And at the back of the train, the upright cars immobile on the track, smoke over the black wreckage of the armored car, but the wheel-gear incongruously untouched, the axles unbroken, sitting beside the smoke.

That second, tiny blips of brown sprang up in the wreckage and smoke, a scattering of them, a big crop, maybe fifty well spaced out, moving.

"*Tzo! Tzo!*" The gunner yelled in front of me, and the gun banged out and kept banging. Shouting ran through the pillbox and the other guns took up the firing. I saw the smoke zips of the tracers curving into the wreckage of the armored car.

The brown blips were moving fast in the wreckage, but their movement, astonishingly enough, was back, away from us. Three of them, fairly close together, suddenly stopped moving, their axis seemed to have changed, they were lying down. One lay still, then the others edged slowly, creeping, the agonized, lopsided movement of a wounded man. "*Tzo!*" the gunner cried out, and a crazy cheer ran through the other gunners at the slits above the noise of the firing. They were killing the Reds, the Reds were falling back.

But I knew it could be deceptive, this kind of apparent victory. This very moment, other parties of Reds could be flanking our position, creeping down the bank over our heads, maybe infiltrating the fort or forts that connected with us by tunnel. That was the trouble with a strong point, it could be enveloped, and in it you were always partially blind, it always had blind spots which the flanking movements could use.

The Captain knew that too. But right now, like a champion fighter, he saw he had an advantage and he was exploiting it as hard as he could. I admired his tactics: he had held his fire until the Reds exposed themselves down in the rail cut. Now he was giving them a good dose of what-for.

He moved fast behind the slits, shouting at the crews: *"Kai-chang! Kai-chang!"* He bounced back and forth between the positions so fast he seemed to be behind every gunner at once, he waved an ammo carrier up to the left gun position, he squinted through the slits and corrected faulty aim, and he yelled *"Kai-chang!"* with such ebullience that even we knew it meant shoot. I had seen leaders like him in wars before; great field commander was the right designation, but the name seemed pale before the reality.

We smelled burning metal as one of the gunners held too long a burst. The Captain shook a hand at the gunner and yelled: *"Boo-yow! Boo-yow!"* and in a couple of seconds, again, *"Kai-chang!"* The gunner obediently cut his fire, then started again.

Over a gunner's head, through the glaring picture-frame of sun, I watched the tracers fanning down the railroad cut, curving into the smoking wreckage of the armored car. The gun shook, the cartridges spun away hot and clanked into the metal surface below. *Crash-crash-crash*, the gun thudded, the tracers seemed to sail into the center of the wreckage where the brown dots had moved like frantic ants.

More brown blips had fallen among the streaks of tracers, maybe forty were visibly stretched out, horizontal, one group of maybe ten lying close together. Many of the dots had disappeared —there seemed to be only about a third as many as at first. Some had got away to cover, around the bend of the track or up in the cut.

Somebody stood beside me, something moving fast. A moving hand, a firm little jaw, a camera this time without the telephoto lens: Martha, shooting back toward the rear of the pillbox. That rapid brain of hers had fixed on the most remarkable person near us, the Captain. She was photographing him while he talked on the field phone—a lean, handsome, intense face, wide-spread black eyes and big cheek bones like wings. A man all concentration, all effort—proof that a Chinese can be a Superman. And I was thinking happily:

"Good—pictures for the story. The Captain is a great story—if we ever get back to write it—if the Communists don't come in here with Army strength and mop up the place, including us."

The Captain was talking fast into the phone, talking loudly too because the guns were still hammering.

Min, who had a sharp ear, was enough recovered now to translate for us: "I think Captain has—good news. I think fresh Nationalist troops on way up here from Kalgan—very close now."

But like most engagements I had ever seen, this one wasn't going to fall into a neat pattern—-a pattern only in that the confusion was the pattern. And the Captain didn't say anything about the good news of the relief troops—if that was what it was and Min had understood correctly. Instead he went back to the gun slits, and in his usual bouncy way, ripped out a chain of Chinese commands, I suppose exhorting the troops to shoot, and to find targets of opportunity, and to aim to kill. Then he was back on the phone, talking fast, calling a messenger and sending the runner out the interior door with a folded yellow paper. When I watched the Captain and he thought no one was watching him, the wide grin evaporated and you could see how deadly earnest he was. I would have wagered right then that he was worrying about where the rest of the Communists were, if there were any more, and that he was straining all the antennae of his intelligence to find out.

Then he was bouncing back to the firing slits, peering down at the train cut with field glasses, the same fixed wide grin on his face, the same encouragements in shouted Chinese. I had seen men like him before, of different nationalities, giving all they had of strength and cleverness in a fight they never questioned; the type A-1 warrior.

Now, having satisfied himself that the target had been shot up thoroughly enough, he shouted a cease-fire in a clear voice: *"Boo-yow Kai-chang!"*

He was shouting something more in Chinese, making a kind of short speech like a pep talk. When he'd finished, six or seven men moved toward the door at the side of the pillbox where we'd come in and stood there facing him respectfully, at attention.

"The Captain asking for volunteers, for patrol," Min explained. "These men volunteer."

The Captain talked to the others in the pillbox, evidently ordering them to keep a sharp lookout through their gun ports—for they did just that.

Then he smiled that big wide synthetic smile and made another little speech to the volunteers, accompanied with many arm movements and a couple of simulated crouches, a quick, acted-out charade of rubber-neck caution. He called out a couple of syllables sharply, evidently a name, for a thin young officer with two stars on his collar came from somewhere and saluted. The Captain spoke to him, made some kind of joke, and he and the officer and the volunteers laughed.

"Captain appoints a commander while he leads the patrol," Min explained. And at that moment, my blond warrior whispered to me: "Could I go—on the patrol?"

"Decidedly not," I answered her without thinking, and not having to think about it. "I don't want you knocked off. Besides, they don't want you or me along—excess baggage like us."

She accepted it without complaining, and we watched the tilted oblong of sunshine fall on the dirt floor while the patrol edged out, one at a time, clutching rifles and tommy guns. Then through a slit we watched the Captain, a dusty green, bobbing back, and the rigid shape of a tommy gun moving up the slope; he was running a few feet at a time and hitting the ground, the light face looking back when he stopped, then the green back hunching for another dash up the slope. Then I saw two other backs and rifles spaced out behind him. And Martha was still making pictures.

There was no radioman with a walky-talky, no aid-man with a folding stretcher on this patrol, the accouterments of an American-type scouting mission. These boys did it the hard way, the short way, the Captain would send runners if he needed to, and if there were wounded, he would improvise. I noticed the ammunition they lugged with them was thin—only a few clips on each man's belt. I knew now why he had been so decisive about his cease-fires when the targets were not good. They had no ammunition to spare up here. This, I knew, was some of the handiwork of the Carl Snoops in Shanghai—and so was the plenitude of the Communist ammunition. Martha read my expression and asked, "What's wrong?" I said: "I was thinking—I know where the Communist ammunition came from." She caught it, and nodded. Then I was sorry I had said it. Now, she wouldn't ever want to go back to civilization.

The thin lieutenant squinted after the patrol, squatting with his carbine beside the left gunner's slit, so he could cover the Captain's progress up the slope to the last possible moment. Then, apparently he could no longer see them, for he got up nervously, propped the carbine against the wall and walked to the back of the pillbox where a few cases of ammunition were piled. He checked the nearest open box nervously. I could see there weren't more than twenty rounds in it.

A startling quiet had fallen over the pillbox, the wreckage of the train, the railroad cut which had been ablaze with explosions so few minutes ago. We could hear distant crying and wailing from down at the wreck, and even a moaning which I think was the desert wind. In the pillbox two men were whispering, the others remarkably quiet for Chinese.

Martha had stopped shooting pictures. I took the chance to check the cut on her neck. It still bled slowly, the handkerchief was all stained maroon. I indicated the improvised bandage to the lieutenant, who now stood beside us, and with sign language indicated the need for a fresh dressing. He nodded his head quickly, waved impatiently back toward the empty ammunition boxes. I went back there and found an American G.I. first aid kit in the usual green metal box. Most of the stuff was gone, but luckily I found what I needed and applied it and the lieutenant plainly disdained so much attention to such a little injury to one of the little-no-good sex. He was as jumpy as a leopard, while the Captain had gone.

It seemed that almost everybody in the pillbox had crowded up to the gun-slits. We were all on edge for the sudden sharp slicing of machine gun fire outside, the popping of rifles—or the crash of another mortar that might signal the Captain and his patrol had run into trouble.

Down in the train cut the wretched backwash of passengers, which had been so still, had begun to move again. Probably thinking the engagement was finished, some of them had come out of the ditches and were climbing back onto the overturned cars, and back through the openings where broken glass glittered. Miserable as their possessions might be, they were going to get them quickly before the looters. The dead bodies, the people pitifully cut by glass, weren't going to slow down Operation Repossession. Those miserable belongings might determine whether they lived or died later. The margin of survival was that narrow in China.

I thought about our own possessions: the sleeping bags particularly. They might be invaluable in this rough country, if we survived the day. But I had seen enough of wars to be distrustful of what appeared to be the end of an engagement. Maybe we could get them later. Engagements didn't end neatly, after the proper climaxes, but were given to unpatterned tag-ends of action that could reopen the whole affair, and sometimes incidentally kill you.

I wondered momentarily if my affair with Martha had spooked me, made me too cautious. And just that moment, she asked me: "Couldn't we go down to the train? The fight seems to be over."

"No, Martha, better wait a minute. These things are deceptive." She seemed dubious, so I added: "You saw how cautiously the Captain went out with his patrol," and that convinced her.

On the slope below us we could see some unarmed soldiers in Nationalist green moving up towards us. They would be soldiers on leave, train passengers still alert enough to want the protection of the pillbox until the issue was clearly settled.

The lieutenant had gone back to the field phone and he was talking nervously into it. Min listened, his eyes brightened and he translated: "Lieutenant receives good news. Sentry in another post makes report that troop train from Kalgan is within sight."

And I took advantage of the chance to ask the lieutenant—who was still a nervous wreck—some questions about the Captain. Harassed as he was, the second-in-command gave me a few quick answers: The Captain's name was Ling Ye-win, he had been trained by the American MAG in Peiping, he had been a brilliant military student. He was twenty-four.

And what had happened to his cousin, the exchange student?

"Killed at Weishien, in Communist attack."

Then the lieutenant was visibly worried, watching over the train-cut as if it might explode, anytime. He had been well trained: he knew well the military man's aphorism—never stop, never relax.

Martha was making pictures through a firing slit again, I came up next to her and watched the wrecked train through the concrete frame.

Down in the glare at the end of the train the smoke had settled and without it the wreckage of the armored car seemed to have taken more shape. About half of the car seemed to be in one piece, it looked like a steel freight car that had been charred black. The other part lay in broken, black pieces as awkward and distressing as elbows out of joint. And with the smoke gone I could see what had happened to many of the Communists who seemed to have evaporated before; I could make out a spreading of seventy or eighty bodies, mostly in brown, some of indistinguishable color. Only a few seemed still to move. Captain Ling's pillbox had done good killing.

That moment I saw some green figures moving into the area, just beyond the black splotch where the explosion of the armored car had scorched the ground. The green dots appeared momentarily, while they moved. Then, the movement finished, they disappeared. They were expert, well-spread out, moving crouched over, taking advantage of cover. Probably they were the Captain's patrol, they had searched the top of the cut and gone down below. Being the kind of leader he was, he probably moved first in line, doing his own scouting.

"Is that the Captain's patrol?" I asked Min, and he seemed startled that it could be. He asked the young lieutenant, and the lieutenant nodded nervously.

The leading green dot popped up again, almost at the edge of the black scorch on the tan earth, and ran for the shelter of the armored car. He reached it and sank down beside, disappearing behind some object. I saw something move there, it would be his arm, signaling the rest of the patrol to come up.

Then my unbelieving eyes saw the gray mushroom of a mortar burst spring up, maybe fifty feet from the spot where the Captain had stopped. Then, immediately, another dark splash springing from the ground. *Crrassh! Crasshh!* The sound of the two explosions came a second later, the two sounds almost together.

The shock of what had happened struck me with the same kind of delay as the sound after the sight. The Captain!—it would probably be Captain Ling, though I felt something like a prayer, an effort of will that it wouldn't be he.

A green blob moved down there, exactly where he had been, with the erratic gait of someone wounded. The blob wobbled irregularly, crawling, and then stretched out and didn't move. The smoke of the explosions still hung over the wreckage, thinning. A green dot came running from the edge of the scorched area and flopped next to the leader.

Down the slope below our pillbox, the three or four Nationalist soldiers-on-leave who had been climbing towards us were now running back toward the shelter of the ditch. In the quiet after the mortar bursts, the scraggly black line of people midway between the train and the ditch bent and broke, a strip of tar disintegrating.

I looked far down the cut again, to the wreckage of the armored car, saw that two more green dots had come up to crouch beside the inert leader. If the engagement was opening again—if the Communists had been waiting to throw their big punch now—those green blobs, exposing themselves recklessly to help the leader, were brave men. The two mortar bursts could be the beginning of a renewed offensive; or the last fling of the Reds before they folded up their mortars and pulled out. If it were the former, we would probably catch shelling up here in the pillbox, too.

But the bursts didn't come, and they didn't come, and the soldiers at the foot of the grade below our pillbox climbed out of the ditch and hesitated between going to the train or towards us again, and farther down in the ditch the black tide of passengers edged cautiously back toward the train. And down where the horizontal green blip of the patrol leader lay on the burned ground, now four green half-blips were beside him, they would be squatting. Then they were carrying him carefully, like ants with food, and putting the green burden down in the ditch gently. I saw them moving and the green blip grew smaller until it disappeared into the tan earth. All seven green blips had come up with their guns and they stood there beside the ditch for a moment, and then, spacing out as they should, they worked along the ditch in single file toward the head of the train, the overturned cars and the engine. In the calm the noise of people shouting down in the cut grew louder again, and I saw the soldiers-on-leave below us in the railroad cut moving back toward the train. Then, near the locomotive on its side we saw the fresh troops moving in, from the direction of Kalgan. They were hurrying in single file, rifles ready. They strung out, maybe two hundred of them, and then they stopped and bunched up as inexperienced troops will. The fact that they stayed bunched up and no mortars, no small arms came to slaughter them, seemed convincing evidence that the Commies had withdrawn.

"It looks as if the raid is over," I told Martha. I thanked today's fortunate combination of chance and intelligence that Martha was still okay. It had been close. I promised myself that there would be no Djin-zuh for her or me. We would go back out of China from Kalgan. This was enough crazy risking of her neck. I had a good story now, I could get it done quickly, and go to Hong Kong with her. I wasn't going to tell her that yet, but I did inadvisedly say:

"It's a good story—a sad story but a good one, the story of Captain Ling."

"Yes," she said, "but there's a better one in Djin-zuh."

"We can talk about it in Kalgan."

"Don't give it up," she said. "Please."

But I had already made up my mind.

17

IT WAS LATE THAT NIGHT WHEN THE SHUTTLE TRAIN CHUFFED into Kalgan.

We had loaded the wounded and dead into the cramped cars, amid the rats' nests of passengers and their scrambled belongings, the smell of sewage and sweat and the moaning and groaning of the injured. One Chinese doctor had come down on the relief train, and two priests, medical missionaries from the Belgian Scheut mission at Kalgan. But the supplies of penicillin and sulfa drugs, and morphine surettes, were pitifully small again, largely thanks to our lazy, selfish, racketeering brothers in Shanghai, and elsewhere behind the lines. Net result: many of the most badly injured never got their cushions against pain, and some died in pain.

Martha and Min and I slept most of the time, the nervous strain of the day, and the physical effort of all the running, and then loading the injured, had worn us out.

Before we left the scene of the raid, we had visited the grave of Captain Ling, for it had been he who died down there in the railroad cut with the patrol. I made a crude cross for the grave mound, and stood beside it with the lieutenant. I carved R.I.P. on the cross, as I had seen soldiers cut those comforting letters for their buddies. It was the best thing I could do for him, to show my respect for him as a Grade A-1 soldier. He wouldn't have minded the symbol of Christ. Ling also knew how to struggle and sacrifice for his beliefs. I stood beside the grave, not speaking, glad that there were such men as Captain Ling in the world, on our side.

Kalgan was a bigger town than I had expected, about 150,000 people, but there seemed to be no hospital beds for the injured. About thirty were carried off to the Scheut mission where room was made for them, but that left maybe forty more. About twenty were squeezed into an Army dispensary, and maybe eight died on the train or the station platform. In this raid, the Reds had done well what they consistently tried, to disrupt the countryside and communications, to drive the people into the cities so they would be a burden on the Chiang government; the heaviest burden of all would be refugee peasants.

Min, at one o'clock in the morning, had a conniption trying to locate the local KMT Office of Information man. He had to deliver the body of Duncan Wong to a safe repository, for later return to his family.

Then, at two-thirty in the morning, he found us quarters somehow in a filthy hostel called the Chahar Hotel. Martha and I had separate rooms which, however, connected. We found our beds were straw ticks covered with a single grimy sheet each, and strewn with specks which turned out to be the dead bodies of bedbugs. We put our sleeping bags side by side on the floor and sprinkled them liberally with bug powder, without a chance to talk much, and in a few seconds fell dead asleep, our hands locked together.

It seemed too short a time before Min was banging on the door and asking if we wanted to go to breakfast. Over a considerable repast of noodle soup and *bao-tze* rolls and eggs cooked somewhere between poached and fried and eaten gingerly on chopsticks, Min, Martha and I had our first chance to talk over our plans.

The food worked wonders for our philosophy. But it didn't change my mind about my plans for us, to go back to Shanghai— get her away from this hairy country, and make it to Hong Kong. We had our story now.

I wanted to be gentle about introducing the plan, because I had a fair idea what her reaction would be. "Well, I've been thinking about the Communist raid back there in the rail cut, and I believe we have a remarkably good story."

I hastened on with it: "Matter of fact, I think the story of Captain Ling will do fine for *Beacon*—it'll be just about what they want. And—" I said to Min, "it's a very good story for the KMT—that the Nationalist troop will fight so hard against the Communists, and that they have such dedicated officers."

Min nodded. "Yes, very good story—good enough to justify entire trip." I could see I wasn't going to have any trouble convincing him we should head back toward Peiping and Shanghai, and give up the trip to Djin-zuh. And so far, I could see no reaction from Martha. I was taking it slow.

"Baby, did the pix look good? Did you get enough—and was the light all right?"

"I followed your advice," she said, "forty-one rolls of film. Almost all thirty-five millimeter."

"Very good."

Then Min uncorked the trouble bottle. "Local Information Ministry man, Chu Hsi, can no doubt find film processor with necessary technical skill. But cannot you bring films back to Peiping or Shanghai—where are many qualified people? We can go back in short time —perhaps within week when rail line repaired."

It was a bomb to Martha. I saw her eyes open wide, but probably not with surprise. She had been expecting this since our discussion of the story on Captain Ling, back at the train cut.

"Scott—you're not going to give up the trip to Djin-zuh, are you?"

"Yes, I am," I said, knowing this was the time to come out with maximum firmness. "We have a fine story which will be exactly what *Beacon* wants—" I saw that she was crushed, like a kid whose Christmas presents are taken away from him, and I added hastily: "The story will tell something important about China, too—about the brave men fighting the war, and why they fight on despite the obstacles." I was overdoing it—it sounded like an inscription on a monument.

The chain reaction had started. Her eyes were glinting now, the yellow fires flashing. "You know better than that," she said. "It's only one man's story, the story of one pillbox, one Communist raid. But you know—it needs more, more body, more scope. We have a chance to check the story, a chance to see other people who lived under Communism and had a chance to choose. Djin-zuh, a village like this. We have a chance to see what happened when the Communists came—and what they thought about it!"

"But Baby," I knew the depth of her passion by now and I wanted to brake the runaway jet. "Look—don't you realize the danger? We're lucky to be alive, now—and the trip to Djin-zuh will be three times as dangerous."

She got up, and I felt as if my words were bouncing from a solid wall of fury—also that the small bundle of anger was going to remove itself beyond earshot if I didn't somehow get through to her. I felt a sudden tongue-tiedness in the face of the fury, in our first real quarrel. But then my words began to spill out fast:

"I don't want to seem chicken—but what's the point of going on to Djin-zuh? We have more than enough for a fine story now, an important story. Should we risk everything to get what will be in effect another story? *Beacon* won't run any more than one on China right now. And they wouldn't ever run two in a row, on China. It's a monthly magazine."

The small package of fury exploded—but with a kind of concussive rather than incendiary effect. She snapped at me: "I just don't want to talk about it. I'm going back to the hotel." She strode off.

"Baby—wait!" But she was practically out of the room.

Min laughed uncertainly. I knew the laugh for a Chinese token of embarrassment, not meant to be insulting.

"Excuse me, Min," I said, getting up to follow her. He bowed soberly, and raised one hand to get my attention while he added one considerable item:

"Mr. Ostermann, one important information at this moment in relations: Djin-zuh is surrounded on three sides by Communists, we will need bodyguard of troops to make way in—may be very difficult to come out afterward."

"I know, Min," I told him, my heart focused only on the thought of the quarrel. I started out of the restaurant sure of one thing now, that Min wanted no part of the trip to Djin-zuh. That wasn't much help, now, but as I left he mentioned one last item that was important.

"Beside," he added, "accreditation for Mrs. Shoop must come through from Peiping before Information Office will permit trip."

That sly reminder stopped me in my tracks. He was right. It was clear that there might be considerable delay before we had that radio authorization, forwarded from Peiping, even if I wanted to take her on to Djin-zuh. Min had given me one more weapon to use in my upcoming dispute with Martha.

I felt sick at heart as I climbed the dusty stairs to my room in the Chahar Hotel—but much worse when I saw that she had closed the door between our rooms. And she had even taken her sleeping bag into her room. Mine was a lonely object on the floor.

I went to the door and tried it. Locked!

"Martha! I want to talk to you," I shouted, but there was no answer. "Baby—open up—we have to talk."

I heard some murmured, almost hysterical complaint from her room.

"Baby—open the door. This is important—about the trip to Djin-zuh." I heard her fumbling with the lock, while I rapidly marshaled my arguments. I would have to be very convincing, but I knew that whatever happened, I was going to take her in the direction of Peiping, Shanghai, and Hong Kong, not the other way, where we'd be risking everything—especially her neck—for no really important reason that I could see.

She probably wouldn't realize the meaning of the risk we'd be taking. She was bright, and perceiving, she had been through some mortal dangers during the raid. But she seemed to have a minimum of fear. She seemed as close to fearless as anyone I had known. She would probably always be like that. Telling her the trip would be dangerous—that she might be ripped apart, killed or ruined for life— probably wouldn't make much difference.

When she opened the door and I saw her face all drawn up, agonized but not weeping, a surge of compassion came over me and I wanted to hold her and comfort her. But she stood there so distantly, there seemed such a great distance between us, that I felt helpless and useless.

I stepped across the distance and put my arms around her. My logical arguments seemed to have forsaken me. One of her arms was around me, but her body was stiff, her face was still tortured, twisted, as if she wanted to kill someone and the murder was being fought out inside her—or perhaps, as if she were killing herself inside, dying in there.

"God damn you!" She spat out the words. "You're like the others! I didn't think so—but you are!"

I was astonished. It was almost maniacal, this stratospheric rage.

"Baby—wait," I tried to hold down her incandescent, ice-cold passion. "Wait." I still held her but she seemed rigid. "Wait— what is it? You've got to tell me. What did I do—so wrong?"

She was saying nothing, her mouth set now, in stiff, rigid lines.

"Come over here, Baby—we've got to talk." I led her, a mute child, to the dusty window ledge and sat her down on it, and sat down on the opposite side. She responded like an automaton.

"Baby," I hugged her now. "Tell me what it is. Come on—I have to know. Tell me what I did so wrong. Even if I'm hopeless I can still improve."

A faint hint of a smile. I was penetrating a little. I knew one thing now—I must really love her. Otherwise, I would have stormed at her in response. And now she was talking, the psychic gates a fraction of an inch open, as if she got the vibration of my thought.

The words came out fast, as if they were bullets rushing through a narrow opening.

"When you said *Beacon* only wanted one story on China, and you asked me didn't I realize the danger. The danger! Since when have you been security-minded? I thought I knew you better—that you were one of the Brave Ones. I saw in you that you always tried hard, harder than anyone, despite your protestations to the contrary. I thought you had it—you were a giver—a clean, hard giver, not a taker like the soft ones.

"In you I saw a writer as a writer should be—a man who had to be near the truth—right in the heat of the truth—the cauldron, the flux, the furnace, and you weren't afraid of the risk of the fire. I saw that you had it in you to write something better than an adventure story—one that would tell the world about China, about the civil war weapon the Communists are using everywhere in the world, to put bigger and bigger sections of the world behind bars, where they could be milked dry and never have the strength to escape. But you were like the racketeers—you were lazy, you were afraid. You didn't even want to go and see what the truth is—when up there in Djin-zuh we would be able to see it clearly, see exactly what it is—to see if what that brave man Ling said was true, if it was generally true about the Communists. To find out for yourself—and I would help you. But you wanted the easy way, the money."

She stopped. It seemed as if all the words were gone. I was thinking: That wasn't much of an easy story. But I said:

"Martha—I'm not afraid—except of losing what you are to me. We have our story. I want to get you out of this alive."

"But," she said, that intense simplicity speaking clearly, "don't you see that the story isn't finished yet. We have to make the extra extra effort—the Nietzschean overgoing—the superhuman effort when it seems as if all the efforts are gone. Even if we don't make it—even if we get hurt, we have to try—and make it better than just good or even excellent. That's what makes the champion. And that's what I see in you. I want you to be the best."

She smiled. It was all gone, her body was not stiff any more. And she knew that she had won, the warrior woman had won. I couldn't help smiling with her.

"Okay," I said, "I just came up to tell you that your accreditation hasn't come through yet from Peiping—but I think it will soon."

I picked her up and carried her toward her sleeping bag. "Min will be one unhappy fat boy when he hears about this in the morning."

"But—he's growing up, too," she said.

I put her on the sleeping bag, and she reached up to pull me down to her. I kissed her and she said simply, "I love you, Scott." And I knew that was what I wanted—that and her being there to help with that dangerous moment. It was the moment of Nietzschean super-effort and overgoing she had in effect promised me. I hoped the moment would not end with the catastrophe which Mr. Nietzsche threatens. But I would be happy taking the risk if that was what she wanted.

18

IN THE MORNING, MIN MADE IT ALMOST OBLIGATORY THAT I take her up to Djin-zuh, for he came around with news that her credentials as a photographer had been approved, the word had come by radio, from Jimmy Yung in Shanghai. Min seemed almost cheery—the rail line had also been repaired to Peiping. But he was his old suspicious self when he asked:

"Do you think—Mrs. Shoop—will be able enough as a photographer?"

I caught the drift and made the answer as positive as I could. "She's a very good photographer. I've seen some of her pictures at Shanghai—and I know she made plenty of good ones during the raid."

He bowed—a winning gesture he must have picked up from Duncan Wong.

"Then at what time shall we make the trip to Djin-zuh?"

"Could we go in a couple of days—will that give you time to arrange the truck, the escort, the jeep or whatever has to be arranged? "

"Yes, it should be okay to make the arrangements in two or three days. We must prepare it all with the *shien-jong* and the garrison commander...."

And he pursued at some length the matter of the Communist guerrillas in the hills around Kalgan and Djin-zuh, the need for a bodyguard along the trail, the roughness of the trail . . . He was reluctant, but he was what Martha would call a doer—certainly not in the racketeer group.

Martha did some studying in a Chinese grammar and dictionary the next two days while I worked. She considerately didn't practice while I was working, but sometimes I heard her talking to the room boys outside the door, and I saw that she had mastered elementary things like numbers and handy phrases with remarkable celerity. She ran a test strip of film to make sure her battered Leica was light-proof, and it checked out. And somehow she found time to get white window curtains of some gauzy stuff and hang them in our room. She bullied and cajoled a couple of room boys into scrubbing the crummy floor until it was clean as a cruiser's deck. She saw to it that I always had a pot of tea at my elbow after a long stretch of work over my notes. Best of all, she was as self-renewing a demon lover as any sex-mad Arab warrior could want in his paradise. And I gave up worrying about the trip up-country. It was good enough to live for this day.

The city seemed calm, considering what our Chinese friends had told us about its being virtually under siege. Soldiers in Nationalist green, the soft caps, the wrap-around puttees and the sneakers, were always visible.

Sometimes we could hear the bugles, the weird calls that sounded off-key, and the tramp of marching men, from the other side of town where we had seen a parade ground and some dirty barracks buildings.

But there seemed to be no excitement along the irregular military front, which apparently began at the pillboxes on the outskirts of town and stretched into the loosely-held countryside. "Front is quiet," Min declared concisely. The trains ran through to Peiping; no bridges were blown those two days.

At the end of the second day I suddenly remembered the Chinese calling card I carried in my wallet. The Chinese characters on the big card, I knew, spelled out Shin-yu, Bud Wade's Mr. Fixit in Kalgan. Bud Wade had said Shin-yu was very savvy and could do anything, and if Bud Wade thought that highly of a man, he must be one of the doers and givers.

As soon as I finished the story, I contacted Shin-yu through the room boy. Shin-yu came in to see us at the room, and he was as savvy as Bud Wade had represented to us. He appeared to be of mixed blood, with the round eyes of a Caucasian, and a bald head. But the Asiatic high cheekbones and smooth brown skin were there. He spoke a good American and apparently fluent Mandarin, and also the local Mongol dialect, for all the house-servants accepted him as their own.

He gave me a card with some Chinese characters engraved on the front—and he had written something in fluent Chinese calligraphy on the reverse side.

"This is a friend of mine in Djin-zuh. It's a lousy little rat-hole, but if you need something and it's available, he should be able to help you. His name is Wu Tao-tzu, you'll probably think he's a weirdie, he's a real pure-blood Mahayana Buddhist—but he's okay."

Shin-yu had one final word of advice: "Better make it as fast as you can into Djin-zuh and out. It isn't very healthy up in that neck of the woods."

"We're going to get in and out as fast as we can," I said.

"And still get our story," Martha added.

Just as Shin-yu was leaving, Min knocked on our door, and we knew it must be mealtime.

When I asked if the trip to Djin-zuh was set up for tomorrow as he'd promised, he was evasive. There had been some delay, the *shien-jong* hadn't completed all the arrangements. It might be three days more before everything could be done. We would have to wait until a unit of soldiers would be moving up to Djin-zuh, and go with them. Apparently the military situation was worsening up there—maybe the local military commander was worried that we might not get in and out. I had noticed a column of battered trucks passing through town this morning, loaded with green-uniformed Nationalist troops, heading north—probably reinforcements. I asked if we could see the *shien-jong* the next day and talk over the arrangements. I caught Shin-yu's eye as I made the request and he nodded approvingly.

Min finally arranged the interview, the following morning, and I got assurances from the *shien-jong* that he would send up a platoon of troops on special assignment to accompany us, probably the next day. I also went around to see Chu-Hsi, the Kalgan senior information man, to get him behind the move.

Late that afternoon, as the mauve twilight began to settle on Kalgan, and a weird bugle call drifted from the parade ground to the north, I suffered some Grade A misgivings about my efforts.

That moment, standing by the dusty window, I wondered why I was working so hard to get Martha and me killed.

Martha had gone out, in a pedicab, to look for some film in the town. It had been a hot, hectic day and I was alone in the room. If I had been the heavy-drinking type, I probably would have tried to drown it all—the headwound be damned.

Then Martha came in, the Leica in her hand, the sunbeam smile bright on her face.

"Guess what—I got film," she announced. "And I'll make you a promise: I'll do everything right, this time, I'll make you some wonderful pictures—and we'll send in the best story ever done on China, won't we?"

I wished that I could share her confidence, that all you had to do was try very hard and great results would automatically follow. But I would give her one thing: So far, her system had produced great results.

"Is something wrong?" She looked into my face and kissed me. In a few seconds, a wash of light seemed to brighten my inner world; it had all changed miraculously with her coming.

She kissed me again and the faint, clean scent of soap, lingering in her hair, touched my senses. "What's wrong, Scott?"

"Nothing, Baby." It was easier to laugh. "I'm just—worried. Maybe the story I write on Djin-zuh won't be good enough—for those great pictures you're going to make."

19

It was a clear, windless six o'clock in the morning when we started up the hill at the northern gate of Kalgan. For once the dust seemed to have settled.

Min, Martha and I rode in the jeep ahead of the truckful of soldiers. In our little bouncing vehicle, naturally the important Mr. Min had the front seat beside the driver, Martha and I rode the spine-shattering rear bench.

We reached the high masonry ridge of the Great Wall, the mammoth brown snake writhing over the mountains east and west. The massive wooden gate, tall as a house, stood open. No soldiers guarded it there, but I could see the turrets of pillboxes glaring down at it from neighboring hills.

I looked back at the old American truck with the tires worn down to spots of gray fabric, the green-uniformed men in the open back rolling patiently with the bumps and potholes in the dirt road.

Behind them lay what I thought might be our last view of Kalgan: a chuffing locomotive in the freight yards, some dusty, slab-sided factory buildings, the long gouge of a dry stream bed bisecting the city, north of that gulch, the clusters of round Mongol yurts like overgrown brown buttons, and to the south, the shantytown of the Chinese settlement. Good-by, Kalgan, you were a poor thing of yourself, but beautiful to me because of what had happened here, now. It had made life worth reaching for, and reaching hard.

We hit a chuck-hole that snapped my jaws together. "It's a lovely road," I said to Min.

"It is much worse farther along," Min answered almost cheerfully.

Almost immediately after we passed through the Great Wall, Min's grim promise came true. On the far side of the first hill, the road faded into a donkey track of irregular boulders. It was a full-time job to keep our duffel bags and ourselves in the jeep, we bounced on every anatomical angle except the right one, and the landscape was only a blur. It could have been much worse: we could have been riding in the truck with the soldiers. We had seat cushions, thin but still cushions, and the soldiers sat on the bare metal floor.

We followed a dry stream bed through the valleys for a while, threading our way through the hills as bare as animal hide. We saw no one, the slopes were empty of people or livestock. Min watched the hills anxiously.

"Nobody lives here?" I asked him.

"Only guerrillas—Communist bandits."

I looked back toward the truck, a tortured creature of twisted axles, cockeyed wheels dropping into holes and angling high over boulders. The soldiers were bouncing and sliding with the bumps, but they too watched the hillsides.

Occasionally we came to tan round pillboxes jutting from the hillsides, Nationalist strongholds, and beyond them, little villages of mud huts, and ploughed fields with sparse wheat or millet crops, whiskers of crops sprouting from the brown furrows. The villages had bigger mud huts at the center, which would be the houses of the *tsun-jongs*, the village head men, and even in the adobe wretchedness, little tradesmen had set up wooden stands to sell patched pots and pans, a few scraps of old clothes or soggy-looking packages of tobacco. The more prosperous merchants showed their wares in display cases of wavy glass. A few of the villages had dinky mud-walled temples, with carved wooden demons around the door. "Chinese not religious," Min commented shortly.

We halted in almost every little town, while Min checked with the *tsun-jong* and asked if the next lap was clear. So far, the countryside had been almost ghostly quiet. It gave me the creeps—because I knew that in any war, silence is the mark of the front. Most of the time, the front would always be quiet and deserted. Then, suddenly and when you least expected it, everything would blow up in fire, concussion and blood. I watched the bare animal hills nervously, knowing that any of those shadows could explode with brown men moving and the rush of small arms fire, ripping steel. At every stop, farmers in felt caps and shoes, and dirty quilted jackets and pants, lined up at a polite distance and surveyed us. They too, like the land, breathed out the menace of the front. These people were bigger and slower than the Southerners we had seen—this was getting to be Mongol territory.

As we moved deeper into the country, we began to see cave houses in the hillsides. If the town lay on a slope, most of the houses would be only fronts plastered against caves in the clay mountains.

"Cave houses arc very adequate," Min explained. "Cool in summertime, warm in wintertime."

"I can see how they'd be cool in summer," Martha said conversationally. "But aren't they cool in winter too?"

"They have stoves," Min answered her curtly. Probably he was hungry, as well as scared to death.

But it was not lunchtime yet when we crested a low brown hill and looked down on a sizeable town spread around the blue trickle of a river. From the distance, the dirt road along the river seemed a major thoroughfare, compared to the donkey trails we had been following. The collection of adobe huts was the largest we had seen since we left Kalgan, maybe sixty or seventy; and up the far slopes of the valley, rows of cave houses ranged along footpaths that were almost roads. On every slope above the town big pillboxes perched, four that I could see. And in the edge of the town where the steep slope began, a block of green-uniformed men were marching. Next to them sat a bare barracks-like building, unpainted as is the Chinese practice. Near it stood a stone structure with a steeple, and, I thought, a cross on the top.

"Djin-zuh—our objective," Min announced.

"Is that a church, there, a Catholic church, with the steeple?"

Min ducked his head a little. "Yes," he said, "Christian church."

"Is it a Christian town, then?" I had begun to suspect that he had chosen a town where we would find an especially violent anti-Communist attitude. I knew how ruthlessly the Communists had attacked the Catholic missions in China and elsewhere. The Information people in Peiping, it seemed, had tried to load the dice in their favor. They wouldn't censor my story—only control the information I got at the source.

"No—not only Christians, all kinds," Min said. But I could tell from the way he hung his head that the town was supposed to be a ringer. This was one of the subtle complexities you don't foresee when you make a plan for front-line coverage—it was one of the exigencies that foul up simple plans, as an enthusiast like Martha might not realize. As with sex, field operations were always turning out to be totally different from what you expected, dreamed or feared. But Martha had been able to make sex better than a male could imagine—and she had taught me by now the power of concentration and effort to overcome unexpected complexities in sex. Perhaps she could do the same in other areas.

By now I had made up my mind that this story was going to have more political connotations than I'd first thought of, when I asked the Nationalists for a trip up-country. I had my adventure story, the Communist raid in the rail-cut. Now, since the Nationalists were so determined to control the information I would get—and expose me only to Catholic Chinese who would give me a loaded, and naturally anti-Communist picture, I was determined to foul them up and get an unbiased story, especially one with political overtones. I was beginning to think like Martha.

"It would be better to write about people who are not Christian," I told Min. "You know, the Chinese Christians have been getting especially rough treatment from the Communists. They're not representative of the average Chinese."

"Very well," Min said solemnly. "But we must not rush matters. At first, we must fulfill the amenities with the *tsun-jong*."

As our jeep bounced down the slope toward the town, Martha smiled and whispered to me: "Well done. Stick with it."

The little town along the creek had an eerie, empty feeling about it—none of the crowds of noisy people we had seen everywhere in Shanghai. People moved slowly along the edges of the mud buildings as if the centers of the streets were sure death. A group of peasants in patched dark tunics and pants watched us respectfully as we stopped in front of the *tsun-jong's* hut, a wooden shack shaped like half a barrel. The peasants had the graver demeanor, the darker skins, slower movements of the North Chinese-Mongol strain. It seemed to me they were especially spooked; they said hardly a word to each other while they watched us.

Two hardy-looking little fat men came out to greet us. One was the *tsun-jong*, polite and bespectacled; the other, a smiling little colonel in a tidy green quilted uniform, the commandant of the local garrison: "Colonel of the Peace Preservation Corps," Min said in introduction. Neither of the officials spoke English, it seemed.

While amenities were being exchanged in the bright desert sun, two men in long black robes came running around the nearest comer. When they saw us, they stopped running and smoothed their disordered vestments and came forward with a hurried attempt at dignity. But they were still panting.

"This," said the taller, older of the two men, bowing to us all, "is Father Cadmus. I am Father Henri, father superior of the Djin-zuh mission. Father Cadmus does not speak English—only Chinese— and of course French, we are a French mission."

I introduced Martha and Min. The two priests bowed politely, but when I told them that we had briefly met a couple of priests of the Scheut mission in Kalgan, Father Henri's eyes lit, he translated into French for Father Cadmus, and Father Cadmus grew just as excited.

"If you would be so kind, we should like to be informed about them," Father Henri's English was labored. "We have been *coupé*—how you say that—in Djin-zuh, many months."

"*Coupé;* cut off," I supplied the word.

"Yes, *c'est ça*. You speak French?"

"Not as well as you speak English, Father." We went into the hut shaped like a barrel, sat at a long rough-hewn table, and Martha and I told the two priests how the Scheut mission had taken the injured from the train wreck and cared for them. Father Henri translated the English into French, Min translated into Mandarin for the two officials. It looked as if we were going to waste hours with mere sociability. But I had to wait for the tactful moment to dig into the matter of finding a more nearly average Chinese town than this one. There must be other towns like Djin-zuh in the vicinity which had been under Communist rule before the Nationalists took them back.

It was time for food and the *gambay* session, the hot yellow *gotlion* in bottoms-up toasts while the first courses of the meals were served. The priests didn't drink, but the rest of us toasted the usual assortment of Chinese and American notables, and time was wasting.

The priests went on at some length about the Communists being antichrist, and told how they were trying to liquidate the Catholic missions in China by impossible taxation. They told the story of the local seminary building, which the Communists had burned down. But that story lost its impact when it developed under question and answer that the mission had trained a local, anti-Communist militia, that the militia had made their last stand in the seminary. The burning job had been a war operation.

The Chinese officials weren't any more productive of the kind of story I wanted. Even after the fifth toast, they hedged when I asked them pertinent questions about taxation, whether the Nationalists made fewer levies on manpower for army service than the Communists, and so on. It was clear to me that I'd have to find people less biased than Catholics or Nationalist officials, to get a valid idea of what it was like to live under Communist rule in China.

I ventured a fishhook: was there any other nearby town the size of Djin-zuh, which had also been under Communist domination? I mentioned size because Djin-zuh seemed about right for our research, not too large to bear research in a week, not so small as to have been ignored by the Communists.

Father Henri's long face bent into a smile. "There are several. But they are hardly, shall we say, accessible."

Min translated this question and answer into Chinese and a laugh went around the table. The jolly little colonel, jollier than ever with six or seven shots of *gorlian* under his belt, guffawed and made a vehement answer in lusty Mandarin. Min rendered it in English:

"Colonel remarks that almost every town in the area is impassable, that is to say inaccessible, because of the Communists—except with heavy military escort. He says that he and his friends very much surprised that we came through to Djin-zuh this morning without a fight. He says Communists hold more territory in vicinity Djin-zuh than Nationalists.

"Fortunately," Min added hastily, and I was sure he was making his own interpolation, "the Nationalist forces hold all of the strong points."

Most of the conversation for the rest of the meal was given to the PRO line on Chiang Kai-shek, delivered by the colonel and translated by Min. The colonel rhapsodized about what a wonderful job Chiang was doing in leading the KMT forces, how he had taken a personal hand in saving the big city of Changchun from Communist attack, by ordering heavy air drops of ammunition, supplies, and such. I could see that even under a good load of *gorlian*, the colonel was going to be cagey. He would take longer cultivation than this, even if I wanted to do a straight military story—which I didn't. Mainly, I wanted more reinforcing fact for the story on Captain Ling, which could be very powerful with extra on-the-spot research.

The two priests told us they had rooms for us at their temporary seminary building, and that was welcome news. We were still caked with yellow dust and our joints were battered. I didn't expect there would be any water, but at least we could sit down by ourselves, scrape off some of the dust, relax and make some new plans. I could see it would take careful thought to get the story we wanted, and still do it in a reasonably short time.

The quarters turned out to be two tiny bare board rooms at one end of a clean-looking seminary shack. Min fortunately said he would stay with the *tsun-jong*, and Martha could have the chamber next to mine.

"We had not known that the group would include a lady," Father Henri apologized. "We have quarters for the nuns. They would be glad to have her with them."

"Thanks very much, Father," I answered him quickly. "But we must be close together because we must confer a good deal on photographs and—and on captions. It would be awkward to have to walk to the nuns' quarters every time—such a distance."

I didn't know whether the nuns' quarters were far or near, but no mere civil war or Catholic seminary was going to keep me from my Sunbeam, whatever flimsy excuses I might have to invent. And the grave, long-faced priest accepted my reasons without blinking an eyelid. "Yes, I understand," he said with a slight bow.

So at last we were alone, my Sunbeam and I—a thousand miles from nowhere. And now it looked as if we might not even get a decent story for our trouble. But at least, we were together.

We stood by my window, looking out toward a dusty level area where squads of soldiers in Nationalist green were marching—and singing. The song was a kind of chant, something like the katydid invocation and response we both remembered from the students' parades in Shanghai. In the stillness of the desert town, with the Communists sitting out there in the hills and looking down our throats, the chanting seemed strangely plaintive.

"It sounds as if they're singing to keep their courage up," I said. But she only nodded. I knew there was a cloud on the Sunbeam brow, but I couldn't outguess her. In a lesser woman the cloud might have been fear, but I was sure that with Martha it wasn't that.

"Scott. . ." she began, "we will get a good story, won't we? We won't have had this trip for nothing?"

"I don't know, Baby. I think Min's going to give us a lot of static if we try to get to a town that's not Catholic. And we might not be able to make a trip anywhere without an escort. The escort has to come from the colonel and the *tsun-jong*. We seem to be stuck."

Her mind charged into the problem as eagerly as usual: "Scott, wouldn't it be worth checking with that friend of Shin-yu up here— the one he said was a Buddhist?"

It was a good idea. Maybe another of Bud Wade's friends would have a solution for our present trouble. I checked my wallet; I still had the card to Wu Tao-tzu.

At that moment, someone knocked on our door. It was a Chinese boy with two tin pitchers of water, sent to us by Father Henri. It was priceless stuff, nectar to our dirt-impregnated pores.

The boy also brought an invitation to tea at Father Henri's room —to meet the other priests and the nuns of the mission. The boy would wait while we washed, then guide us to Father Henri's quarters.

✳

The tea was another social affair, if any gathering in the little dusty town surrounded by Communists could be called social. The tiny room was jammed with priests and nuns, the nuns dowdy French and Belgian women, most of the priests Chinese converts who had taken up the cloth. There was no room to sit down, it was a Mongolian version of a New York cocktail party, with jasmine tea instead of martinis. And as I might have done at the Madison Avenue counterpart, I took advantage of the occasion to conduct some business.

At the right moment I asked Father Henri about Wu Tao-tzu. He took the card I extended and he was not impressed.

"We know Wu Tao-tzu," he said. "A Buddhist." He said the word as if it alone were sufficient to condemn the man.

"Could you show us the way to his house?" I asked directly.

"Yes, yes, of course." Politeness obliged that answer. "Perhaps it could be done tomorrow. For tonight, we have had prepared a supper for Madame Shoop, Mr. Min and you. We hope you will make us the honor of being present."

*

Supper was an ascetic affair at the bare table of the priests: mostly-European style bread which the fathers had baked in their own oven, and a few scraps of stew meat. Four of the priests told us the mission story: how the Communists had literally liquidated a church building, saying the Church owed back wages to the labor they had exploited, and the building was being seized in payment. A working party had dismembered it, carting the stones away. And the back wages had never been distributed, as far as could be found out. They went like taxation into the party coffers.

The same, they said, had been the fate of the livestock—oxen, mules and horses, which the mission had owned—they had been seized by the local commissar to pay assessments of wages allegedly due to labor exploited by the missionaries.

It was interesting, it was worth note-taking, it would supply background for my article, certainly. But it was hardly a story of what was happening to the average town in China.

I was telling Martha this when we got back to our rooms that evening. But I could see the slight jut of her jaw as I spoke. I had noticed how absorbed she had been in the stories of the priests earlier, and I knew she had an opinion.

"Scott," she began firmly. "Why wouldn't it be a good story to write about a Catholic town occupied by the Communists? Wouldn't that be an interesting story for the people back home?"

"It probably would be a good story if this were Europe," I said. "Because most everybody is Christian there. But here, Christians are such a minority.

"It might be an interesting story, but it isn't on the beam. I mean, not exactly the focus of the truth. What I want is to know what happens to the average poor Chinese slob, not a Christian, under the Commies—whether he gets treated better or worse, whether he makes more or less, whether he has less friends or not—all that stuff."

"But," she countered, "we know the Communists give you less food, less freedom, less of everything except security, the kind of security you have in jail. We know that, from Europe."

"Yes, that's what seems to have happened in Europe—but does that make it true of China? Maybe Communism in China is different. Some of the authorities—like Vinegar Joe Stillwell and Teddy White and Colonel Carlson—say the Chinese Commies are only agricultural reformers."

"That's not true." She was vehement about it. "All you have to do is read Lenin on the subject and you can see that all the Communist cells everywhere are wired for the same electricity. Russian, Yugoslavian, Chinese—it doesn't matter what national color they have. The doctrine is the same: Communism, the new religion, above every individual or national idea."

She surprised me. I had thought that I was pushing beyond the restrictions the Nationalist press people were trying to impose on us by steering us toward Catholic sources. For once, she wasn't trying as hard as I wanted to with a story. Her reasons were good, but the fact remained: she was ready to settle for a story on Chinese Catholics. She was going on:

"It's all there in print if you want to read—all the Communist doctrine. This is the revolution that shakes the world. It's a holy war of ideas, totally opposite ones. Catholics on one extreme, Communists on the other. One side will win out. And the one that wins will shape the minds of all the people still to be born."

I said, "Martha, you know that's not true. Not Communists versus Catholics—that's too limited a frame. It's Communism versus Democracy, economic and political democracy. You know that. You mustn't settle for less than the truth."

I was surprised. I was beginning to sound like her.

But she was just as stubborn: "So I think the Catholics should be interesting to study here. Catholics are just the most vehement capitalists. They have a faith too, just the opposite of the Communists."

I looked into her intense small face, that seemed so much more intent in the flickering candlelight of my room. "Look, Baby, I've read some of the books about China too—though you've evidently read more on Leninism.

"But here's the important thing: here we are in a spot where we can see something for ourselves—not go by what we read or by hearsay.

"And we don't want somebody with an axe to grind to tell us what the score is. This is our chance to see what happens to the poor average ordinary slob of a peasant under Communism. This is the important thing, it should be the most interesting story to most outsiders—if anything about China is."

She nodded, her aggressiveness suddenly gone. "You're right, Scott. I'm glad you'll fight to get the best story. I say—that's the spirit. Keep it up."

Suddenly, speaking of the poor slob of a peasant had given me an idea. If we couldn't get to another town, why not find one peasant in Djin-zuh who was not a Catholic, and do the article just about him and his family? He could be a microcosm, a prism to reflect what happens to an average Chinese family under Communism. It would give us good pictures—and a chance to dig harder for facts, because our attention would be concentrated on the one small unit.

I told Martha about the brainstorm, and she agreed it was a good one. "But," she said, practical as she usually was, "how are you going to find the peasant?"

"That's where the unspeakable Buddhist, Mr. Wu Tao-tzu, comes in—I hope. He should be able to help us."

20

BUT THE NEXT DAY, WHEN WE ASKED FATHER HENRI TO GUIDE us to Mr. Wu, he made excuses: he was going to be very busy at the church school all day. We could have sought the *tsun-jong's* help, hut that little fellow was genuinely occupied with a sudden crisis which made me more than ever eager to get the article under way and done with.

The crisis came up because during the night a large group of Communist troops had been spotted in the Djin-zuh vicinity. One of the Nationalist pillboxes had reported a Commie group much larger than the usual guerrilla band and possibly as big as a battalion, moving over a distant hill. The resultant flap oscillated between the colonel's headquarters at the parade ground and the *tsun-jong's* barrel-shaped hut in the main street. The field phones jangled, patrols went out; but no contact was yet made with the enemy.

We could have gone to look for Wu by ourselves, but Martha had a better idea. "Min should be willing to help us find a family to write about," she suggested. "As long as we don't have to make a trip to another town."

I agreed. "We'll just tell him it has to be a non-Christian family. He shouldn't object."

And he didn't. He said he thought the family profile was a good idea, and promised that as soon as the *tsung-jong* was free he'd ask for help in locating some likely families we could choose from.

In the late afternoon, the colonel and the *tsun-jong* agreed that the scare of the new Communist force in the hills had apparently faded. The *tsun-jong* promised to consult with Min about the story we wanted to do, the first thing in the morning. But another day was shot, precious time wasted. I wondered if my anxiety showed as much as Min's; his eyes were racked, white, pulled tight with worry, almost as they had been at the time of the raid on the railroad.

The next morning, though, Min had talked with the *tsun-jong* about our story, and by ten o'clock we were walking along a dusty path on the hillside above the town, on a tour of a line of adobe-fronted cave houses. There had been no Communist scare this morning, so the *tsun-jong* had come along to superintend.

We visited seven or eight families, with much bowing and scraping because of the *tsun-jong*. The caves the peasants lived in were much alike: semi-circular in shape like a Quonset hut, with a big mat-covered bed platform called a *kong* at one end. One corner of the platform was taken up with a stove, which had the dual function of cooking food and heating the bed. The whole family, which usually seemed to be at least five people, slept on the *kong*.

The families were all wretchedly poor, with patched tunics and pants of dark padded cloth, and felt slippers they called *shed-zuh*. Their clothes had the look of having become part of the body because baths were so infrequent, and their ears seemed permanently crusted with dust.

Two of the families had bad cases of trachoma, the eyes of kids and adults swollen, weeping and red exactly as if they had been badly bashed. The *tsun-jong* explained that the trachoma germs were spread by the use of the same wash-basin by the whole family.

The fronts of the houses were about standard, tan adobe walls flung against the caves, with a couple of windows, and the more affluent families had windows of real glass. Most had covered the openings with cardboard.

The front yards were fenced with high adobe walls, with one corner set aside, the *tsun-jong* explained, for the collection of human manure which was used to fertilize the crops. This, he told us with a detachment evidently learned in some institution of higher learning, accounted for the high incidence of hookworm, sprue and other parasitic diseases which afflicted almost all the peasants.

I wanted to settle on a family as quickly as I could, because I was jumpy about those hills around us, and their hidden load of Communists. The two families with trachoma seemed so miserable I didn't want to bother them, a third family seemed loony in their misery; the mother, with rags tied around her head, sobbed hysterically all the time we were talking to her, and teetered on her feet as if her sense of balance were gone. Even in the language I didn't understand, her answers seemed wild and erratic. When we had left her cave, Min pointed to his head and made a small circle with his index finger, speaking the international sign language.

Another matriarch, when we questioned her, seemed to have been too wealthy, at least before the Communists, to be representative. Her family had owned parcels of land totaling eighteen hundred *mo*, which would work out to three hundred acres. By Chinese standards, she had been immensely wealthy. Naturally, the Communists had singled her out for persecution as an arch-Capitalist. She was poor now, because her land was still in Communist hands, and she wept during the interview because her husband, she said, had been beaten to death by the Communists. It was a sad story, but not the one we needed.

We settled on an alert, forty-year-old peasant named Fon Chung, who had been approximately an upper-middle-bracket farmer in China before the Communists. He had owned about twenty-six acres of millet land before the Reds came. He seemed to stand for a large group in China—although of course by direct comparison with an American farmer, he was dirt poor.

Fon had a family of six children, all girls. Two sons had died, one of typhus, the other killed by the Communists, Min translated, and of course I suspected that Fon might have been handpicked by Min and the *tsun-jong*—but at least he wasn't Christian and he hadn't been rich.

He was a good-looking man, despite the permanent crust of dirt in the ears and eyebrows, and his ragged, worn quilted jacket and trousers. He had regular features, well-spaced eyes, and the polite, grave manner common to Northerners in China. His level eyes and thoughtful answers to questions made you feel he was honest. His wife was attractive and his kids seemed well-behaved. Fon, I thought, would do well as our subject.

That afternoon we sat around Fon's cool cave and went after the story as intensively as we could. The *tsun-jong* left us. Martha shot several rolls of film, Min translated, grew short-tempered after a couple of hours until I told him the quicker we could get the facts the sooner we'd be able to head back to Kalgan—and with that reminder he became very willing.

The story was working out very well, though slowly. As one must do with these profiles, I went back over Fon's history, way back to his boyhood, and the process was laborious with the translation and the differences in things like our calendar versus the Chinese calendar.

Though he was polite, I could see that Fon was growing restive towards the end of the afternoon, and Martha reminded me: "Maybe he has work to do." It had been stupid of me not to think of this. I asked Min to check it, and he reported after protracted question and answer that Fon did have some oats he was tilling, but he said politely, his friend was taking care of the work this afternoon. He said the Communists had taken almost all of his land away and given it to good party members—it was all—like the territory around us— in Communist hands. The two acres—twelve *mo*—left to him in town were all he had. The work went hard because he had no oxen, everything had to be done by hand. The Communists had grabbed his livestock and tools—confiscated them. I asked Min to tell him we would like to see him at his convenience an hour or two a day for the next few days. So the story would go even more slowly than I had expected—but I could fill out the rest of the time by talking to Fon's relatives and friends. That would have to be done to check the facts, anyhow.

After the day's work, when Min, Martha and I were picking our way down the hillside toward the seminary, I remarked to Min that if things went this well from now on, we could probably wind up our research and our pictures in a week.

"A week!" He was incredulous. "I had thought it might be done in two days. A week might not be in time."

"In time for what?"

He pointed down toward the rectangle of the parade ground. It was almost solid green with a mass of assembled troops, possibly five or six hundred men in ranks. On a board platform facing them a stubby figure was evidently haranguing them. At a respectful distance behind them on the platform stood five or six other men in green—probably staff officers, with the colonel out in front giving the men a pep-talk.

"The situation grows critical." Min's eyes had that white, drawn look. "There are signs Communist armies approaching from north."

"I know that. But why do you say a week will be too long a time? Is there some special reason you think so?"

"Plenty of good reasons." His face was dark, I couldn't tell whether he knew something he wasn't telling us, or if he simply had the wind up and would take any excuse for a quick exit.

Below us at the parade ground the stubby little man in green stood rigidly before the troops for a second, saluting, then turned and walked off the platform, his staff marching behind him. We heard the tweeting of whistles, and guttural marching commands, and saw the ranks of green begin to move. The tramping of their feet came up to us, then that same determined chanting we had heard before: it sounded as if they were singing down in their throats, trying to be as bass-toned, rough and terrifying as they could, and not quite making it.

"Well," I suggested, "why don't we stop by the colonel's headquarters and see if we can get any late news. Wouldn't that be a good idea?"

"Then we shall," said Min gruffly.

The colonel was closeted with some of his staff when we reached the stucco shack that served as headquarters. But Min had an audience with the adjutant, and reported to us with a grim face:

"Dun Liao Di fell to the Communists this morning."

"What's Dun LiaoDi?"

"It is a town only three miles from here. A large attack on Djin-zuh may come at any moment. It is believed a Communist division is close."

His information sounded factual enough. "How many Nationalist troops do we have here?" I supposed the colonel would have a regiment—maybe thirty-five hundred men.

"I believe two thousand men," Min said as if it were my fault. "The Communists far surpass us in numbers."

While we walked on toward the seminary, I tried to make a plan to hold our little venture together: a way we could get the story and stay in one piece. The name of Wu Tao-tzu stuck in my mind; he should be able to help. If he could speak English, we might get him to help as interpreter; Martha could do some of the interviewing with him interpreting, that way we could clean up the research faster.

Martha had roughly the same idea at the same moment. "I could talk to Fon's wife and his relatives while you talked to him. Tomorrow—if we could get another interpreter."

"I was just thinking of that," I said. "About Wu Tao-tzu. Maybe he could do it. Do you think you could help us to find him?" I asked Min.

Min was far off, flying like a bird over the mountains to the relative safety of Peiping. "Who?"

"Wu Tao-tzu. We have his card, remember, from Shin-yu in Kalgan. We thought he might help us as an interpreter, it would speed up our interviews."

"Yes. But when shall we be leaving Djin-zuh? I must make a plan to ask for an escort from the colonel. It is urgent."

"If we can get another interpreter, we can speed up our research—perhaps we *can* leave here in two days."

"Good. Then shall we find an interpreter tonight?"

"Yes. Wu Tao-tzu—"

"I understand, he may be the interpreter." Getting through to Min in his present mental state was a job for radar, but it seemed that at last I had penetrated. "Tonight, after supper, we shall search for him."

✻

We found Wu's house on an alley called Da Jing Ya Go, meaning "Gold Tooth Trench" and it was that, a path along a jagged tan spur. The house was the standard tract model for Djin-zuh: high adobe wall at the outside, a false house front of mud slapped on a cave. But he had a real glass window, and several candles inside the whitewashed arch—more illumination than most of the cave houses had.

Three wooden chests stood at the head end of the cave, with drawers, also more furniture than in the houses we had previously seen. On the center chest stood a handsome ceramic Buddha, about three feet tall. And, wonder of wonders, there were books, mostly paper-bound volumes, ranged in rows behind the Buddha.

"My library," Wu said in good English after we had introduced ourselves and he had given us a flamboyantly courteous welcome. "You see, I teach the Buddhist Way." He smiled and bowed. "These are for my students—and also so that I may enlighten myself over and over as long as it is necessary."

Wu was tall and thin, probably younger than he seemed, he had a shaved head, and wore a yellow robe, in the fashion of the Buddhist bonzes I had seen in Siam.

When we had sat down he joined us and said, still smiling: "I knew of your arrival, but did not know that you were friends of Shin-yu or of Mr. Bud Wade." The American name didn't sound strange on his lips, it had become Chinese in sound and was more like Budd'ade, who might be a disciple of Buddha. "What service may I have the honor of performing for you?"

We told him about the story, how Martha and I were writer and photographer on it, and how we had trouble getting the priests at the Djin-zuh mission to guide us to him—how the military emergency had precipitated the need of an extra interpreter at Fon's house.

He smiled knowingly. "I shall be glad to act as an interpreter. And furthermore, if you should desire it, there is a poor house exactly like this one which you may have during your stay. It is poor, but clean, and servants will tend it for you." Somehow, he had sensed the awkwardness of our relations with the priests. I told him how much we appreciated the offer, but that we expected to stay in the town only a couple of days more, if we could finish our research in that time.

"I understand," he said, still smiling. "But if the need should arise, the poor house is available. And incidentally it is not too far removed from the house of your subject, Fon."

21

WU'S UNDERSTANDING HAD ANTICIPATED WHAT WAS TO happen when we got back to our quarters at the seminary that evening. A Chinese boy was waiting outside the door.

"Father Henri—cha," he said. The priest was inviting us for tea.

"*Shemma shir hou?*" Martha's Mandarin was good enough to ask when.

"*Shian-dzai,*" the boy said.

"Now," Martha translated.

On the way over to the priest's quarters, I could see that Martha's face was unsmiling under the brilliant starlight. "Will we have trouble about our quarters?" she asked.

"It could be, Baby."

"Do you think Father Henri knows that we sleep together?"

"I don't think he's thinking about that. I think he's worried about something more fundamental to him—his doctrine."

When we had been through the amenities with the tea, we saw that my guess was right.

"Why is it that your publication is so interested in the non-Christian Chinese?"

"Father," I said. "In the interests of truth we should study the people who are average Chinese as well as the special cases of the Catholics and other Christians." I was thinking: it's going to be a job to get all this into my adventure story about Captain Ling and the Communist raid. But it will also make the story important. I was learning from Martha.

"Yes," the priest said solemnly. "I understand." He didn't say anything about our bed and board with the mission, but I thought: tomorrow we must move to the house Wu has offered—even if our stay in Djin-zuh is just for a day or two more.

✳

Back at our rooms, Martha was even more depressed, it seemed to me, than the circumstances warranted.

"What is it, Baby? Something I don't know about?"

"It's nothing." But the tightness of her lips told me it was a lot more than that.

"Tell me, Baby." But she got up without answering and walked to the window. In the flickering candlelight she seemed thin as a wraith. From the direction of the military headquarters a forlorn bugle-call, full of minor notes, drifted in our direction.

I got up and walked to Martha and put my arms around her. She looked up at me and her lips trembled.

"I feel—guilty," she said. "Since the trouble with Father Henri."

"But Baby—it isn't our relationship, yours and mine—that disturbs him. It's the way we're researching the story."

Suddenly she hid her face against my chest, and I could feel her choking back sobs.

"There, Baby. Everything will work out all right. We'll get out of this."

She still hid her face. "But—" Her voice was muffled against my chest. "I think I'm pregnant."

"You're what?"

"I think I'm pregnant." The sobs broke through now. Her small body shook in my arms.

"My God," I said, and stupidly enough: "Are you sure?"

The responsibility of getting her out of there, out of Djin-zuh and Kalgan and Peiping, came down on me with the suddenness of a drop-hammer. But even under these circumstances, the shock and surprise were not unpleasant. Subconsciously, I must have wanted this more than anything else.

"No, I'm not sure. But I've missed my time. And I never do."

"Poor Baby." Her body shook, and I knew she was resisting tears, and also that she would not give in to them. "I'm glad, I'm very glad about it—and I'm going to get you out of all this, and quickly."

I stroked her golden crown of hair. "Sweet Baby—I know exactly what we're going to do—and it will be good."

"What?" The voice was like a hopeful child's. The sobbing stopped, but she still hid her face against my chest.

"We're going to move to the house Wu offered us, right away. And I have another idea that will make everything better for us."

"What is it?" Still the muffled voice, but now there was hope in it.

"It's a secret. A surprise. But it'll be good for you—for us."

She moved her face away from my body but still wouldn't look up to me, she didn't want me to see her face with the tear-stains. She hid behind a handkerchief and blew her nose.

"Tell me what the surprise is."

"No, Baby, you'll see in a little while. Meanwhile, let's get our stuff together right now and go on over to Wu's. We can make all our explanations to the priests tomorrow."

✳

Wu accepted us as if it were nothing unusual to take in boarders at ten o'clock at night in Djin-zuh, in fact he smiled as if he had expected us.

By candlelight, he showed us the inside of the cave house, which was clean and whitewashed like his own. If he had any questions about our marital status, he didn't mention them. Maybe he assumed we were married. He introduced us to a Chinese boy with the shaved crown and orange robe of the Buddhists. The boy would cook and keep the house for us, he said. I explained we would probably be there for only one day more, if we could arrange to get an escort for the trip to Kalgan. That, he said, was acceptable, he was glad to be our host for any length of time. The boy smilingly promised he would have a *ding hao* breakfast for us—and bowed out of the room.

"Now," I said to Martha, "Master Wu and I are going to talk about the surprise for you."

I took him by the arm and we went out. I could tell from the small sunbeam face as we left that she had faith in me.

Under the clear bright starlight I asked Wu my favor: since he was a priest, a *samga*, could he marry us in a Buddhist ceremony?

He responded with a good acceptance of life, the intuitive generosity.

"Yes," he said. "I have watched you with her. I know your attitude is correct."

"It's as correct as I can make it."

"Yes," he said gravely. "I look for devotion as the requirement of marriage—more than passion. Devotion is founded on admiration and compassion—you have both in good store, toward the woman. You know that the Great One teaches physical desire, passion, to be the great delusion of mankind. But you have found the truer value of attachment to a woman—devotion. I can see the manner you have with her."

I nodded, knowing that I might have climbed the Platonic stairway of love from the physical to the spiritual, but that my admiration and compassion for her, fortunately, had physical roots, and they were at least ninety-nine and forty-four hundredths per cent of our relationship. Thank God for that, I said to myself—and more's the pity that the good man will never know this celestial kind of mathematics. Passion will never teach him to be virtuous in his life, he will have to accept virtue on faith, without knowing its real well-spring: passion.

I told him only that I wanted the ceremony for Martha—that this was a time of great danger and I wanted her to feel recognition as my wife.

He said calmly:

"I shall plan for it in the early morning. Certain preparations must be made in any case. If it cannot be done, I will send word to you before the morning."

He bowed and went off, and back in the candlelight of the cave, I found my Sunbeam unrolling the sleeping bags on the clean *kong*, and singing, off key as usual, but delightfully to my ears.

"Is the surprise all arranged now?" She came to me and put her arms around me.

"I think so. For the morning, first thing."

"Tell me what the surprise is."

"No," I kissed her. "If it didn't happen, you'd be very disappointed."

"Is it a way to get out of here?"

"No. Though I have ideas on how to do that, too." I picked her up and carried her out the door and in again and laid her down gently on the sleeping bags. Before I kissed her she said:

"Scott, don't skimp on the story because we're anxious to get out of here—promise?"

"Okay. But I'm going to work like a demon to finish the research tomorrow. So are you."

Her most charming smile, the shy one, broke over her face. "Yes, sir."

She held my face against hers and asked me:

"Is this our very own house?"

"Yes, Baby, our very own."

"Then I'm happy." I put out the candles and came back to join her in the dark. It was cold and our warmth was perfect.

"Scott," she said, the voice in the dark that I knew so well, so well that her voice alone filled in her body and all of her, in my mind. "Let's pretend this is our very last night on earth."

"Okay," I said. "But why? We'll get through this, out to Shanghai and Hong Kong, and write the story, and live happily ever after. And have many more children after Junior." I didn't believe it, but why give in to *Weltschmerz*?

"But right now everything seems just right. I wish it could go on just like this, forever."

I held her tight. "Yes, Baby, just like this—forever." Good things, the best sensations, were beginning to develop as we stayed close together.

"Yes," she said. "Yes-like this, forever, forever."

✳

Afterwards, I watched her float away in sleep, and I closed my own eyes. But sleep wouldn't stay with me that night. About three a.m. I put on my clothes and went out our front gate and sat on the edge of the sloping path called Da Jing Ya Go and watched the stars. They were beginning to wash out as the sky got ready for dawn.

I had been thinking that a new and wonderful event was emerging in my life, a new value, something that I must save and hold, the baby seed that was developing in her, a life from our life. She and that baby seed must get out of China, I must get them out. I would protect them, but she would also be with me, she would share the risks I would take to write good stories, true and honest stories. She would be there to keep my courage up, to remind me that I had an important job to do, and remind me that the real happiness is in fighting—fighting for what you believe in, with every ounce of nerve and energy you can muster—that the real game is in the trying and the fighting, even beyond your strength. And if you are lucky to have a woman who will fight beside you, you are truly fortunate. And now, there would be a small one to remind me of all she had taught me—I hoped.

I tried to think through what would happen if we set out with a truckload of soldiers for Kalgan. Could we get through the hills as easily as we had reached Djin-zuh? Or would we run into patrols from the regiments that seemed to be coming down from the north?

One thing was in our favor: Kalgan lay to the south. We might be able to get through without any trouble at all. But every day would make the trip more dangerous. Now I knew we would be finished with our story research soon—maybe in a day or two.

An idea which had been much in my mind was somehow getting word down to Shin-yu in Kalgan, trying to get a plane sent up here to fly us back, maybe all the way to Peiping. Then we could easily connect with a flight to Shanghai—and out. But the question was whether we could get word to Kalgan. If we could get the military to send a radio message, if there was a plane available in Kalgan, if Shin-yu would send the plane up for us—

I realized how critical time had become. To get the colonel to detail a platoon of soldiers and a truck—that would take some time, and some doing. Maybe longer than a day, a couple of days, maybe much longer. It would take some time and some doing to get the colonel to okay a radio message to Kalgan—though maybe in his state of nerves, Min would be sufficiently eloquent to swing the deal.

But, I was wondering, if Shin-yu did get the message and could and did send a plane, could a light plane come in—and more important, take off with a load? And an L-5 would be overloaded with pilot and two passengers—and Min would be wild to get aboard at any cost. But could a bigger plane than an L-5, maybe an L-16, get in and out, say at the parade ground?

Then I heard the distant thunder, a faint booming like kettledrums, coming from the mountains to the north. It kept on irregularly, exactly like the first rumbling of a summer storm. I watched the edge of the peak behind me for the edging of light that could be flashes of gunfire against the black. But none came there to silhouette the hill—only the gradual lightening of the sky with the onset of dawn. The fighting hadn't reached this area yet.

I saw lights moving down at the headquarters building of the Peace Preservation Corps, flashlights. I heard an engine sputter, choke and start: probably a generator. I saw a flash of yellow light as a door opened and closed. The buildings were usually kept blacked out, and wisely so. A jeep engine started, and the vehicle putted down the hill. I could hear the moving of feet. But by this time the thunder of distant gunfire had faded.

I watched the camp come to life as the sky gained a shade of gray and the buildings took edges in the light that was like fog. Somewhere a bugler sounded one of his weird minor-key calls.

Then I grew aware that someone was standing beside me. It was Wu, his robe brilliant in the pre-dawn light, his face beneficent. For a moment I sank inside as I thought he was going to say the ceremony was impossible, then I realized that smile meant everything was all right; it was early morning, and he had promised the big event for now.

I stood up and shook his hand and he said:

"Preparations are being made for the marriage fete. You and the woman may be at my house within the hour, perhaps."

I said we would, and he sat down beside me, the pleasant smile on his face.

He said: "Have you heard the guns in the north?"

"Yes."

"They are the voices of hate, soon they will be here, in this village. For this reason, we must conduct the marriage quickly. The Dhammapada says, 'Hatred ceases by love, this is an old rule.' By an act of love, I can help to destroy hate."

It sounded convincing enough, and I didn't much care at this point, as long as it could be done. "It will mean much to Martha," I said, and that was the important truth: after racking our situation back and forth in my mind for hours, I wanted any kind of a ceremony for her benefit, and any official-sounding hocus-pocus,

I thought, would make her feel better and surer. As for me, what we had been to each other was enough, I needed no official sanction.

✳

The ceremony was a lovely one. First, Martha and I were purified by the drinking of rose tea, then Wu and the novice who tended our room officiated at the improvised altar where Buddha stood.

From somewhere, Wu had secured some flowers to deck the altar, and some branches of trees to wave over us so that the clean wind would also purify us. God knows where he got his rose tea, possibly it had been hoarded in a jar for such an emergency; I hadn't seen any roses in Djin-zuh or the vicinity.

Wu and his novice, with white cloth bands wound around their heads, knelt before the altar, clapped their hands sharply, and chanted alternately, a practiced solemn tone which had a hypnotic rumble to it.

Martha and I sat at opposite sides of the room, facing each other, and we nodded when Wu gave us the signal to nod. Wu and the novice addressed the altar with wooden paddles, clapping them together in rhythm. Then the novice carried cups of yellowish wine between Martha and me, so that each of us had sipped three cups which the other had sampled. It was like the Shinto custom of sealing the bond in saki.

Then the marriage was done, and we went with Wu to our cave house, where the novice had prepared a wedding breakfast of tea and *man-to*, home-baked bread. Martha, in her wrinkled khakis, was still more radiant than any bride I had ever seen before, with her gold curling crown brilliant in the early sun, her face a flower.

"You have made me very happy," she told Wu, with a formality of phrase uncommon in her. But when the quick repast was over and we were walking down the Da Jing Ya Go to meet Min and begin the day's work, she kissed me gently and said: "Scott—darling — you didn't have to go to all that trouble. I feel legitimate enough without it."

I gasped. "Sometimes you astound me, Martha. You think so much the way I do." She pressed my arm, and it was a happy moment walking with her in the bright, six a.m. sun. I couldn't remember any happier moment, when I had been so closely identified with a person I loved.

"Anyhow, I've got two more surprises for you this morning," I said.

"Tell me."

"The second surprise depends on the first."

"What's the first?"

"The first one is a plan to get out of here, but quick. We should be able to get through with the research today. I'll get Min to send a radio message to the *tsun-jong* in Kalgan, asking him to contact Shin-yu and have him send up a plane to pick us up. He could land on the parade ground—and maybe fly us all the way back to Peiping. From there on, it'll be easy to get back to Shanghai—and out."

I could see that she was dubious, but I ploughed ahead as if everything were in the bag. "The second surprise is that once we're out of China, we'll get divorces and have a second ceremony, the Christian kind."

She stopped and drew me down to kiss me on the cheek, and she whispered in my ear:

"I don't believe you, but it doesn't matter. You don't have to be officially called my husband. I know you are in fact."

Min fell in rapidly with the suggestion of asking the colonel for a radio message to Kalgan. And the colonel, surprisingly enough, agreed to do it this morning. Min evidently asked him to specify in the message that a plane big enough to carry *three* passengers besides the pilot be sent, because the colonel laughed heartily, and repeated one of the few words I had absorbed in Mandarin, *san*. I had at least learned how to count.

I tried to will that there should be a plane in Kalgan or due in Kalgan, as we trudged up the hill toward Fon's cave house, to begin the day's work. It was not yet eight o'clock.

"We shall know this afternoon about the plane," Min said. "The colonel will ask for a reply." That word made our spirits zoom.

Martha and I jumped into the research job as if it were the first or last of our lives, and even Min seemed eager. The research clicked along nicely. Martha, with Wu interpreting, interviewed Shu-ding, Fon's wife, in our cave house, and also sought out and talked to Fon's mother and some of his friends. To make up for some of Fon's lost working time, I gave him some money so he could hire another farmer to do his chores for the day.

With time so precious, I skipped some of the background questions, and concentrated on the most important issue in his story: how had he fared under Communism, how did the Communist regime compare with the Nationalist?

The story of Djin-zuh, as Fon unfolded it, followed lines familiar in Europe. As soon as the Commies came in, they had set about liquidating the middle class, the bourgeoisie—and of course, the big landholders, the capitalists.

They did this by the same device the priests had told about at the mission: the Communist committees for "Settlement of Accounts and Public Revenge" assessed all landowners for back-pay allegedly owed to farm laborers as far back as 1927. In Fon's case, this came to seven thousand Chinese dollars, or about one thousand U. S. at the rate of exchange that year. Of course, Fon didn't have it, so in payment the committee took his two horses, his two oxen and his cart.

Furthermore, the Commies confiscated all private land holdings of more than twelve *mo,* or two acres. That meant Fon was deprived of two plots of land totaling twenty-six acres. The land was supposed to be distributed to the peasants, but, said Fon with a wry smile, it all ended in the possession of good party members, and the other poor were still left out in the cold. It was good confirmation of what Captain Ling had said—that the economic benefits of the Communists were reserved only for good party slaves.

"Were you happier under the Communists or the Nationalists?" I asked, and Min snorted before he translated. Fon nodded as he heard the question, and a slow smile spread across his face. Then carefully, in slow Mandarin, he answered and Min translated:

"He says 'Too many spies' under the Communists. *Kampu* Communist political activists: that means party members, always informing on everybody. Two *kampu* members told the Communist *tsun-jong* this Fon had twelve silver dollars which he had hidden from Public Revenge Committee. *Tsun-jong* ordered beating in public with clubs—and thirty days in jail."

Each translation seemed to make Fon more anxious to talk; now he went on without prompting on the subject: happiness or lack of it under the Communists.

He automatically acted a series of charades, quite animated for a Northerner: he mimicked an orator bellowing and waving his arms, he was a soldier or a Communist goon prodding and threatening someone, he was an inoffensive peasant being beaten, he became an executioner with a pistol and a man kneeling to get the shot in the back of the head, then falling pitifully.

The narrative in translation was that as soon as the Communists came in, they started mass meetings every day. Most of the people couldn't read, so they had Communist orators who kept the assembly at attention for hours while they harangued, even in the coldest weather. The soldiers herded the people to the meetings and threatened anybody who wanted to leave before they were over.

The orators dinned into the heads of the people the motto, "No Communism, no China," they promised the workers and peasants back-pay for the years they had been exploited—but the money they raised by assessments went into the Party funds, rather than to the peasants—unless they were good Communists.

The people who were forced into the pep-meetings had to sing songs about the Party, said Fon. And the *kampu* kept turning in people who were supposed to be traitors, minions of Capitalism; there were public trials which usually ended in quick execution in the public square.

So it went—we were getting to the meat of the subject, and I tracked down details so I could check Fon's statements. I believed Fon, his manner seemed honest and genuine, but everything must be checked, and getting details was the best way. A man can invent generalities, but his imagination isn't usually up to manufacturing minutiae that check with each other.

I took Fon up to Wu's cave, we had a lunch of oat gruel and *manto*, and it was good because with Wu interpreting this time, I could go back over some of the crucial things Min had been translating for me this morning. To give Min his due, it all checked out.

Then Min came back from lunch, and he told us he had stopped at the Peace Preservation Corps headquarters to check on the radio message to Kalgan. No reply yet.

That afternoon with Fon we progressed to the second regime of the Communists: when they had been driven out by the Nationalists for a year, and returned in force to annihilate the defending forces — the small Nationalist garrison, and the Djin-zuh militia the Catholic priests had organized.

This time, the Commies had plenty of rifles and some machine guns. Fon didn't think there were Russian arms among them at that time; plenty of Japanese arms, and American rifles the Communists had taken from the Nationalists "and from other sources" Min translated, and I was glad Martha wasn't within earshot. No good reminding her why we were in such grave danger at the moment. Fon's son, Fon Jun, had been killed in the fight, he had been drafted into the Nationalist forces, although only seventeen. Fon's face was drained as he told about finding Fon Jun's body in the snow, almost frozen stiff, two bullet holes in his head. When the Communists were driven out the second time, Fon had enjoyed his revenge. It was a cold winter night, he had caught a Communist soldier in an alley as the Communist forces were evacuating the town, and cut his throat. But, he said, afterward he was sorry; the man probably had nothing to do with his son's death.

So it went into the afternoon, our research effort, and Fon's story unrolled. We got to know the man, and also worked into details like the relative taxes and military levies of the Communists and Nationalists. The Communists' were much worse, Fon said in Min's translation; but that was one item I would have to check with Martha's research, tonight. It was adding up to a great story— provided we could get out with it.

Some of the time we sat in the sun beside Fon's front gate, where we could look down the slope and see the parade ground and the Peace Preservation headquarters. A company practiced marching, and sang their dismal chant, and once, a truck with about a platoon of soldiers and a jeep with officers bounced up the far slope to a pillbox. But there didn't seem to be any signs of a big flap. And my hearing strained for the faint sound of gunfire to the north, but none came.

About four o'clock, Min said he must go down to the headquarters and check on the radio message. He came back disconsolate, there had been no message yet.

With the sun working westward into the Gobi sky, I began to have misgivings about tonight and tomorrow, and whether we would get out at all. It could be that the colonel hadn't even sent the message. We should check with him; if he wouldn't send the message for some reason, we should get after him to get together a bodyguard of troops and a truck and try to run us down to Kalgan tomorrow. Worry kept tripping me now as I went on with the questioning of Fon. Min, too, was absentminded. Sometimes he didn't even hear my questions, I had to repeat them.

Finally I said: "Min—it's on your mind and mine too. Could we check and see if that message has really gone out to Kalgan?"

He was right in gear for that. "Yes," he said immediately, "it is a good idea."

"And if we can't get a radio message through, we should try something else."

"Yes." We excused ourselves from Fon, who needed a break. The poor fellow was exhausted from the mental strain of constant question and answer. He could till hard land endlessly with a hand plough, and spend hours treading the paddle-boards to bring water to the fields, without tiring, but the unaccustomed routine of an Occidental-style business office had worn him out in two days.

At the Peace Preservation headquarters, we found the colonel closeted with some officers as usual, but the adjutant agreed to check with the radio shack and he came back eventually with the news. I could tell from Min's Cheshire cat smile that it was good.

"Plane will come in tomorrow to pick us up. At seven o'clock in the morning."

It was good, it was wonderful, I even shook Min's hand in a powerful overflow of spontaneous emotion. Now we could go back to poor Fon and ask him some more questions with renewed energy, and clean up the story.

First, though, Min and I had the same idea: what was the military situation? If that grew worse, it could foul up all our plans.

Min checked with the adjutant, whose face seemed blank when he answered, only a few words. "No enemy contact reported today."

I had one more thought that ought to bring us peace of mind. "Could you ask him what those guns were this morning?—Sounded like artillery fire, up north."

The usual translation process followed, the adjutant's thin face was blank as usual. "He says he doesn't know," Min relayed.

We bowed our thanks, the adjutant bowed in return, and we were off to join Fon in his cave home. This time five of his six little no-goods, pretty little slant-eyed beauties of the sex that nobody wants in China, were quietly in attendance. The eldest of the group, Fon Wen-li, who would have been twelve or thirteen, had served him tea, which he certainly needed after the experience of the magazine interview. Now it had picked him up and he was ready to go when Min explained that we would be leaving in the morning and must finish our work now. We sat on the *kong* platform and made notes and were nearly finished when Martha came in about six o'clock with Fon Shu-chen, Fon's wife, and his smiling, moustached buddy, Jong Sun. Martha said she had legged it around the hillside to the houses of Fon's friends and second cousins, made two notebooks full of notes and pictures too; she looked tired, but she was happy. "I was working very well," she said.

"That's good, Baby," I told her, loving her earnestness and single-mindedness. "But don't you want to know the good news?"

"Is the plane coming to pick us up?"

I nodded vehemently. But the news didn't seem to add to her already happy mood. "Aren't you glad, Sunbeam?" I asked.

"Yes."

"Min and I practically blew our tops when we got the word. Think of it—we can be in Peiping, probably, tomorrow afternoon."

"That's very good. Tomorrow should be good. But you can't count on it. Right now everything is fine, too, and that's enough."

I put my hand on hers and squeezed, and later, after we had thanked Fon and his wife and were walking up to the path toward our cave hand in hand, she pulled me down to kiss me on the cheek and said: "I love you, Scott. I'm happy with you. I have everything I wanted." For her, it was a long speech, except when she talked on the subject of Communism.

22

THAT NIGHT AFTER SUPPER THERE WERE A COUPLE OF CHORES to be done. One was to go over our notes and make sure we were covered on everything. The second came out of the first: while Martha and I were checking over our notebooks and the captions for her pictures, I was taken by too-frequent scratching and investigation showed a matter of small gray items called lice: I had probably picked them up sitting on the *kong* platform at Fon's. Thank God, Martha was clear of them.

It was a normal occupational hazard of working on a story like this, and Wu considered it that, too. He sent his novice to get some water and some strong soap from one of his mysterious sources, and he suggested an extra remedy that sounded something like modern black magic: gasoline. I promised him I would try to negotiate some of that later in the evening; I had seen a stack of green American-style jerry cans in a fuel dump behind the colonel's headquarters building. Meanwhile, fortunately, we still had our reliable G.I. bug powder.

I gave Martha the clean water and the soap first, both being so precious here, and by eight o'clock we felt renewed and recreated. When the rumble of the guns began in the north we were almost ready for it, a regular evening noise, but this time I found myself thinking hard, let them not get any closer tonight, no closer please, with the plane coming in the morning.

Martha didn't show any change when the murmur of the guns began, she kept on with her self-assigned chore of readying our small amount of personal kit for tomorrow. I tried to work over my notes in the candlelight, making sure they were readable, and she began to sing a little off key: she sang flat, it was a monotone, but it always sounded good to me. It was a tune I didn't know, anyhow, something about a happy jumping flea, so the melody didn't matter.

> Here's to the happy jumping flea!
> You can never tell a he from a she;
> But he can tell them,
> So can she.

"What are you thinking about, Baby?" I knew she didn't like me to ask that, but I wanted to be close to her.

"Nothing." I might have expected that answer too, but I did feel closer to her now. I went to her and put my arms around her waist.

"Baby," I said, "let's get out, in the air. It should be good in the twilight." I could see in my mind the perfect shade of night out there, the dusty purple of the desert.

"We should stop by the seminary anyhow, and make our apologies to the priests." That sounded like a good practical reason.

But she had a better one: "Yes, and we could find Min and check up on the military situation—if any." Her face broke into that quick smile and I squeezed her and kissed her before we went out.

✳

It was darker than we had thought it would be in the evening air. Over the Gobi to the west the shades were deepening to mauve and violet and overhead the stars on the pale night sky seemed bright already.

I held her hand as we walked down the grade and we were both watching the north where the guns rumbled, but they were not close enough to flash against the carved mountain silhouette.

"People always seem to fire more guns at night," I said. "I think it's because they're scared and the guns, especially the big ones, give them courage in the dark."

"It makes sense," she said. "Like the soldiers singing, in the daytime."

Now, when we were passing the drill ground the shape of it was white in the faint light, no figures of men to darken it. We could see cracks of light where the headquarters building stood, and a field phone rang and we heard talking, the calm kind as if nobody important was listening.

Tomorrow, I thought, the plane would be a spot on the parade ground, a moving one, it would move with us and take us out of these mountains to Peiping. I willed that the night should be quiet and the plane should come, and that the Communists should not.

At the seminary Father Cadmus told us that Father Henri had gone to the church with some of the other priests to pray. We walked over there.

It was our first time in the church, we had seen it only from a distance, and the fathers, knowing we were not Catholic, had not taken us there.

We opened the massive wooden door and saw the row of priests kneeling and the altar glittering with the candlelight. Their backs were toward us at the far end of the church. Father Henri knelt on a higher level. The rich sound of the Latin prayers hung on the air and someone rang a bell. The inside of the church was very bare, just the stone walls and the rows of plain benches, and the candles at the altar. Father Henri had told us the Reds had taken most of the fixtures during a drive to get metal for the army.

We closed the door, went back to Father Cadmus and asked him to convey our thanks to Father Henri for his hospitality, and found Min at the house of the *tsun-jong*. Min was more than eager to try the adjutant again for information, but the adjutant still looked blank about the cannonading in the north.

"He believes it is major engagement of armies up there," Min related. "But locally, front is quiet." If the adjutant knew what was happening in the north, he wasn't telling us. But at least, there had apparently been no change of plans about the plane's arriving in the morning, at seven.

On our way up the hill, I noticed that faint flashes of light were rippling the black sky to the north now, just over the rim of the mountains. And the gunfire sounded louder. I wasn't going to mention it, but she did.

"Scott, what do you think is happening up there?"

"Major engagement of armies," I tried to make a joke of it, mimicking Min's important tones.

"No, really, tell me." She was serious.

"Baby, if those guns were close enough to be dangerous right now, they'd be a lot noisier, and brighter."

"How far would you say they are?"

"If there were fewer of them, and they were closer, I could tell you exactly: with my stopwatch. But not now."

"I'm glad they're not close enough." The smile was there again, in the starlight.

But inside our cave house, as we lay on our sleeping-bag mattress, under the clean quilt Wu had provided for us, I could tell even in the dark that she was worrying. The muttering of the gunfire seemed to have grown considerably louder; even in the cave, with the door closed, it was audible.

I held her naked body close, she was smooth and good to the touch, but I could tell as if I could see, that her face was cloudy.

"What is it, Baby?"

"I don't know."

"Are you worried? Not scared, certainly?"

Silence, maybe while she thought about it. "Yes, I am. Scared, I guess."

"After all we've been through—you should be scared tonight: without a Communist in sight."

"Maybe that's it. We can't see them, but we know—they're getting closer. Maybe tonight—" She let it trail.

I stroked her cheek. "Is it the baby that makes you jumpy?"

"I guess. But it's—everything, too. It all seems so close. You think you're not afraid of dying, it wouldn't even bother you. But when it's close, it's different. It's not what you thought it would be like."

"Baby, you talk as if this *were* our last night on earth. Don't you remember—last night was. Now we're on the second go-round, and tomorrow the plane'll come in, pick us up and take us to Peiping, and you'll say: 'Remember how I worried, that last night in Djin-zuh,' and you'll laugh and say you were a comical girl that night."

"It doesn't seem comical right now." From her tone, I wondered if there were tears in her eyes.

"Look, Baby," I started to tell her, and everything seemed to be coming truly, "don't *you* be scared—you've been the one who brought strength to me, strength I didn't think I had. You made my work seem important to me again, you stuck with me whatever happened. You gave me something to live for—everything. A sense of importance . . . being in an important fight, which is what we all need, more than anything. Don't let me down now, my—Amazon!"

I heard her laugh, and I could see her smile as if the light were bright day. Now, I thought, she'll be all right, and she was. She put her arms around my back, our two bodies began to work into the smooth, massive patterns of oneness that made the strength flow between us and through us like waterfalls running sideways and up and down and every direction, pinwheels of waterfalls darting fast as light and stronger than gunfire or atom bombs, and infinitely brighter, as it had been since we had met and was now and would be in our seed tomorrow.

And afterward, we talked about the baby's name, would we call him Scott? I said no, Scott was a last name and I was tired of honoring the English side of my family, now that I had another Kraut in the family we should call him Hans or Fritz or something like that.

"No, I like the name Scott. It has—dignity."

"That's what I mean, it's too—" I started, but she had gone asleep. I lay awake, listening to the guns in the distance, and willing that in the morning everything should go all right, the plane should come on time and not crash on landing or take off, that the Communists should not come before or during, or for that matter, any time.

✳

I woke up about four because there was only the sound of silence, the guns had stopped. Not a murmur, even of the wind, came into our room.

I got up, dressed, and went out into the courtyard inside the mud wall, and out the gate where I could see the sky to the north. It was still and silent, the North Star bright, the pointers of the Big Dipper aiming at it from just over the rim of the mountains. But this time, no faint impacts of gunfire splashed the sky, only the first tide of the growing dawn. It was as steady as if it had been painted.

I looked down at the Peace Preservation Headquarters and the parade ground and saw that they were quiet. But something in the night made me restless. As long as she was secure in the bed and asleep I might stay here on watch.

My nerves suddenly twanged. Two sharp cracking sounds had jolted the night air. Rifle shots from the hills to the east? Then there were more, five or six—and the heavy, solemn *bap-bap-bap* of a BAR. But I could see nothing up there on the slope. My blood raced, my heartbeat was thudding. I looked at my watch: four thirty-five.

Down at the parade ground, I saw two men in the gray predawn light run across the ground in front of the headquarters shack, the door banging behind them. The bulb was still on inside, it flashed yellow. They jumped into a jeep, it started and raced across the ground toward the grade to the east. They had to go up a winding donkey trail and the progress was suddenly bouncy. The car had to travel in low ratio on that slope, the gears screamed at the speed.

I combed through the thin shadows on that hill but could see nothing else moving, only the jeep clattering up the slope. And my nerves reached out again beyond the jeep noise for the punctuating sound of rifle or machine gun fire, but none came.

A field phone rang somewhere in the army buildings, but no one moved among them, or on the drill ground. Nothing was happening. I watched the jeep struggle over the eastern hill, and heard the noise diminish, then stop, somewhere on the other side. Maybe this was nothing, my imagination was working too furiously. The shooting might have been soldiers triggering at roaming guerrillas or a moving shadow. And a jeep might normally hurry up a trail, without a crisis. I tried to sit on my nerves: after all, it was surprising there hadn't been more of this sporadic small arms firing at night.

I thought about going down to the headquarters to check, but then a couple of soldiers ambled among the buildings, their uniforms vivid green in the yellow dawning light. One of them carried a bugle and he walked leisurely to the flagpole in front of the headquarters shack and blew a complicated call I took to be reveille. I heard people stirring in the dingy barracks buildings. A detail of eight or nine soldiers came out and raised the white sun flag. Beyond the parade ground, down by the Belgian church steeple, thin white smoke rose from the mud-daubs of houses, and a rooster crowed. Everything, I thought, is going to be all right after all, and she'll have our baby.

Then the novice in his brilliant orange robe was standing beside me and smiling and saying, "Sah—teach a-ru invite you, missy bleak-fast." His English lessons with Wu were progressing well, and he was proud. I thanked him and went in to wake my Sunbeam for what I hoped would be our last meal in Djin-zuh.

✳

While we were finishing our noodle soup and *man-to,* Min came hurrying up to Wu's cave.

"Will you be ready to depart in a short time?" he asked without any preliminaries.

"We're ready now."

Wu rose and motioned to him to sit on the bench, "I must go and make preparation for the landing," Min said abruptly.

I could hear the chanting of marching men down on the drill ground, indicating things were normal, but I knew Min would probably have the latest news bulletins about the Communists.

"How is the military situation?"

"Adjutant says small patrol action during the night. Everything okay now."

The priest walked to the door and looked up at the bright sky. "One of your wise men wrote: 'The day is my brother.' I hope this day will be a brother to us."

The kind, wide-boned face was smiling as usual when we thanked him for all he had done.

"You are a good man," I said, "truly."

He bowed. "Kindness is not the monopoly of one race." Then he was immediately practical: the novice would help us carry our baggage down to the parade ground.

Martha and I and the novice went down to our cave to collect our stuff and we could see the round figure of Min down in front of the headquarters shack. A coolie was struggling up behind him, hauling his barracks bag. I looked at my watch and it was six twenty-eight.

Then I heard it, the faint high sigh of a shell far off, and unbelieving I saw the gray splash of the explosion on the far side of the town, landing on a house, the smoke dark with flying debris, and I heard the crash that reverberated in the valley.

"Is it—artillery?" Martha asked, her eyes wide open, catching the sun.

"Yes," I said, though it could have also been a rifled mortar, the poor man's artillery. This was no time for technicalities.

Down in the alleys where the shell had landed we could see little gray gobs of people running. Their shouting carried that long distance. A knot of people had sprung up in the alley near the explosion: probably somebody hurt. From the way we had heard the shell passing before it exploded, I guessed it must have come from the north and east.

In the yellow streak of the main street more dark figures moved, keeping smartly to the edges of the buildings.

"We'd better get on our way." I indicated the direction of the parade ground. We started down the slope, and Wu came up running in his orange robe and stopped by our cave and stood watching us go. He didn't wave.

The phone was ringing in the headquarters shack and a group of soldiers stood on the edge of the parade ground staring in the direction the shell had landed, as if they were sightseers.

I looked across the flat to the southeast where the shell had landed. The smoke had gone and one corner of a roof was mashed in as if the heel of a big hand had hit it. No more shells had come in, no sighing, no crashing.

Min waved to us and he seemed to be motioning us to hurry down. A tall thin man in Nationalist green came out and talked to Min, I thought it was the adjutant.

We were moving down as quickly as we could, and a bugler came running to the base of the flagpole and sounded a hurried call. Men in green poured from one of the buildings and fell in a double rank, and we heard the tweeting of a whistle and a few barked commands. A truck came out of nowhere, the engine roaring, then it slammed to a stop and the rank of men double-timed to it and climbed into the back and the truck sat there. It looked like the old wreck of a vehicle that had carried our bodyguard up from Kalgan. It had stopped now right in the middle of the parade ground, and inside I was saying move, truck, for God's sake don't sit there, the plane has to land there.

When I looked back at the headquarters shack Min had gone and a jeep and driver had come where he had been standing. Probably he had gone into the shack after the adjutant. The fat colonel came out of the shack, banging the door, jumped nimbly into the jeep and the vehicle charged across the parade ground toward the barracks building, leaving a wedge of yellow dust behind it.

I was helping Martha down a steep jog when I heard the sound again—the sighing, the quick silence and the crash of the shell. It seemed to come from the same direction as the first and I saw that it had landed in a line with it, which was good artillery procedure, one over and one under, but what were they trying to bracket?

The black genie of the explosion stood for a moment and then began to sink, but this time it seemed to have hit in an open place, something like a courtyard. In between the two explosions I could see a larger building that was of wood, and I wondered if the artillery spotter had mistaken that for an official building.

Then we were just above the parade ground, and skinning down a wash onto the flat, I was slipping and sliding and grabbing the typewriter and the notebook and the duffel bag to keep them from tumbling. Martha kept her precious camera bags around her neck and I caught her when she slipped, to prevent her choking herself to death. And the little novice, anchor-footed like a mountain goat, moved gracefully with a duffel bag balanced on his shoulder and Martha's airlines suitcase clutched in his hand.

Another bugle call had sounded and as we reached the flat I saw a mass of men in green running from the buildings and beginning to fall into ranks. Non-coms barked orders and blew whistles, and the colonel's jeep bounced out into the flat where the platoons were forming. The car stopped and he shouted something, a long sentence, in a loud voice. A tall officer with metal pips gleaming on his shoulder ran up, the colonel shouted at him again. I looked at the nearest rank of troops and saw that they had old rifles, Arisakas or Lee-Enfields or old Springfields, and their uniforms were sorry, none had helmets and some were hatless and most wore felt *shed-zuh* below their puttees instead of shoes. The Peace Preservation Corps were no elite troops; like many Chinese soldiers, they fought on hope.

Min was rushing out of the headquarters shack. He stopped as if he had been hit when he heard the noise and we heard it too, the double fluttering of the shell wings overhead, lower than the last. He crouched to the ground and the two projectiles exploded, sounding closer than the last time but still well away on the other end of the town. Three, four, five winging shells, three four five crashes that shook the air, they were firing the battery.

Min had stood up again but his eyes were drawn back like a cat's ears. "We're being shelled!" he shouted.

"I know." For some reason I was shouting too. I looked across the parade ground and saw that the truck loaded with soldiers had gone from the middle, thank God. It was struggling up the same donkey trail I had watched the jeep climb this morning. Some of the platoons in ranks were double-timing after the truck, jogging off the far end of the parade ground. Some of the other ranks stood in lines, then somebody was barking commands. The plane could never come in with the troops there. Move, move, troops, please move, I said inside.

"What's happening?" I yelled at Min. "Is it a big force over there?"

"Adjutant says the north pillbox has fallen. They surrendered."

He hadn't answered my question but what he said was important enough. The north pillbox I didn't know, but wherever it was exactly didn't matter. It meant the enemy was coming in and the closer he got the better his artillery observation would be and the shells would come more accurately.

The ranks of men still stood at the center of the drill field, most of them. Was that all the trucks they had, just the one truck? Then I saw two old vehicles lumbering from between a couple of the buildings. Two ranks of men were climbing aboard one of the trucks while it moved, a pile of green humanity, falling together, and someone was shouting there, loud-voiced, probably commands.

The shelling had slacked, no shells singing with angel-devil wings, no air-shattering crashes of explosions. The fat colonel's jeep whipped up beside us, squealed to a stop and he jumped out without noticing us and went into the headquarters shack, banging the light wooden door.

I glanced at my Sunbeam: excited, but not scared, She looked up at the sky; nothing there, no plane, not even a cloud, nothing, just the pale, burning, morning blue. My watch showed six fifty-eight.

Min was hurrying toward the headquarters shack. I called after him: "Any word on the radio about the plane? Is he coming through?"

"Okay, everything okay," he mumbled as he went in the door.

On the drill field, suddenly, many of the troops seemed to have evaporated. I saw a couple of platoons like green cords twisting up the tan-colored slopes to the west and north. That was good, the plane would have room to land.

A sudden sound, my nerves felt it like a punch: small arms, a cascade of rifles, the short rattles of machine guns. And they sounded close. I had dreaded this most: if the Red rifle companies got to the town, maybe the plane couldn't land.

More ripping of gunfire, and a fast-paced machine-gun at the top of the cacophony; would it be a Red burp gun? Where was the sound, from the north?

I felt a hand in mine, her flesh. I looked at her and tried to smile, but she was motioning up at the sky. I saw it too: a light plane, the sun glinting on the windshield for a second, then on the wing as it turned. It was spiraling down toward us. I heard the engine; the gunfire had lulled.

He came in faster than I thought he would. In a few seconds he buzzed the field, an L-16, painted blue. It looked bright and new. He circled once low, I could see the pilot silhouetted in the high canopy as he passed.

No shellfire, please. For a moment, no small arms. Till he got in and out, with us. Why weren't they firing, now? I didn't care why, just let them not.

The colonel barged out the door, Min behind him. Min carried his duffel bag. The colonel nodded to us this time, he jumped into his jeep and it roared out into the middle of the field where he stood up and bawled out some order. The ranks of men on the field double-timed for the edges, the colonel's jeep bounced off the field and between the buildings on the other side.

Suddenly the air seemed quiet, dead still. I squeezed Martha's hand, hard. The coffee-grinder sound of the little engine seemed loud, then it stopped as the plane curved around low to the northeast, coming in for a landing. We could hear the wind in his struts. He blimped his engine to keep it alive. I was biting my lips, Min covered his chin with one hand and sweat beaded on his forehead.

The plane was low over the buildings, light flashed on the fuselage as he fishtailed to lose speed, the nose and the engine and the wings grew suddenly larger, he whipped over our heads, the landing gear hit with a rumble and a splash of dust, he was on the ground, swerving around a group of soldiers. He spun the plane around, gunned his engine full blast and scooted towards us in a dust cloud. He had seen the shellfire and he was hurrying.

He stopped close to us, the engine turning over, the plane seemed high off the ground, bigger than I had thought. I saw the head and shoulders of the pilot, a big man, with a dark patch over one eye. Could it be Bud Wade? I couldn't tell with the motor idling, the blur of the blades ticking over.

Then he was getting out, flinging a wooden chock in front of one wheel. And that second, a shell came, low and loud: *schweeeeee-*

crraash! It was like a truck skidding around a corner, it was near us, and the explosion was closer, somewhere among the houses to our left. Another shell, another. Men in green were running across the drill field at this end, but not towards us. Some running for cover. I saw a smoke splash standing to our left, maybe a quarter of a mile away.

I saw the pilot's shoulders hunch down instinctively with the first blast, then he straightened and he was coming toward us. It was Bud Wade, but he wasted no time talking.

"Gas!" he yelled. "I need gas!"

I dropped my bag, typewriter and notebook. "I know where there is some. Behind that shack."

We started to run. Nobody was around us, except Min, who crouched for protection on the ground next to his duffel bag, and the novice in the orange robe.

"Come on!" I yelled. I saw Martha beginning to run behind us, and shouted at her. "Stay here. We can get it." But she didn't stay, she being Martha, she ran with us.

Min wasn't coming. He was moving toward the plane, dragging his barracks bag. The orange robe of the novice flashed in the corner of my eye, he was with us.

Nobody was in front of the headquarters shack, the door was closed, but I could hear voices inside. Then we were running along the side of the building and I could see the pile of green jerry cans with barbed wire around them—and a sentry standing by the wire with a rifle and bayonet. I hadn't thought of the sentry, that there would be one. He lowered his shoulders and pointed the gun at us.

He yelled at us and we stopped. Bud answered him in Mandarin. They yelled at each other for a minute, Bud waved in the direction of the plane, then he moved gingerly up to the sentry with an identification card extended. The sentry lowered his rifle and stood aside. But too much time had been wasted.

One jerry can of gas was about all each of us could lug on foot: four of us, twenty gallons. It would be a struggle for Martha, the damned cans weighed fifty pounds each.

"How much do you need?" I asked Bud.

"Fifty gallons." He chattered at the sentry, waved toward the plane; the man shook his head, he wouldn't leave his post to help us.

Bud hoisted a can, hauling it as fast as he could. "Isn't there anybody around this damn burg? Where's your Chink friend?" He was fuming. One of my Chink friends was in there with us, pitching, the little novice.

Another shell shrieked and skittered overhead and crashed somewhere to our left. We couldn't move fast, we had to hobble with the awkward loads. I couldn't help Martha, she didn't ask for help.

Small arms were popping somewhere on the slopes to the north, louder than the last, close enough to make me sweat. If snipers could bear on the plane; or if there were machine guns—murder.

We rounded the corner of the shack and could see the plane again. "Maybe we can make it on twenty gallons," Bud yelled. "Should be half a tank left in one wing."

"Can't we-at least make it to Kalgan with the gas we have?"

"That's what's wrong. Reds are infiltrating the field there, that's why I couldn't get a full load gas this morning."

We were running ahead of Martha without thinking about it. We reached the plane and Bud jumped into the cabin to get a funnel. Min still sat in the back seat of the cabin.

"Come on, help us load!" Bud yelled at him, but he slumped there without moving, I knew he was petrified.

Bud was up on the fuselage, his toes in the steps while he poured gas. The novice and I stood waiting at his feet: you can pour gas only so fast with one funnel. Then I saw Martha straggling toward us, the jerry can seemed to be more than she could manage but she was doing it, I had forgotten about her.

I ran to her to help her. As I ran, the door of the headquarters shack opened and three officers stood there. One of them was the adjutant.

Then one of them on the end was falling slowly, and the other two moving away somewhere fast, disappearing, and I heard pops of rifle fire the same moment.

Martha was ahead of me now and stumbling, the gas can pitching onto the ground and bouncing. She fell and rolled.

It can't be, it can't be; I ran to her and saw the bullet hole in her chest, high up on the khaki shirt, oozing red. I turned her part way over and the bullet was in her somewhere, it hadn't come out. Her eyes looked at me listlessly.

"Baby, Baby!" I could hear rifle fire cracking somewhere behind me but it was faint and it didn't matter.

"Did you get the—fistures? Did you get the fistures?" she mumbled. Her eyelids slowly closed as if she were sleeping, going to sleep.

I picked her up and staggered toward the plane. I saw Bud looking at me, he was still pouring from a jerry can, and the popping of the guns I could still hear faintly. I saw Bud duck his head and a freight train sound passed overhead and crashed to the left and a big column of black stood up there but it was all distant and it didn't matter.

I got to the plane and Bud was still pouring gas. I moved past his leg where the cockpit door was open and put Martha on the floor there. Her head lolled back and I put my arm behind it to cushion it.

Min was sitting in the comer of the back seat. I climbed up in the cockpit holding Martha and put her into the back seat next to Min so that she sat up but her eyes were still closed. Her face was smooth, inert, like a stone idol and her eyes were closed as if she were asleep. I could hear another shell going overhead like a freight train and the explosion, somewhere among the houses.

Bud was vaulting into the front seat. He ripped the tape from the first aid kit under the dash and passed it back to me.

"Don't give up yet." The words slipped through his teeth as he pushed the throttle knob full forward. The plane whipped around and I could see three blobs of figures running across the far side of the parade ground, stubby-barreled guns in their hands— Communists in dust-colored uniforms.

I took Martha's arm and felt for the pulse. The pale wrist was cold, the veins seemed deep dark blue. The plane was lurching and bumping and I couldn't feel the bulge of pulse. We jounced over something hard with a sudden crashing sound, and I fell forward past the seat and onto the floor beside Martha's feet—the small squarish boots of oiled leather. I struggled half way up and was sprawled over the folded back of the front seat. I could see Bud's long-fingered right hand playing the stick with the sensitivity of an orchestra conductor, his other hand shuttling over the dials and switches. The plane veered and yawed across the dry turf, and any other pilot than Bud would have yelled at me to get back in my seat. But I could see the corner of his eye watching me to make sure I wasn't going to be hurt, while his attention was directed elsewhere, and his piano player fingers tended the controls.

I could see one of the brown figures aiming at us as we rolled past. He had stopped running, he seemed to be bending over something, and I saw puffs of orange in front of him—and I heard the fast, ripping sound of an automatic weapon.

I heard the clatter of something breaking behind me and saw some movement snap through the canopy overhead. A tear had appeared there in the plexiglass, the plexiglass was torn raggedly. Small arms fire had come from another direction, from somewhere behind me, from the other side of the plane. But the plane kept going, the tan-colored ground was slipping by, we were gaining speed, and I felt the cushion of air as we were buoyed up free of the ground.

"You all right?" I heard Bud shout as he hauled back on the stick.

"Yeah." I had to shout over the engine roar and the whistling of the wind through the broken canopy.

I saw the barrel-shaped mud huts on the edge of the parade ground slipping by—the bare ridge, and I knew we were turning south toward Peiping. Bud was flying the plane with one hand, and I could see his eyes flicking around the plane. He leveled the aircraft and kept it roaring at full throttle.

"Flies all right," he shouted, and in the same second he had screwed his mouth around and spoken to Min: "Help him with the girl." It was a command.

I was kneeling beside her now, my head sideways on her chest, listening for her heart. Warm blood ran down my cheek, and I pressed my ear hard against the wet khaki shirt. I couldn't hear anything against the roar of the engine.

I ripped the cloth and I could see the blood was only oozing. It was smeared and I grabbed some gauze and tried to clean the blood away, and I could see that this was seepage from a bullet wound higher up, the wound still faintly pumping blood, alive with blood. My heart jumped at the thought: her heart is going, still, it's going! She was alive, there was hope.

Now Min had actually loosened himself from his safety belt and he was kneeling beside me. He had heard his master's voice in Bud and he was fumbling with a packet of sulfaguanadine powder. He extended it to me and I yelled to him as if he were the only person in the world: "She's alive, she's alive!"

A faint smile came to Min's cherubic face and I think in that moment it was the most beautiful, most beatific face I had ever seen. Maybe she was badly hurt but she was alive and we were getting her out of this toward a hospital and Peiping and safety and Shanghai.

Min got out a bandage while I dusted sulfa powder on the wound. It was not bleeding heavily.

"How bad is it?" Bud called from the front seat.

"I don't know. But it looks like small caliber."

"How's her breathing?"

"Can't get it."

Bud fumbled under his seat with one hand and now he was extending an oxygen mask and small walk-around oxygen bottle to me.

"Force her breathing."

I clamped the rubber mask and raised her arms, and I saw the mask move on her small face. She stirred and the regulator needle moved. She was breathing deep, now I saw the eyelids open slightly and saw the dark blue color there. She was breathing regularly and her eyes were opening wider. I took the mask away and she was still breathing—and my own life seemed to be coming back to me.

"Is the slug still in her?" Bud was asking.

"I think so." I moved her shoulder—there was one wound in her chest at the front, nothing in her back.

"We'll get her to a hospital quick," Bud said. "Within an hour we'll be in Peiping."

Bud looked back and now he was studying her closely. "It's high up—it might not even have hit her lung." I was giving her an ampule of morphine.

"It seems nothing broken," I said. "Her arms move all right. And Martha said foggily, faintly: "Move all right."

I put my face next to hers and kissed her cheek. Blood from my face smeared on her. I took her hand and held the fingers, and the ring I had given her.

I told her: "You'll be all right, Baby—all right."

"All right," she repeated faintly. And she raised her head and asked me a question, a rhetorical question: "You got your story?" I nodded. I bowed to her.

I taped a bandage on the wound. We hit a bump as I finished and I fell beside her. For a moment I couldn't move and I was beside the small feet in the still, oiled leather boots, and I remembered how they moved in the precise, efficient way I loved so much. I held my face against her boot.

"Better stretch her out on the seat," Bud was saying, breaking in.

"I'll sit on the floor," I told him. "I'll stay with her."

"Min can sit up front," Bud said. Min nodded and now he was helping me to put Martha across the back seat.

Her eyes were open and she was watching me feebly. I leaned forward and told her: "Baby—one hour and we'll be in Peiping. You'll be okay." She smiled and I took her hand and held it. Her hand seemed warm now. That touch was the touch of life. More than that, it was strength and courage for the battle we have to fight.

Bud seemed to sense my feeling. He lit a cigarette and it drooped from his lower lip, and his face creased in something between a grin and a grimace.

"Take a brace, boy. Got to keep trying. Danged if I don't think we'll make it to Peiping." Ahead of us I could see the faint glow of the city where some of the lights were still burning.

Afterword

RT Would Go
A Crusade for Ideals and Survival
Ray E. Boomhower

In the months following the Japanese attack on the U.S. Pacific fleet at Pearl Harbor in the Hawaiian Islands on December 7, 1941, millions of American men pondered what would become of them as their country took its first tentative steps in the worldwide conflict. One of those who wondered what his future might be was a young reporter working on the rewrite desk at the New York office of the International News Service, Richard Tregaskis of Elizabeth, New Jersey.

Tregaskis had suffered several shocking developments since the surprise Japanese raid. He had been rejected for service due to his height (he stood more than six feet, five inches tall) and weak eyesight and had learned he had developed a debilitating chronic illness, diabetes. To get to the fighting, Tregaskis became determined to become a foreign correspondent for the INS, a news agency founded by newspaper magnate William Randolph Hearst. He kept after his boss, Barry Faris, to send him off as to cover the war, believing that the "closer I cam to getting killed in this career, the better my story would be, if I survived."

One rainy March evening Tregaskis learned that Faris wanted to see him the next morning. Tregaskis respected Faris, who, although physically undistinguished, could do any job in the newsroom. He particularly admired the veteran journalist for "his fondness for direct action—the shortest way to a point. This was characteristic of all great newsmen I knew—and it was the quality they had in common with the great military leaders I came to know, the leaders among the brave men."

Faris was polite and to the point, asking Tregaskis if he would rather go to London or Australia. Knowing that Faris did not "brook a 'think it over' kind of answer," Tregaskis seized his chance and made up his mind, picking Australia. Tregaskis was on his way to combat, pleased that "out there in the void of the future was a shape I had dreamed of: men at war in a crusade for ideals, and for survival."

From the Doolittle Raid, the Battle of Midway, and the invasion of Guadalcanal in the Pacific, to the invasions of Sicily and Italy, as well as the drives into France, Belgium, Germany, and back to the Pacific, Tregaskis followed the troops, paying the penalty many others paid in the war, including being gravely wounded by a German shell in Italy. "I gave that effort a lot of my own blood and I didn't hold back when it came to risking my neck to do what I was supposed to do," he recalled.

In doing so, Tregaskis discovered that he possessed an innate affinity for covering combat, writing his sister Madeline shortly after he had finished his Guadalcanal book that it was funny the way "this war business hits you, after you've been meddling around with it for a while. Action, and particularly some new variety of action, gets to be like a drug. You feel let down without it and with it you feel a sort of unhealthy excitement. And frightening—shooting at people and that sort of thing—comes to have a compelling interest, although you're fully aware of the unpleasantness of it." He even began to look forward to the next assignment, hating to miss any upcoming big battle, even if he had an opportunity to return to his family in the United States.

Tregaskis's willingness to go where the action was heaviest impressed me greatly as I researched his career for my book *Richard Tregaskis: Reporting under Fire from Guadalcanal to Vietnam.* The reporter's courage in combat also amazed the soldiers, sailors, airmen, and Marines he covered. One awed soldier told the correspondent, "How you guys go ahead and stick out your necks when you don't have to—well, it just beats hell out of me!" Tregaskis had a simple answer: "But we certainly do have to— that's our job."

Asked by the editors of a national magazine to return to the Pacific late in the war to follow the crew of a B-29 Superfortress as it prepared for bombing missions against Japanese cities, Tregaskis was asked by an editor, "Do you really want to go?" Without hesitating, Tregaskis gave an answer that any reporter who covered World War II would understand: "I don't want to go, but I think I ought to go." He went.

Richard Tregaskis Books

SOUTHEAST ASIA: BUILDING THE BASES
THE HISTORY OF CONSTRUCTION IN SOUTHEAST ASIA
CHINA BOMB: A NOVEL
GUADALCANAL DIARY
INVASION DIARY
JOHN F. KENNEDY AND PT-109
LAST PLANE TO SHANGHAI
SEVEN LEAGUES TO PARADISE
STRONGER THAN FEAR
VIETNAM DIARY
THE WARRIOR KING: HAWAI'I'S KAMEHAMEHA I
WOMAN AND THE SEA: A BOOK OF POEMS
X-15 DIARY

Other JMFdeA Press Books

CHASING THE SURGE
THE ENERGY INSIDE VALSIN'S CHOICES
PERSIGUIENDO LA OLEADA
SASSY FOOD

www.ingramcontent.com/pod-product-compliance
Lightning Source LLC
Chambersburg PA
CBHW051217190726
48288CB00006B/1999